I0451939

REBEL GREY

STELLA DREXLER

An imprint of Diogenes Club Press

Worldly, Whimsical, and Weird Books

www.diogenesclubpress.com

Dallas, TX

Copyright © 2013 by Stella Drexler

All rights reserved. This book, its logos, symbols, images, and likenesses are copyrighted by Author name. No part of this work may be reproduced in any media or format without prior written consent of copyright holder except for limited selections intended for journalistic review.

DC Dreams, an imprint of Diogenes Club Press
8619 Reva St. Dallas, TX 74227
www.diogenesclubpress.com

The characters and events in this book are fictional. Any similarity to real persons, living or dead, is coincidental and not intended by the author.

ISBN: 9781622010233

Library of Congress Control Number: 2017955990

CHAPTER ONE

Razor City, sometime in the near future....

A powerful dance beat pounded through the club. In the center of the floor, dancers spun and twisted and thrashed together to the music. They all wore dark clothes. Some wore masks to hides their faces. Others wore bright, colorful paint. They looked like horrible, insane clowns, beautiful monsters, dangerous animals poised to strike. Their arms and legs struck out and twined together in an eerily rhythmic pulse. They might have been many parts of a single terrible, confusing creature.

A scream ripped out across the floor. It was lost in the earsplitting melody. It became part of the music. The dancers broke apart as three men tumbled into the crowd, throwing kicks and punches in a vicious, intense brawl. No one stopped them. A shower of blood flashed for the briefest moment in the strobe light. One of the men fell, clutching at a knife in his belly.

The light flashed again. His face twisted in a horrible grimace. It went dark. He lay upon the floor in a pool of dark liquid. No one rushed forward to help him, but the small table of bounty hunters on the edge of the floor lifted their heads. They eyed each other cagily, but they didn't rise to scoop him up. He was no one. Even King Scarlet didn't want him. Petra doubted anyone would miss him. She wondered if anyone knew his name.

It didn't matter. If they had, he was probably lucky to have died on the floor in a pool of his own blood, in the middle of the swarm of dark, twisted dancers. A burly bouncer in grey coveralls materialized out of the fog and flashing light. He gripped the dead man by the arms and dragged him off to the edge of the floor. The bouncer propped him against the wall. The dead man's eyes were open. They were as black as a bottomless pit. He stared blankly out at the crowd.

Petra swiveled away from him to face the bar. Her stomach roiled, but she lifted her chin. She'd seen much, much worse since Scarlet and his men had taken control of Razor City. She didn't speak up. No one ever spoke up. When they did, they went the same way. She was better off minding her own business.

In a place like this, you got good at minding your own business. The Uprising's rebel propaganda littered the floor and tables. Outlaws lurked in the corners, avoiding the sharp eyes of the bounty hunters scanning the crowd for faces they recognized. Men exchanged thick envelopes for locked briefcases.

Women lounged around the room, exchanging themselves for money, drugs or other favors. Others covered their faces and danced to the endless, pulsating beats until they forgot the war and Scarlet and the crushing oppression all around them. They might have been rebels, hunters, outlaws or the King's Nobles. No one asked your name in a place like this.

It was the sort of place you went to when you had scores to settle and people to meet. It was the only place inside Razor City's limits that King Scarlet's Marshals didn't dare enter. When they did, they were never seen again. And no one came looking for them.

Petra was there to work. She motioned the publican for another drink. He hesitated a moment, but Scarlet had bigger problems than underage drinking. She slapped a bill on the tarnished brass bar and stared up at the television monitors above the publican's head. There were dozens of screens and dozens of images: cartoon characters chasing each other around a barren landscape; a couple twined together in a heated embrace; a masked man slashing through a high school; detectives leaning over a dead body; King Scarlet, standing before a large, shining steel building, smiling out at her and speaking animatedly to the crowd gathered around him.

His propaganda machine was well-oiled and finely-tuned. King Scarlet was an impressive man in his early forties. His charcoal suit was perfectly tailored to his tall, lean figure. He wore his dark hair combed back from his handsome, sculpted features. It barely moved in the slight breeze that rustled the trees over his head. He looked beautiful and untouchable.

And there was nothing but cold cruelty in his dark, almond shaped eyes.

Petra frowned at the screen. A headline scrolled across the bottom of the screen in cheerful yellow letters: *Razor City patriarch Ezra Scarlet attends the opening of the Razor City Home for Lost Children*. Lost children? Razor City's children weren't lost. Or at least, they hadn't been. Not until Scarlet and his Nobles had taken their parents and families from them, accused them of treason and imprisoned them or worse.

Behind the king, a young man stood motionless. He was as tall as Scarlet and resembled him so closely, Petra knew he could be only Prince Dante, the King's infamously cruel and haughty son. He looked so cold and still, he might have been only a statue of a young man. His dark, stormy grey eyes peered around at the reporters, onlookers and lost children as though they meant as much to him as a bug he might squash beneath his perfectly polished black boot. His dark, shoulder-length hair blew around his beautiful face, making him look eerily vulnerable and sinister at the same time. He didn't bother to brush it back.

He was notoriously camera shy. She'd never seen him before, but she knew all about him. Everyone in Razor City knew about Prince Dante. He had a reputation for spreading terror and destruction wherever he went. With an army of bodyguards and the King's might behind him, no one dared stand up to Dante. They just got out of his way and let him smash up whatever club, hotel room or innocent bystander had attracted his ire.

Petra hated him. She turned away from the screen. She didn't want to watch the King and his son dedicate a home to the children of the families they'd torn apart. She didn't want to see their supercilious smiles or hear their empty words. It was all lies. Razor City was a city of lies.

A fist flew at her face. She reared back, but it didn't strike her. She relaxed and took the drink in her employer's outstretched hand. "That's real cute, Max."

Max smiled. "Good evening, Petra." He was a tall man in his mid-twenties. He wasn't handsome, but his face was smooth and even-featured. There was an odd sort of appeal to him. It might have been the slight air of danger about him.

Petra didn't trust him.

He lifted a thick, pale eyebrow. "So, you have it?"

She tasted the drink carefully. It smelled like battery acid. She didn't swallow it. She placed the glass gently down on the bar in front of her and glanced at Max. "You have the money?"

"Yes."

It was the sort of place where no one noticed an exchange of illicit goods or services. Still, Petra wasn't a fool. Nowhere in Razor City was truly safe. She slid the thick, compact square disc under the bar and dropped it in his opened palm. "I think you'll find the information useful. It's proof your competitor is funding the Uprising."

"What kind of proof?"

"Emails to and from an anonymous address that detail the transactions."

"Did you trace the address?"

She lifted an eyebrow. "No."

"Can you?"

"You really want me to try? You really think either of us is safe having that kind of information?"

Max was silent a moment. "No. Probably not." He frowned thoughtfully. "But it would get me in good with Scarlet if I could hand him one of the Uprising."

"I probably wouldn't be able to. The Uprising uses signals bounced off other signals all over the place. It would take a super computer to track them." She cut him a wry look. "You got one of those?"

"No."

"Right. Well, neither does anyone else. The Uprising has kept underground for this long for a good reason. They're good."

"You don't even care who they are? You don't even want to try?"

"Why would I? It's not my problem. I'm not interested in taking them down. I'm not interested in joining them."

Max nodded. "You're interested in my money."

"Right."

He passed her a thick envelope under the bar, and she tucked it into the pocket of her long, red leather jacket. He glanced at her. "You sure I won't get caught with this?"

She shrugged. "Not unless you're dumb enough to flash that disc around. No one will even know I was in the system. It's not exactly a high tech operation over there at the machine shop. It's just a small local network. I covered my tracks. You got what you wanted." She flicked her fingers in dismissal. "Leave me alone."

Max didn't like this. He frowned. "That's not very nice, Petra. Don't you want to finish your drink and have another with me?"

"No."

She felt his hand on her knee. "Come on, Petra. I know I paid more than this job was worth. I know it wasn't that hard for you. I expect you will make it worth the money."

Petra did not wait for his hand to slide higher up her thigh. She drew her hand from her pocket and jabbed the barrel of her small, single shot pistol into his side. This was the sort of place where you came prepared. "Don't make me use it, Max. Not here. You know I'll be out the door and in the wind before anyone even notices you're dead."

Max held up his hands in surrender. "Come on, Petra. There's no need for that. I thought we were friends."

"We aren't. Keep your hands off me. I did the work. You got what you wanted, and I got my money. Now go away before I get angry."

He glared at her, but he didn't need to be told twice. He hopped off his stool and disappeared into the thrashing crowd. Petra lifted her chin and turned back toward the bar. She didn't regret the termination of her business relationship with Max. In a place like Razor City, you had to know when to cut your losses.

He was a pervert, anyway. He had to be more than ten years older than she was. She pushed the drink he'd brought her away. She wasn't an idiot. There were men like him all over the city, and she knew better than to take a drink from one of them.

He'd better not have shorted her on the cash.

She motioned the publican for a fresh drink. On the screen above his head, Prince Dante peered out at her. For a moment, she felt as though his large, almond-shaped grey eyes could see straight through the television, as though he was looking directly at her. She grimaced and gave him an obscene hand gesture. She hoped he could see her. She spun around and hopped down off her stool.

A tall, dark-haired man in black leaned against the bar, smiling at the pretty young red-headed woman perched on the stool beside him. Petra heard her laugh heartily at something the man in black said. The woman tossed her red hair and laid a hand on his thickly muscled arm. Her fingernails pressed into his flesh as though she were marking him. Petra rolled her eyes and paused right behind her, crossing her arms over her chest.

Key Kelly leaned down to murmur at the pretty red-head. She turned her head to look at Petra. Her eyes were as cold as ice. Petra lifted her eyebrows at her. If she thought she was going to argue about being dismissed, something in Petra's gaze changed her mind. She hopped off her stool. She tossed her hair and strode away without looking back.

Petra scowled. "Having a nice time?"

"Quite, thank you."

"I thought we were here to work."

"You're here to work. I'm just here to make sure Max doesn't get out of line."

"He did get out of line. Luckily, I can take care of myself because you seemed quite caught up."

Key smirked. "Are you jealous, Petra?"

She tossed her long, pale blonde hair. "No."

His face changed so abruptly, she nearly jumped when he stepped forward and caught her arm. "What happened?"

"What?"

"Your gun. Did you something happen?"

Petra had almost forgotten she was still holding it. She tucked it back into her pocket. "No. Nothing. I'm fine. I took care of it."

Key crossed his arms over his broad chest and leaned back against the bar. "Petra, is there something I should know?"

"Max is just a jerk, okay? He got his merchandise. I got the money."

"Good." He caught her arm. "Come on. Let's go before it starts to get dicey in here. I've already seen some bounty hunters looking keen on the guy in the corner over there."

Petra glanced over her shoulder at the thin man in ripped jeans and a grubby tee-shirt. His eyes were huge and dark. They darted around the club with a cagey intensity that suggested he'd just realized he was in the wrong place at the wrong time. His face was probably on the wall of every bounty hunter outpost in Razor City. He had the look of a very hunted man. He looked as though he wanted to run but was too afraid to call attention to himself.

"No wonder. He looks as if he's afraid of his own shadow. What the hell is he doing in here, anyway? Everyone knows what kind of place this is."

"He was handing out Uprising pamphlets in the bathroom." Key eyed him in interest for a moment. "Come to think of it, I'm pretty sure I saw him on a wall somewhere."

Petra lifted her eyebrows. "Are you thinking of collecting?"

He shrugged. "We could use the money."

"Come on. We didn't come here to pick up an errant bounty. Besides, the hunters would probably jump on us before we ever got to him. We don't need them to start looking too closely at us. We're probably better off letting him take the heat off us until we can get out of here."

Key smiled. "Maybe we should stay. We haven't seen a good fight in a while."

Petra glanced at the thin, frightened man. "It doesn't look like it would be much of a fight. That guy looks like he would go down in one punch."

"Don't underestimate the Uprising. They're very well trained. Many of them are killers. They've been preparing to take down Scarlet for ten years."

Petra crossed her arms over her chest and rolled her eyes. "Of course they'd say that. It keeps people scared."

"It keeps some people hopeful. And more people are joining them everyday. It's looking like they might actually have a chance."

She scoffed. "No, they don't. No one's going to stop Scarlet. He owns this city and none of us can do a damn thing about it."

Key looked at her with a curiously pitying expression in his brilliant blue eyes. "Petra, don't be like that. Ren didn't believe that. He thought there was a chance."

She glared at him. "And where did that get him?"

Key sighed, but he didn't reply to this. He reached for her. She shrugged him off and spun away from him with a toss of her head.

She went alarmingly rigid.

"Petra, what is it?"

"Spears."

"What?"

"It's Cage Spears."

Key glanced around the club, but he did not see the man of whom she spoke. "What? Where? Are you sure."

"Yes. I'm sure. It's him. I would know him anywhere."

"The Nobles don't come in here very often. When they do, they make an entrance. They make sure everyone knows."

"Not always." She lifted her hand to point at the man across the room, standing on the edge of the dance floor. He didn't seem to be watching the dancers, though. His dark eyes were sweeping slowly around the club as though he were looking for someone or something. He was a handsome man in his mid-thirties with shortly cropped blonde hair, but he was so cold, so austere, he might have been a statue.

Key was surprised to see him there. "What's he doing?"

Petra glared across the room. "Probably looking for someone else to frame for treason."

She was moving toward him before she even paused to think about what she was doing. It took Key several seconds to realize what she intended to do and dart after her. He caught her arm and dragged her back. She threw off his arm and spun back toward Spears.

"Petra!"

She struggled, but he was much larger and much stronger than she was. "Let me go, Key."

"You can't go over there."

"He is the one who sent Ren to prison. He framed him. Ren could die because of him."

"You can't just go over there and confront him, Petra. He's got bodyguards, and he could bring the bounty hunters down on us in a heartbeat. It wouldn't do any good. You aren't going to get your brother out that way. You'll just get hurt or thrown in prison yourself."

She glared at him. "You think I'm trying to do some good? What good have I ever done anyone?"

"Petra, this isn't the way."

"What other way is there? Work with the Uprising? Hope the guards won't kill my brother before the rebels finally move on Scarlet and either become the new dictators or be crushed under the Marshals' boots? Come on, Key. There isn't any good in Razor City anymore, but that doesn't mean Cage can't get what's coming to him."

He looked appalled by this speech, and she ground her boot into his foot. He growled in pain and released her. "Petra--!"

She wasn't listening. She darted through the cluster of dancers. Two large, dangerous-looking men stepped into her path before Petra could reach Spears. The Noble barely glanced her way. "Cage!"

His dark eyes flicked to her as though she were nothing more than an irritating insect. His bodyguards looked at her coldly, but they didn't seem to think she was much of a threat. Spears probably got shouted at in the streets and in clubs all over the city. The men looked prepared.

"You son of a bitch!" She launched herself forward, hoping to take the bodyguards by surprise. She tried to dart between them, but they were ready for her. They each shot out a hand in a single fluid motion to catch her arms. She bared her teeth at them. "Let me go."

They didn't speak to her, but their cold, alert eyes were warning enough. She wasn't getting through them. She wasn't going to let that stop her.

"You put my brother in prison!" She wasn't even sure Spears could hear her over the pounding melody. "You framed him!"

He could hear her. He lifted his chin. "I am sure he was guilty." He spoke softly, but his voice carried over the music with a chilling clarity. "People often fail to accept that their loved ones are guilty, but they nearly always are."

She struggled to reach him, but his bodyguards were prepared. "My brother was innocent!"

Spears lifted an eyebrow. "You don't speak out against King Scarlet in Razor City unless you are looking to get arrested. Your brother must have been looking."

Petra screamed in outrage. The sound wove into the music. She reached out for him again, clawing at the air as though she might draw his blood through the sheer force of her anger. The bodyguards were utterly unimpressed. Spears peered back at her so calmly, she thought the tight, roiling ball of rage inside her might explode. It didn't. She wished it would.

It wasn't fair. He shouldn't be able to look so cool and so unbothered by her loss. He should have to pay. All of Scarlet's men should have to pay.

She felt Key behind her. She could feel the tension in his body, but he looked as relaxed and undaunted by her outburst as Spears and his men. Spears' eyes swiveled to him. "You would do well to get your friend out of here." His voice was still eerily tranquil. "I'm sure you wouldn't want to see her in trouble, too."

Key inclined his head almost imperceptibly, but Petra could not mistake the expression in his eyes. There was nothing to be accomplished, not in this place, not tonight. She didn't care. She wasn't trying to accomplish anything. The man had taken her brother from her. She just wanted to take something from him in return. She didn't even care what it was.

"Are these people bothering you, Mr. Spears?"

Petra paused and glanced up at the large man in grey coveralls she'd seen drag off a dead man and prop him against a wall. There was no expression in his curiously blank, colorless eyes.

11

Spears shook his head. "I think they were just leaving."

"Yes," Key said in a low voice. "We were."

"No, we aren't." Petra bared her teeth at the security guard. "I just want a few moments alone with Mr. Spears."

She felt Key sigh behind her. He stepped forward and seized her arm. The grey security guard took her other. She kicked her legs, but the bodyguards stepped back to evade her. She yowled angrily as Key and the colorless man lifted her up and carried her out into the alley.

The air outside was chill and rank. As soon as her feet hit the ground, she spun around, but the security guard looked at her with an icy, immobile expression. "Get out of here, kid." His voice was a low rumble. "You're better off out there. Don't come back until you can control yourself. We can't have people attacking Nobles in here. We've got enough problems. It ain't good for business."

She hissed at him. He slammed the door closed in her face. She yanked on the large handle, but he'd locked it from the inside. She cursed and spun to face Key. He stood in the alley with his hands in his pockets. His sandy hair blew around his face. He looked remarkably calm. She glared at him.

"So that didn't go well."

She scowled. "You could have been more helpful."

"I think I was quite helpful. Just not in the manner you wanted me to be. Come on. Let's get home."

"He shouldn't be able to just walk in there and be so calm. He should have to pay for what he did to Ren."

"This isn't the way. Get a hold of yourself. You got the job done. We've got the money." He wrapped an arm around her shoulders. It should have been a soothing gesture, but his grip was firm.

She hesitated and glared at the door. "It's not right. Nothing in this city is right anymore."

"We have to get to the compound before it gets too late. They outlanders will be on their way into the city center. We don't want to meet them on the way."

Petra sighed, but she didn't argue. She nodded. He gripped her hand, and she did not resist as he pulled her along through the winding backstreets of Razor City. They glided silently through the shadows and debris. Even the vagrants ignored them. They looked away as though to avoid attracting the young man's and woman's attention, as though they feared Key and Petra might fly at them or attack.

No one trusted anyone in Razor City.

A scream rent the quiet of the night. Key paused and threw back an arm to stall Petra. She leaned against him and peered around his shoulder toward the flickering neon lights of the main street ahead. Key's fingers bit into her wrist. He crept forward, as light and quiet as a cat.

The street beyond the dark, dank alley was deserted but for three of Scarlet's Marshals, dressed in brilliant crimson suits. A young woman cowered between them. They weren't touching her, but their menacing posture suggested they intended to as soon as terrorizing her lost its hilarity.

Petra grunted in disgust. "Come on. Let's keep moving."

Key half turned his head to look at her in surprise. "You're not going to do anything?"

"Against the Marshals? Like what? She's got no chance. What do you think you're going to do?"

He scowled. She tugged on his hand, but he resisted. He took a step toward the street.

"You want to go help her? Fine." Petra released his hand and spun back toward the alley. "I'll see you back at the compound if you survive."

He didn't move. He cursed under his breath and turned his head toward her. "This isn't right, Petra."

"You do what you have to do to survive, Key." Her stomach roiled with nausea. "You don't have a choice if you want to stay alive." She took a step toward him. "You're the one who was just stopping me from fighting."

Her words didn't matter. She saw it in his eyes. She felt sick. She felt like screaming, but this was Razor City. You didn't fight Scarlet's men in Razor City, no matter how appalling and gruesome their crimes, no matter how wrong it felt to leave an innocent girl alone in their midst. Not if you wanted to stay alive.

She wished she were somewhere else. She wished she and Key and Ren were in a different city in which Scarlet's men didn't roam free, where they didn't do whatever they wanted to whomever they wanted with no consequence. She wished she were in a place where speaking out and fighting back against the horror and corruption didn't get you imprisoned or killed.

They weren't somewhere else. They were home in Razor City, and the only way to stay alive was to not get caught lurking in alleys contemplating rescuing a stranger from the king's private police force. You didn't stick your neck out for a stranger in Razor City. Sometimes, you didn't even stick your neck out for a friend.

"Key."

His brow furrowed, but he nodded shortly and caught her hand. They avoided the main streets where the Marshals patrolled, supposedly keeping the peace. There was no peace in Razor City.

Key tensed as they left the protected area of the King's territory. There were no Marshals or Nobles in the areas outside the city center. There were other dangers. The outlands were dilapidated and hostile. Smoke lingered in the air, wafting from the smoldering remains of warehouses and abandoned houses that had fallen to the vandals and outlaws.

There was noise here. Lots of it. It was as though a sound barrier lifted as they darted out of a dark, silent alley and crossed the invisible line between the King's province and the outlands. There were shouts, screams, whoops of laughter or cries of pain. A band of outlaws in leather jackets and ripped jeans prowled along the division, wary to cross. They looked as though they were waiting for some innocent to wander too close, waiting to yank them out of the circle of the King's light and into the treacherous shadows of the outlands.

Key and Petra avoided them. She clutched his hand almost painfully, sliding along the wall to remain in the deepest gloom. The street lights were burnt out in this part of the city, and the houses were quiet, dark and still. No one but the outlaws and the rebels lived in the outlands.

In the distance, in the no-man's land between the outlands and the city center, a dark, quiet monolith rose above the decrepit, abandoned houses and buildings around it. Petra relaxed. She felt Key's hand tighten convulsively in hers. The old city mall was as forgotten as the world in which it had once held a place.

"Just a bit further," Key breathed.

Almost home. The streets ahead were ravaged by the war that had torn apart the country. Vagrants' bonfires flickered among the ruins of what had once been houses, shops and cafes. The buildings that still stood were blighted by the graffiti that warned passersby of the small tribes of vandals and outlaws that had taken up inside them. There were no alleys through which to creep unnoticed through the gloom. They would have to run for it.

Key met Petra's eyes. She nodded. They ran. Just ahead, they heard shouting and loud, wicked laughter. It was coming closer. Key grabbed Petra's arm and yanked her around the side of a crumbling brick building that had once been a pizza shop. The large, round neon pizza sign above the door still buzzed, but the neon bulbs had long since been smashed by bats or slingshots or errant bullets.

Key pushed her back against the wall, standing in front of her as if to guard her as a young woman raced past. Her face was red and twisted in terror. Moments later, two men flew past in pursuit. Petra started as if to follow them, but Key pressed into her to keep her in place. "No," he hissed. "We're almost there. We have to get home. You said it yourself. It's the only way to survive. We can't rescue every foolish person who gets caught up by the Marshals or the outlaws."

She hissed air out through her teeth, but she hung her head. "I know."

"It's terrible."

"It's a terrible place."

When the shouts faded, Key stepped away from her and caught her hand. "Come on. No stopping."

"No stopping."

They raced through the streets. They didn't stop. The old mall loomed up before them, set back from the main thoroughfare. The large, razed asphalt parking lot was empty but for a few school busses with shattered windows and flat tires. Petra had never known how they'd gotten there. They had simply always been there, as long as she and Key and the others had taken shelter in the mall. She didn't mind them. They seemed to deter any errant vagrants from wandering inside.

The mall was dark. The windows had long since been blacked out and boarded over. There was no sound from inside. Key tugged her toward the side of the building. They ducked into a narrow cement tunnel. They didn't run. No one would come for them now. They were safe.

Petra breathed a sigh of relief as they strode along the lighted passage toward the thick steel door up ahead. Key smiled. "We made it."

"Another day."

"Another day."

At the end of the tunnel, he bent down and lifted a hidden panel on the right side of the door that concealed an electronic keypad. He punched in the code and yanked open the door. He held it open for Petra. He smiled. He didn't like going out into the city if he could help it, but he almost never let her go alone. He was as relieved to be home as she was.

Inside, the mall was as noisy as the club, and its tribe was as motley. Music pumped through the cavernous common room. Kids in bright, mismatched or ripped clothes with painted faces or wild haircuts skateboarded or roller bladed on a huge ramp on the far side of the room. Others gathered in small groups at tables spread around the main floor, watching the skateboarders or the others dancing to the pounding music on a large, well-tread dance floor. More played games in the corner. The younger ones chased each other around, shrieking and whooping with laughter. On the east side, a long, flat counter ran the length of the room, and several kids served drinks or food to the others.

They were all laughing, smiling or otherwise enjoying themselves. Inside the mall, it was as though the war had never happened. They were safe here, and they were together. It had happened, though, and the children and teenagers inside the mall had lost their parents, aunts, uncles or siblings to the devastation or to King Scarlet. They were the real lost children of Razor City, and this was their home.

A tall, thin teenaged girl in an olive green fatigue jacket over ripped jeans strode over as she caught sight of them from a table of the older kids. Her long, honey blonde hair was tied back in a tight braid. She'd been with the Uprising. She always wore her fatigue jacket when she visited the Uprising. Petra smiled as she approached them.

"Key. Petra." Beth's voice was as serene as a still brook. It wasn't the sort of voice that belonged in Razor City. "You're just in time for dinner. Jayne barbequed tonight. I'll have Cera bring you some plates."

Key waved his hand. "It's all right, Petra. I'll get them."

Petra glanced at him, but he smiled and strode away before she could reply. Beth lifted an eyebrow. "Long night?"

She wondered how her best friend always seemed to know exactly how she was feeling. "It did not go as expected."

Beth frowned. "Did Max try anything?"

"Yeah, but he found out real quick not to do it again." Petra frowned. "Spears was there."

Beth blinked. "Cage Spears? He was at the Blade?"

"Yeah."

16

Petra's expression must have revealed her feelings. Beth wrapped an arm around her shoulders and led her toward the small group of teenagers with whom she'd been sitting. Petra paused to hold her back. Beth lifted her eyebrows. "I'm sorry. Did you do something you ought not to have done?"

"Yes. But not what I wanted to do."

"What did you do?" Her voice was not as serene now. She looked almost angry. Beth was almost never angry.

"I just wanted to talk to him."

"Damnit, Petra, we've talked about this. We have to keep our heads down. We don't want Scarlet and the Marshals to start noticing we're out here."

"He is the one who framed Ren! He's the reason he is in prison."

Beth sighed. "I know that, but you can't do it like this."

"How else, then? What do you think is going to happen? The Uprising is going to save us all? You think they will win against Scarlet and set everyone free?" She gestured around them at the kids. "The Uprising hasn't brought any of these kids' loved ones back. They haven't brought Ren back. Your parents are still in prison. Their parents are still in prison or still dead. The Uprising hasn't done anything but stir up trouble."

"I know you're upset, Petra." Beth didn't seem offended by her friend's remarks. Her own anger seemed to have cooled. Her voice was soothing, and Petra felt herself calming almost against her will.. "I'm sorry about Ren. I am sorry for all of us and for everyone whose lives Scarlet's ruined."

"You should be angrier, Beth. You deserve to be angrier. I'm angry all the time."

Beth smiled sadly. "I know. But getting angry isn't going to help anyone."

Petra sighed. "You're right. You're right, Beth. There's no point. Everything is lost."

"That is not what I said."

"If everything rests on the Uprising's shoulders…then everything is lost. My brother might as well be dead."

"Don't be so dramatic. It won't be like this forever."

"That's easy for you to say."

She blinked. "Why?"

"Because you have hope. You have something to live for."

"I have something to fight for. And so do you, Petra." Beth turned her toward the main floor. She gestured as Petra had done. "Look around us. You did this. You and Key, Ren and I. We did this together. We have a place for these kids, a place where they can be safe and happy and healthy. We are their family now. They are ours. What chance do any of them have if you give up? You have to keep surviving."

Petra considered this. The kids looked happy. They looked as though they hadn't a care in the world, as though they'd forgotten about the pain and the death around them. It was a kid's paradise. In this place, the party never ended. No one told anyone what to do, and no one belonged to anyone unless they wanted to. It was a kid's dream, but at what cost? It hadn't been worth losing their families.

"Yeah," she murmured doubtfully.

"They are safe and happy because of you, Petra."

"They wouldn't have needed us if not for Scarlet and his Nobles."

Beth sighed. "Perhaps, but that doesn't change that they do. And that you were there for them when they needed you. Don't stop being there now. Don't let the pain suck you under until you completely lose sight of what we're doing here."

Petra thought about this. "Yeah. I'm sorry. I just...I don't know what to do. I can't help Ren at all."

"You might not believe it, but there are people who are working on it."

"I just wish I could believe they could do something."

"You just have to have hope, Petra. It's all we have in this world."

Petra nodded. She smiled at her best friend. "Thanks, Beth."

"Does that mean you feel better?"

"No, but it means I won't complain to you anymore tonight."

Beth smiled. "Well, if that's the best I can expect, I'll take it. So...since you're here, I assume you were not arrested by the Marshals."

"No. I was kicked out of the Blade by the weird bouncer, though."

"Well, it's not the first time that's happened."

Petra smirked. "No. It's not the first time. It probably won't be the last, either."

"But you got the money."

"Yes."

Beth nodded. "And you made it back without any trouble, I assume, since you both look relatively unscathed."

"Yes. We made it. One of these days, we're going to have to get some cars."

"You know there isn't any gas left in the city. Scarlet's men have taken it all, and there isn't any more coming in."

"There's gas. You just have to know who to ask."

Beth didn't reply to this. She didn't seem to want to talk about it. She didn't seem to like to talk about what the Uprising did and did not have in their hidden compound somewhere in the outlands. She liked to keep that part of her life separate from her friendship with Petra. She claimed it was to protect the mall, but Petra suspected it was more to protect the Uprising. Even within the tribe of lost children, there were those who could not be trusted. Petra knew Beth trusted her. She just didn't want to know. It was safer that way.

Beth had been sitting with four of the older kids. She tilted her head in their direction. "Come on. You should eat something."

"Yeah." She sighed, but she threaded her arm through Beth's and walked with her to join their friends at the table. She could use something to eat. She could use another drink, too. She hoped Key wouldn't bring fruit juice.

"Hi, Petra."

Petra reared back. A tall boy with dark hair and sky blue eyes appeared in their path as though he'd materialized from thin air. He smiled at them. He had a nice smile, but Petra's guard shot up as though he'd bared his teeth in a leer. She glanced at Beth. Her best friend's expression hadn't changed, but her green eyes narrowed almost imperceptibly. Beth didn't like Shaw, either.

"Hi, Shaw." Petra's voice was unenthusiastic.

If he noticed, he didn't let on. "I heard you were out in the city."

"Yeah. I was working."

"I'm glad you made it back okay. Actually, I wanted to talk to you about that. I've been working on this new program. You might find it interesting. I thought you could help me find a buyer--"

Beth stepped in smoothly, taking Petra's arm. She smiled at him. "Petra's had a really long night, Shaw. She really just needs to have some dinner."

"Oh. Yeah. I could join you--"

Beth's smile didn't waver. "We have some things we need to talk about in private. I'm sure you understand."

Shaw opened his mouth to reply, but Beth steered Petra away without a backward glance. Petra smiled gratefully at her friend. "Thanks, Beth."

"It's Shaw who should be thanking me. You looked like you needed someone to take your anger out on, and he was looking appetizing."

Petra snorted. "Yeah. You might be right. There's just something about him I don't like."

"Yeah. I know what you mean."

"He seems awfully keen to get into the inner circle."

Beth smiled. "Well, we are the coolest."

Petra laughed as they reached the table where the older kids sat. She wasn't so sure how cool they were, but she supposed she didn't blame Shaw for wanting to eat with them. Inside this compound, they were the top brass.

"Hey, Petra," Lux, a tall, muscular black girl with long, black dreadlocks greeted her with a jerk of her chin. Lux's large, dark eyes were rimmed in a shimmering red kohl. They looked huge and uncannily alert. Even as she spoke to Petra, her eyes scanned the room with a sharp, narrow gaze. She was the head of security for the compound, and she took her job extremely seriously. She was dressed in black tonight. She'd been patrolling.

Petra nodded to her. They were friends, but Lux wasn't the sentimental type. She seemed more interested in ensuring everyone was behaving themselves than socializing. She would probably be back out on the perimeter as soon as she'd finished eating the huge pile of food on her plate.

As usual, she had been paying attention. "What did Shaw want?"

Petra rolled her eyes. "He wanted to talk about some program he's working on. He wants me to find a buyer for him."

Lux's eyes snapped to the tall, dark haired boy. "I don't trust him."

Beth waved her hand. "He's fine. He's just lost. He's trying to find his way."

"We're all lost," Petra replied darkly. "But we're not all jerks."

20

Lux grunted, but she didn't say anything else. She turned her attention back to her plate.

Petra slid into the empty seat beside Jesse. He greeted her perfunctorily and turned back to the small computer in front of him. His gingery blonde hair needed a cut. It hung in his face and concealed his narrow profile from her. He was extremely skilled with computers and electronics. He wasn't a hacker like Petra, but he could do things with hardware that blew her mind. When the lost children had needed a safe shelter from Scarlet's men and the outlands, he'd discovered the looted and abandoned mall and gotten it back up and running. He'd even found a way to funnel power from the city center. If not for him, they would probably be living in the burnt out houses and shops where the vagrants gathered around bonfires and fought over scraps of food.

Key brought two plates of food and sat down beside Beth. She smiled up at him, and her translucent green eyes almost sparkled. Petra lifted an eyebrow, but she didn't say anything. She'd always suspected her best friend had more than friendly feelings for Key, but Beth had never talked about it with her. Petra hadn't brought it up.

"Thanks," Petra said, and for the first time that evening, she felt almost peaceful. Razor City was a dangerous, terrible place, but she and the lost kids had food and shelter. They didn't have to fear or want for anything as long as they remained in the walls of the compound. If Scarlet and his people knew about it, they didn't seem to care much, as long as the kids stayed out of trouble. Petra sighed and bent over her plate.

A young, pretty girl in her early teens approached the table with a couple mugs of beer. "Thanks, Cera," Key said to her. She blushed crimson red under a thick mane of black hair. She bobbed her head and scurried away before Petra could thank her.

Petra rolled her eyes, but she smirked a little into her mug. Key was popular with the girls in the compound. He was popular with most girls. He barely seemed to notice.

He smiled around at them. "Anything happening here?"

Lux shook her head. "It's been quiet. A couple of the younger kids got into it, but Eloise broke it up. No sign of outlaws, rebels or Marshals."

Key nodded. No one else seemed interested in talking. Jesse was ignoring his plate. On the other side of him, Rip was fiddling with one of his inventions. Petra didn't know what it was, but it looked like some kind of brass and glass pistol.

Rip was good with machines and especially weapons, but sometimes he didn't think things through all the way. More often than they didn't, they blew up in his face and injured him or destroyed his laboratory in the section of the mall that had once been the food court. When his work was good, though, it was really good. Beth had never confirmed it, but Petra was sure Rip was making weapons for the Uprising. If he was, it would probably tip the scales. She just couldn't be too sure in whose favor.

"Did you get the money?" Ellis was the youngest of the group of older kids. He didn't speak much, but when he did, everyone listened. He'd been a child prodigy, and he could fight as well as Lux. Petra didn't know much about him. No one knew much about him. She liked him anyway. He was as good at keeping other people's secrets as his own.

She nodded and handed him the envelope. "I haven't counted it. It had better all be there."

Ellis opened it. He only had to glance briefly at the stack of bills before he nodded in satisfaction. Max might be a pervert, but he hadn't stiffed them. "This will keep us in supplies for a couple months." He lifted his head to glanced between Petra and Key. "And by the look of you, you managed to stay out of trouble."

Petra exchanged a look with Key. She smiled a little. "Yeah. For the most part."

Key smirked and lifted his mug in salute. "To another day."

Another day. In Razor City, sometimes it was all there was left to hope for.

CHAPTER TWO

Meanwhile, at King Scarlet's luxurious palace...

Prince Dante's bedroom was as large as an apartment. The King's palace was an enormous, lavish affair. The ceilings above were tall and vaulted. The stars barely twinkled through stained glass skylights. A four poster bed with black silk sheets stood in the center of the room. Dante had slept late. He always slept late. The thick, blood red counterpane was still rumpled. He frowned slightly at it. He jabbed a button on the wall beside the double oak doors.

"Sir?" The young woman's voice was soft and hesitant.

Dante smirked. "Get up here, Claire. My room needs cleaning." There was a moment's pause. He scowled. "Now!"

Claire didn't reply, but seconds later there was a quiet rap on the door. He yanked it open. The maid was younger than he by a few years, no older than sixteen. She had been the daughter of one of Scarlet's favorite Nobles until the King's closest friend and advisor, Warin Scanlan, had fingered them for treason. When her parents had been imprisoned, Scarlet had offered the girl a home in his mansion in exchange for her servitude. It was the best Scarlet offered to the displaced children of Razor City. He'd been fond of her.

"What took so long?" Dante barked.

Claire stared at him in surprise. He relished the frightened look in her pale blue eyes. She looked thinner than he remembered. Her short, red maid's uniform hung off her meager frame. He recalled that her father's sentencing was in a few days. She was probably worried about him. She had a very good reason. Dante already knew his father intended to execute the traitor. He almost always executed treacherous Nobles; it wouldn't do to allow the others to believe they could cross the King and live to tell about it.

King Scarlet liked to send strong messages.

Claire bobbed her head. "Sorry, sir."

"Well? This room isn't going to clean itself."

She spun and hurried toward the bed. He watched her straighten the sheets for a moment with narrowed eyes, then nodded in satisfaction. The girl would make the bed perfectly. She always made it perfectly. She had learned long ago not to annoy him. He turned back to the large, wrought iron vanity mirror on the north wall.

He looked good. He never looked anything else. He tucked the tight, black, long-sleeved tee shirt into his black jeans and tossed his dark, shoulder-length hair. It fell perfectly back into place. It always fell perfectly back into place. He smirked at his reflection.

He wanted a drink, and he wanted a woman. He would have both. The city gave him exactly what he wanted. He glanced over his shoulder at Claire. She leaned over his bed, tucking the sheets tightly under the mattress—exactly the way he liked them. He considered her a moment. No. She was too thin. She was too young. He liked women with curves and experience.

She didn't know that, though, and it had been a boring day. He strode up behind her. She straightened in surprise. "Sir—"

He chuckled in her ear as she bumped backward into his lean chest. "Claire." His voice was a low purr. He felt her trembling against him. "That sheet is a little crooked."

Her body quaked. Her voice came out in a squeak. "I'll fix it, sir. Please let me fix it. Please."

He laughed and stepped back. "Don't worry, Claire. You're a little scrawny for my taste." He spun away and grabbed his black leather jacket from the hook beside the door. When he looked back at her, she was staring at him with huge, watery blue eyes. He smiled. "It had better be perfect when I get home."

Her reply was a terrified yelp. He didn't wait to listen to it. He strode out of the room. He ignored the two Marshals in red suits standing guard outside the door. When they followed him, he gave them no indication that he noticed them at all. They might as well have been invisible. He was accustomed to the bodyguards his father insisted accompany him wherever he went.

They did not speak to him. He didn't like them to speak to him. In fact, he didn't like anyone to speak to him unless he spoke to them first.

"Dante."

He spun to face Warin Scanlan on the stairs. He frowned. His father's friend was still dressed in the black suit he'd worn earlier in the day for the children's home dedication. His face was lined, and he was thin. He looked ten years older than Scarlet, though they were the same age. They'd been friends since childhood, since before the war and the inception of Razor City. His sandy hair was receding. He almost never smiled.

24

Dante lifted an insolent eyebrow and crossed his arms over his chest. "What do you want, Warin?"

"Where are you going?"

"Out."

"Out where?"

"None of your business."

Warin's deeply lined face scrunched into a frown. "Your father does not wish for you to leave the house. There have been a number of rebel uprisings and outlaws crossing into the city limits."

Dante laughed. "I can take care of myself." He pushed aside his jacket to reveal the long-barreled pistol on his belt. He smiled smugly.

Warn scowled. "It is dangerous for you out there, Dante. Your father is not going to be happy about this."

Dante shrugged. "Then don't tell him."

"You know I can't do that."

"Why? Because you're his little errand boy? His lap dog?"

The older man took a step toward him. His eyes narrowed into a furious glare. "I am his partner."

"His partner." Dante laughed. "Right. You're equal to my father like a dog is equal to his master."

Warin's eyes flared. "You know nothing about it! You're nothing but a spoiled brat! Your father and I started this city. We're the ones who made order from chaos when the war destroyed everything, when there was no one to help the people."

"No. You followed him and rode his coattails while he built this city. When the government fell, he was the one who had the power and influence to stop the looting and the chaos and bring the city back together again. You had nothing. It's under his rule. Not yours." Dante lifted his eyebrows. "Are you suggesting you would prefer to take over for him?"

Warin's expression changed abruptly. He looked suddenly frightened. "No! No. I am simply reminding you that I have been beside him from the beginning. I have helped him."

Dante snorted. He turned away from Warin and flicked his fingers in dismissal. "Then go on. Go back to him. Kneel at his feet. And leave me alone. I have things to do."

"You will not always be the King's son, Dante," Warin called after him as he started back down the stairs. "You will not always be the prince. There might come a time when you have to stand on your own, to be responsible and behave like an adult. You'll have to live on your own merit instead of riding his coattails and getting away with anything you want."

Dante lifted his head from the bottom floor to glance back up at Warin. His father's advisor glared down at him from the second floor loft. Dante looked back at him with an expression so cold, the air might have turned to ice around him. "When? When you take over? Please. No one can touch my father. He's the king. And I am the prince. I do what I want when I want, and no lapdog is going to tell me what to do."

"Fine. Just remember, Dante. Things change."

"And you're going to be the one to change them?"

"No. I'm happy. But there are whispers in the wind, and the word on the streets is some people might be looking to make some changes. It might not always be like this."

Dante shrugged. "Whatever. Nothing's changed lately, so I don't see it happening any time soon."

"You better enjoy it while it lasts."

The prince lifted his chin and grinned at him. "Oh,. I think I will." He was still laughing as the heavy front door closed behind him.

* * *

At a seedy bar in the city...

The Edge was noisy. Dante liked it noisy. The beautiful blonde girl under his arm was talking, but he couldn't hear what she was saying. He liked it that way. She was probably telling him what she intended to do to him that night. She was probably telling him what she thought he wanted to hear. She didn't know anything about what he wanted to hear. He laughed. For a moment, she looked taken aback, but then she stretched her full, red lips into a sensual smile. Her teeth were pearly white. Her dark eyes, though, still looked confused.

He leaned down and kissed her. When he pulled back, she looked a lot happier. Her smile was genuine. "You want to be with the prince tonight?" he asked.

The girl smiled and ran a long, red fingernail down his chest. Her voice was a low, husky purr. "Yes." She was probably a couple years older than him. She was the best-looking girl in the club, but there was something empty about her. Her eyes didn't flash or gleam. She smiled when he smiled. She laughed when he laughed. He didn't even remember her name.

He caught her finger abruptly, pushing it away from him. "Why?"

She blinked in confusion. "What?"

"Why do you want to be with me tonight? Because I'm the prince?"

She looked as though she wasn't sure how to answer this. Then she smiled and pressed her body against him. "You're also very hot."

Dante scowled and pushed her away from him. "Leave me alone."

"What?" She looked completely shocked.

"I said go! Leave me alone."

Her beautiful face twisted into a snarl. "You crazy son of a bitch." She glared at him and reached for her glass as though she intended to toss the amber liquid into his face.

One of Dante's bodyguards stepped forward and caught her arm. She looked up at him in surprise. She'd almost forgotten they were there, too. The large, bald bodyguard with a scar down his cheek shook his head. She vaulted out of her seat as though she'd sat on a pin. She glared over her shoulder at Dante, but he wasn't paying attention. He sipped his drink and slammed the empty glass down on the table.

She was the third girl he'd chased off that night. "You know, sir," Sean, the bald bodyguard said in a low, toneless voice, "you might have better luck if you stopped running them off."

Dante slammed his hand abruptly on the table and glared at him. "Did I ask your opinion? When I want it, I will ask. And I can't think of any reason why I would." He glared petulantly around though the flashing lights of the club. "I'm tired of these women. They just want my money and my title. Their eyes glaze over. They don't even hear what I'm saying. I might as well be speaking a foreign language. I just see dollar signs in their eyes." His head spun. He felt woozy. His vision blurred, but he blinked suddenly in surprise, squinting across the room.

"Sir, are you all right?"

"What's Cage doing?"

"Sir?"

Dante lifted his hand to point at the pale-haired Noble. "Cage." Even to his own ears, his voice sounded slow and slurred. "What's he doing?"

"He's speaking to someone, sir."

"Who?"

"I don't know him, sir. I don't recognize him."

Dante squinted through the gloom, but he couldn't see the man to whom Cage Spears was speaking. He seemed to blur around the edges. "I don't trust him."

"I don't understand, sir."

Dante waved his hand dismissively, and his vision cleared a little. He slammed his hand down on the table again. "Another drink!"

Sean and his partner glanced at each other. "You have had several, sir," Errol, the shorter, squatter guard with short, black hair said. He sounded almost nervous.

"When I want you to give me suggestions, I will ask!" Dante snapped. "I'm the goddamn prince. Get me another drink!"

Errol and Sean glanced at each other again, but Sean lifted his hand to gesture at the young, pretty waitress who lingered nearby, awaiting the prince's orders. She brought him another drink in seconds. He leered at her as she leaned over him and winked. He seemed not to remember he'd already seen her several times that night. "Thanks, doll."

He slapped a hundred dollar bill on the table. She looked at it hesitantly for a moment. He looked at her expectantly. She glanced over her shoulder at Sean and Errol. Sean nodded to her and gestured her away. She snatched up the bill and fled the table before Dante could call her back. He forgot her as quickly as she'd gone. He sipped his drink and smirked imperiously around the club.

A short man in a tattered suit staggered up to Dante's table. He looked as though he'd had a lot to drink. His small, dark eyes were blood-shot and watery. "You!" he snarled, lifting a hand to point at Dante.

Sean and Errol stepped forward, but Dante gestured them. He looked at the man in interest. "What?"

"Prince Dante, you son of a bitch!"

28

Dante pointed a finger at himself. "What? Me? What did I do?" The man lurched forward. Sean and Errol moved as though to stop him, but Dante waved his hand again. "No, no. Let him talk. I want to hear what his problem is. I haven't heard a good one in a while."

"Your men took my son from his bed! You accused him of treason!" Spittle flew from the drunk man's mouth. Dante wiped at his chin and sneered.

"He was probably guilty, then."

"He was innocent! He was just a boy! He did not even know what the paper was!"

"Ah, he was reading Uprising propaganda, then. You know the penalty. If you kept a better eye on him, you would not have lost him to the rebels."

"He was just a boy!" In the blink of his eye, he was holding a knife. He lunged toward Dante, but Sean and Errol leapt upon him and wrestled him to the ground. He continued to shriek.

Dante curled his lip. "Pathetic." He flicked his fingers dismissively. "Get him out of here."

Sean glanced at Dante as he lifted the sobbing, drunken man to his feet. The prince didn't like the look in his eyes.

"What?" Dante snapped imperiously. "You feel bad for him? He attacked me!"

"He lost his son." Sean's voice was so quiet, it barely carried over the music.

Dante slapped his hand on the table. "What did you say?"

Sean's jaw was rigid. "Nothing, sir. I am sure the boy was guilty."

The prince lifted his chin. He glanced around the club. His vision spun and blurred. He blinked to focus his gaze. "Where's Cage?"

"He's gone, sir. He left."

"I don't trust him."

"As you said, sir."

Dante surged abruptly to his feet. "This isn't any fun anymore." He wobbled slightly. Sean leaned forward to catch his arm. Dante glared at him and shrugged him off. "I can walk. I'm not a kid."

"I am sorry, sir. I only meant to help."

"Then take me home. This place is boring."

"Yes, sir."

Errol lifted a hand to speak quietly into the microphone on his sleeve. "This way, sir. The car is waiting outside."

Dante lifted his chin, but he didn't argue. He allowed the two bodyguards to lead him through the flashing club into a long, narrow hallway. A black, unmarked door led out into the dark alley outside. Dante's car wasn't there. It was quiet, but there was a soft, relentless buzz from the broken neon sign above the building across the way. Most of the bulbs had been shattered. Only the large red O still glowed.

"...this is the new one?"

Dante thought he recognized the voice murmuring in the shadows down the alley. He spun slowly toward it.

"...just out." He didn't recognize the second man, but he was sure he knew the first, even if he could not place it.

"Let me see it...it's good. It will inspire many to join the cause."

Dante frowned and lurched toward the two men. Sean and Errol weren't paying attention to him. They spoke into their radios and stepped toward the entrance to the alley to watch for the large, black car that would take the prince home. They didn't notice when he wandered away, into the shadows of the alley.

When the first man spoke again, Dante recognized him instantly. "How soon will they be available?" Cage Spears asked. He held something up, but Dante couldn't see it in the dim light. Cage stood just on the edge of the halo of the red neon light. Dante couldn't see the other man. He frowned and staggered forward. His mind was sluggish and slow, but he knew something wasn't right. These people shouldn't be here.

"Prince Dante! Your car is here."

Cage and the man with him jumped as headlights flashed in their faces. They split apart instantly and streaked into the shadows. Dante started after Cage, but he had disappeared into the darkness. The prince couldn't even be sure he'd seen him at all.

"Prince Dante."

He spun back toward the car. "Yeah. Okay. I'm coming."

* * *

The same night at the King's palace...

Cage Spears stepped out of the shadows of the grand foyer of King Scarlet's mansion. Dante stumbled backward to avoid colliding with him. His eyes narrowed. "How did you get here so fast?" Dante barked.

Cage did not reply. His dark eyes were curiously watchful and uncannily alert. He watched the prince as he swayed in place. Dante lifted a hand to point at him. "Hello, Dante."

"You. I know what you are up to. You're working with the Uprising."

Cage lifted an eyebrow. He looked completely unfazed by the accusation. "You're drunk, Dante. That's ridiculous."

"I saw you in that alley. I know you had rebel papers."

"You don't know what you saw. You can barely stand up."

"I am not that drunk. I know you were there. In the alley with that rebel."

"So what? I was gathering information about the Uprising for your father. I do work for your father. You know that."

He didn't look worried, but he should have. Dante narrowed his eyes. He lurched toward Cage and reached out so quickly, the older man barely saw him move. Dante snatched the corner of glossy black paper from his pocket. He held it up to his eyes. His vision was blurry, but he could see the large, blood red letters emblazoned on the black cover: *Scarlet's City of Blood*. He waved it in Cage's face.

"Then what is this?"

Cage grabbed at the paper, though his face remained as cold and serene as before. "I have to show that to your father."

"Oh. I'm sure that's what you were going to do with it. What do you think my father would say if he knew you were hiding it?"

"I'm not hiding it. I'm just gathering information. We have to know what we are up against. We have to know how the Uprising are recruiting so we can counter it."

Dante scoffed. "You're lying. You're one of them, aren't you?"

Cage frowned. "Dante, you don't know what you're talking about. You're drunk."

"I'm not that drunk."

"You're imagining things. Go to bed. Sleep it off."

"I am the prince! I won't be spoken to like a child." He glared at Cage. "I am the prince. And you will do what I say, not the other way around."

Cage lifted his chin. "I am your father's man, Dante. Not yours."

Dante smirked. "Not anymore. What do you think my father would say? What do you think he would do to you if I told him I caught you conspiring with a rebel at the Edge?"

"I was not conspiring."

"That's not what it looked like to me. I'm sure I saw you planning something. You might have even given him money to fund the rebellion." He was warming up to the idea. He didn't care if Cage was guilty of working with the Uprising or not. He probably wasn't. It didn't mean he couldn't take advantage of the situation. He wanted to see Cage break. He'd never seen the Noble so much as raise his voice. Dante didn't like a man whose buttons he couldn't push. He held up the pamphlet between his fingers. "And then I found this on you."

Cage narrowed his eyes. Dante was enjoying himself. "What do you want, Dante?"

The prince lifted his chin. "I'm not sure. Not yet. But I will think of something. And you will do it." He tucked the pamphlet into his jacket pocket. "Because I still have this."

"Scarlet will never believe you."

"No? Why not? I'm his son. Besides, you know as well as I that it doesn't matter if you're guilty or not. You know what he does to anyone he thinks might turn on him. You know what this will mean for you." He smirked. "You know where you will end up. You'll do what I say. When the time comes, you'll do exactly what I saw. Like my little lapdog. You're mine now, Cage. I own you."

Cage did not reply to this. His expression did not change as he watched Dante stagger up the stairs. Cage could hear the prince's low, cold laughter echoing even as he disappeared up the stairs.

* * *

Another day in Razor City...

The King's Ransom was quieter than the Blade club. There were no rebels or outlaws lurking in the darker corners exchanging papers or envelopes stuffed with bills. There were no dancers in masks. There was no one dancing at all.

Quiet, bluesy jazz music played just over the voices of the small groups of men and women sitting at the bar or in blood red velvet covered booths around the room.

The place was swarming with Marshals. They lounged about the room in groups or alone with young, beautiful women. Some of them stood around, eyeing the patrons with narrow, watchful eyes.

Petra shouldn't be there. She really shouldn't be there alone. It was too dangerous.

Her heart thumped nervously. It wasn't safe in the city for her or any of the other lost children. It wasn't safe for anyone who wasn't one of Scarlet's men. It wasn't even safe for the bounty hunters, but they didn't look worried or afraid. A small group of them strode into the club. They looked as though they'd just come in off a hunt. Their clothes were ripped, and a few of them were bruised, limping or nursing broken fingers or arms.

Petra eyed them warily. They wore guns on their belts. Even the Marshals didn't seem interested in approaching them. Petra ducked her head as she sipped her drink. Her face wasn't on any WANTED posters yet, but she knew the King would be happy to get his hands on her. She didn't work for anyone in particular, but she suspected she'd done enough jobs to have drawn his attention. She was lucky neither the King nor the Marshals had ever seen her face.

Tonight wasn't the night she intended to show it to them.

A tall, thin woman with a short, platinum blonde Mohawk glanced toward Petra. Petra's stomach flipped. The blonde woman didn't wear a badge or carry a gun like the other bounty hunters with her. She had a knife strapped to her thigh. It was huge and sharp. There was a scar on one side of her face, from her white hairline to the bottom of her lip. Despite it, despite the patch that covered the scarred eye, she was beautiful.

She met Petra's gaze. Petra held her breath as the woman approached her.

She didn't speak to her, not at first. She paused beside Petra at the bar and motioned the publican for a drink. He brought her a beer. For a moment, she sipped it pensively, then she turned her head and looked at Petra. "Hi."

Petra stared at her. She didn't know what the hunter wanted, but she didn't want to give the woman any reason to look too closely at her. "Hey."

The bounty hunter lifted an eyebrow, but her voice was low and almost gentle. "You look a little young to be in here."

Petra lifted her chin in irritation. "I'm old enough."

The blonde woman didn't smile. She looked at Petra seriously. "Listen, you still have a chance, kid. You still have the opportunity not to have to spend the rest of your life hanging out in places like this."

Petra blinked at her in surprise. "What do you care?"

"I was like you once. I'd given up. I thought there was nothing I could do but give in." She sighed and glanced around. "Look at me now. I spend my life lurking around places like this, going fight to fight. Hunting bounties. It's all I can do. It's too late for me. You still have a chance. Get out of here while you still can."

Petra stared at her. She opened and closed her mouth. Then she scowled. "Maybe I like places like this."

The blonde bounty hunter chuckled dryly. "Fine. I'm just trying to help. You think there's no point now? You think you've given up now, just wait. Wait until there's no hope left. You still have some now. I can see it in your eyes." She reached up to flip the black patch up onto her forehead. The eye underneath was milky white. "See mine? There's nothing there anymore but pain and death."

Petra shivered. The blonde woman turned away from her as quickly as she came and strode back toward her partners at a table in the corner. Petra didn't feel any better when she'd gone. Her stomach roiled. She considered getting up and leaving, forgetting about her meeting and the client.

It was too late. Petra's client was already striding over to her on unsteady high heels. She was a haggard-looking woman in her late thirties. She wore too much makeup, and her dress was too tight. Her bleached blonde hair fell around her shoulders. Some grey showed through the dark roots on top. She looked like the kind of woman who hadn't accepted that her prime had ended years ago. Petra felt a stab of pity for the woman. At least the blonde bounty hunter knew what she was.

The woman sat down next to Petra. Petra didn't know her name. Her client didn't know hers, either. It was safer that way. Her client eyed her doubtfully for a long moment. "You're a bit young, aren't you?"

Petra rolled her eyes. She heard this a lot. "How old was Steve Jobs when he invented the Apple computer?"

Her client stared at her blankly.

"Oh, just because the government fell and the world is in chaos doesn't mean the past never happened." Petra could see this meant nothing to the woman. "Anyway, I'm old enough to know what I'm doing. What is it you need me to do?'

The woman sighed. She tapped a long, red fingernail on the bar. "My husband. I think he's been cheating on me."

Petra stared at her. "Why don't you hire a private detective? That's not exactly what I do."

The woman looked offended. "I tried to hire someone. They couldn't find anything. I think he's been talking to someone on the computer."

Petra sighed. "All right. Have you got his passwords?"

"No. The other guy I hired couldn't find them, either. That's why I called you."

"Do you at least have his email address?"

The woman nodded. She fumbled through her handbag for a moment and drew out a pen. She scribbled an email address on a napkin and slid it across the bar toward Petra. Petra stared down at the napkin for several seconds. Finally, she laid her hand on the napkin and slid it back to the woman. She shook her head. "I'm sorry. I can't take this job."

"What? What do you mean? You said you would take any job. You came highly recommended!" She sounded as though she might become hysterical.

"I'm sorry." Petra's eyes drifted over her client's shoulder. The blonde bounty hunter with the eye patch sat in a small group with a few other hunters. They looked as mean and dangerous as she. They were taking shots and laughing raucously. The blonde woman's good eye, though, looked as dead and empty and cold as her blind one. Petra looked back at her client. "This isn't the sort of job I do."

Her client opened her mouth in a sort of angry snarl. "What am I supposed to do?"

"Why don't you talk to your husband? Or better yet, find someone to talk to yourself. Maybe it would be good for you."

The woman shot out of her seat so quickly, Petra grabbed her drink to keep it from overturning. The compound could use the money. Maybe she shouldn't turn her away. If she was angry enough, she could bring the Marshals or the bounty hunters down on her. They might not know her name or her face, but that didn't mean they wouldn't pounce on the chance to bring her to King Scarlet.

If the woman had been a Noble, Petra wouldn't have turned her away. It was never a good idea to turn away a Noble, no matter what they asked. Petra sighed. "I'm sorry," she told her. "I hope you find what you're looking for. I just can't be the one to do it for you." She rose from her own seat. The woman opened her mouth as though she intended to reply, but Petra strode quickly away before she could raise an alarm to the Marshals or the hunters.

She wouldn't, though, not unless she wanted them to start looking at her. No one was innocent in Razor City. Petra didn't turn back around to see what the woman intended to do. She hurried toward an exit in the back. She would feel better once she was in the shadows of the alley on her way back to the compound.

She pushed open the back door. No one tried to stop her or call her back. No one seemed to notice her at all. When she stepped out into the dark alley, she breathed a sigh of relief. She wished Key was with her. The walk back to the compound wasn't long, but it was dangerous. She shouldn't have snuck out without him. She would have liked to have him here with her now. She would have to do it on her own.

She didn't get far.

She heard a moan from the shadows. It sounded pitiful. There was an odd sort of rustling, as though someone was crawling through the debris on the ground. She hesitated. Key would have looked to see if the person needed help. She would have argued with him and forced him to leave them behind.

For some reason, she didn't turn away. She dug into the satchel on her hip and pulled out a small, glowing red light. She held it away from her body. She gripped her gun and crept toward the sound several feet away. She knew she shouldn't do it. It could be a trap or a trick. It could get her killed.

"Hello? Is someone there? I can't see you. Please help me."

She jumped when he spoke. She stepped closer. The red light suddenly illuminated the body lying on the ground. It was a man. A young man. He was curled into the fetal position, and he looked as though he had taken a beating. Even in the red light, she could see spatters of blood around him. His black shirt and pants were slick.

She bent down cautiously several feet away from him. He lifted his head to look around for her. Even through the curtain of his dark, shoulder-length hair, she recognized his gorgeous, sculpted features and storm cloud grey eyes. She opened and closed her mouth in shock.

Prince Dante?

CHAPTER THREE

In a filthy alley outside the King's Ransom on another day in Razor City...

Petra dropped the red light and backed into the shadows.

The prince pushed himself up into a sitting position. It looked as though it hurt to move. Even in the dim, blood red glow, his expression was scared and hunted. "Where are you? I can hear you, but I can't see you. I'm hurt. Please help me."

He didn't sound like the arrogant, imperialistic plutocrat she'd seen on television. She hesitated. She edged slightly closer. Her mind raced. She wasn't sure exactly what she intended to do, but an insane idea was forming in the back of her mind. She ignored it for the moment.

Dante pushed laboriously to his feet. For a moment, he wobbled unsteadily. Then he stumbled. Petra made her decision in a split second. She rushed forward and caught him around the waist. She staggered under his weight, but they didn't fall. He leaned into her to steady himself. He moaned softly as though the effort had been painful.

In the faint, bloody light, he looked down at her. He was nearly a head taller. His eyes were stormy, brilliant grey. They looked curiously soft, curiously gentle. He looked nothing like Prince Dante Scarlet. He looked like a lost, scared little boy. Petra's heart skipped a beat.

"What happened to you?"

He shook his head. His fingers bit into her arm. "I don't know. I don't remember."

Petra frowned slightly. "What are you even doing here?"

"Do you know me?"

She paused. For a moment, she wasn't sure what she should say. "You don't remember?"

His eyes were huge and frightened. "I don't remember anything."

"What do you mean you don't remember anything?"

He pressed a hand to his head. "I don't know. I don't remember. They must have hit me in the head."

"Who hit you?"

"I told you! I don't remember! Please! Do you know me?" He gripped her arm so tightly, she was sure his fingers would leave bruises on her pale skin.

She replied before she thought it through completely. "Yes. Of course. It's me. Petra."

"Petra?" He said it slowly, as though he was trying to hear something familiar in the sound. "I know you?"

She nodded. "We live together."

"What?" He sounded completely shocked. She rolled her eyes.

"Not like that. We live together in a compound with some other kids."

"Oh."

"Come on. I'll take you. We'll be safe once we get there."

He sighed and leaned against her. "Okay."

Petra's stomach roiled uneasily. The prince looked so different. He looked scared and tired and hunted. There was something young and vulnerable about him. She knew what she was about to do was wrong, but it didn't matter. She didn't have a lot of choice, not anymore. This was Prince Dante, King Scarlet's son. No matter how sad and trusting he looked, he was the enemy. She could think of several uses for the King's son.

There was too much to lose to let the opportunity pass.

"Come on. The compound is just a little ways away, but you have to be quiet. We have to be careful. It isn't safe on the streets at night." She peered up at him. He looked back at her as raptly and innocently as a child. "Do you understand?"

"Yes."

"Can you move all right?"

"Yeah. I think so. It hurts, but I think I can manage." He was staring down at her with an odd look in his eyes. He smiled wanly.

Her stomach roiled again. "Ribs?"

He pressed his head to his side. He huffed out a breath. "Yeah, I think so."

Petra sighed. "Okay. We'll take it slow." She reached into her satchel and fumbled out her cell phone. She punched Key's number up on speed dial.

He answered in seconds. "Petra? Are you okay?"

"Yeah. I'm bringing…" She paused and met the prince's tempestuous grey eyes. They made her feel strange. "Grey. I'm bringing Grey home."

"What?" Key demanded on the other end of the line. "What the hell are you talking about? Who's Grey?"

"He's been hurt. He'll need medical attention. Meet me in my room."

"Petra, are you bringing someone here?"

"Yes."

Key sighed. "Are they safe?"

She chuckled wryly. "No. Not exactly."

"What? What do you mean?"

"You'll see."

"Petra, are you up to something you ought not to be?"

She considered this. The prince didn't look as though her conversation was worrying him. He just looked lost. "Yes, but we don't have a lot of choice. You'll see when we get home. We're coming through the back entrance. Can you be waiting there for us? I don't want anyone else to see him…like this."

He sighed heavily. "You'd better have a really good reason for this, Petra."

"I do. See you in fifteen minutes."

"Grey?" the prince asked as she hung up the phone. "Is that my name?"

Petra stared at him a split second. Then she smiled. "Yeah. It's…what we all call you. On account of your eyes."

His brow furrowed, and he opened his mouth to reply to this.

She pressed a hand to his mouth. "Shh. Don't talk anymore. You need to save your strength for the trip home."

"It's dangerous?"

"Yeah."

"Why?"

She almost laughed. It would be dangerous for Prince Dante to wander the streets of Razor City alone. It was suicide for Grey, who had no idea who Prince Dante was. If someone came across him in this state, he'd be lucky if they didn't kill him. And if they didn't kill him…

Well, they'd probably do exactly what she was doing right now. Find a way to use him.

"The outlanders come out at night. Sometimes they rob people or hurt them."

"Is that what might have happened to me?"

She didn't want to think too much about what had happened to him. This gentle, innocent man had been Prince Dante, the King's ruthless, vicious son only moments ago. He had probably deserved it. It probably hadn't been as random as an outlander attack. She didn't bother to tell him the outlanders rarely wandered this far into the city center.

"Yeah," she told him. "It might have been."

Whomever had attacked the prince, they had surely known exactly who he was. In fact, she ought to get him quiet and get him out of there as quickly as she could. There could be someone coming back to finish the job any second now. She was amazed he'd been left alive. If he'd remembered anything, he might have been able to tell her why. Perhaps they were both better off not knowing what had really happened.

He didn't speak again as they stole through the alleys, slinking through the shadows toward the compound. She was glad. Her heart pounded as she struggled to keep him moving quickly toward the edge of town. She didn't think she could fight off any thieves, outlanders or bounty hunters who recognized them. It would be worse if they encountered any of the King's Marshals. Her charade wouldn't hold up for long. She needed it to hold up at least as long as it took to get him under lock and key before he remembered that Grey didn't exist.

There was a shout in the street beyond the darkness of the alley. It was a girl. Several men laughed in response. It was mean laughter. Petra had heard it before. The prince hesitated. He lurched away from Petra toward the voices. "What are you doing?" she hissed.

He peered out of the shadows toward the voices. Four of the King's Marshals surrounded a young girl. Petra had seen it before. Grey had never seen it. He started toward them with a scowl.

Petra caught his arm. "No! You can't go out there!"

He turned back to look at her. The expression in his grey eyes took her by surprise. He looked angry. He looked as though he intended to rush out and save the day, completely mindless of the danger and his injuries. "We have to help her."

"No. You can't." Petra clutched his arm. "Those are King Scarlet's men. They're his private army. You can't save her, and they'll kill you for interfering."

"But she's in trouble."

"She'll live. If you go out there, you'll both be dead."

His brow furrowed. He looked toward the street then back at her. "We can't leave her. It isn't right."

Her fingers bit into his skin. "You don't have a choice, Grey. It's the way it is here."

He pushed his hand through his dark, mussed shoulder-length hair. He glared at her with stormy eyes. "Am I the sort of person who would just let this happen?"

She thought about this for a moment. She wasn't sure how to reply. She didn't know what sort of person Grey was. She knew Prince Dante was the sort of person who would have been there, in the thick of things, egging the men on or joining them. She didn't know anything about what Grey would do. "You're the sort of person who knows not to stick his nose in business that could get him killed. You're smart enough to stay out of it." She hoped he was, anyway.

He scowled. "I don't like this, Petra."

"You don't have to like it. But if you want to live, you have to leave it alone and come with me. I'm sorry." She stepped up to peer up into his face. "It's horrible. But it's the way it is."

He glanced away angrily. "How can we live like this?"

"It's the way it is in Razor City. King Scarlet and his people do whatever they want."

"Scarlet?" Something flashed in Grey's eyes. He frowned as though he was trying to remember something.

Petra's pulse raced. "What? What is it?"

"A face. A man. He's angry." His eyes cleared, and he looked back down at her. "I think I remember him."

Her breath caught in her throat, but she didn't reply to this.

"He seems like a real jerk."

Petra laughed wryly. "He is. Come on, Grey. Please. We have to get back. I have to get you looked at."

"Are you taking me to a doctor?"

"A medic. He's as good as a doctor. He'll take care of you." She tugged urgently on his arm. "Please. I'm sorry you have to let that happen out there, but we really, really have to go. I'm sorry."

He sighed, but finally he relented. When he turned back toward her, she was shocked to see a single tear streak down his cheek. He dashed it away angrily and nodded sharply. She steered him back toward the edge of town, but a strange sensation crept over her. She had thought Prince Dante was as bad as his father. She had heard the rumors and the stories of the misery he visited upon anyone foolish enough to get in his way. She realized now that she really didn't know anything at all.

There wasn't time to think of it now. She could ponder the impact of nature versus nurture another time.

Grey was limping heavily by the time they reached the old mall. Petra struggled under his weight. He'd looked wiry and slender on television, but he was more solid in person than she'd expected. She was relieved to see Key waiting for them around the back of the compound. When he saw them, he rushed forward to take Grey's weight from her.

The dim, flickering light above their heads illuminated the prince's pale face. Even with the bruises and blood dripping from his brow into his grey eyes, Key could not mistake him. He paused and stared between them in shock. "Petra?" he said. He glanced at the prince. "Grey?"

Petra's eyes bore into his. "He was attacked outside the King's Ransom."

Key stared between them for another indecisive moment.

"A little help, please, Key?"

"Oh. Right. Sorry." He stepped forward and ducked under the prince's arm. He didn't ask any more questions, but he scowled at Petra. She would hear about it later.

Grey frowned and reached out his hand. "Petra."

She looked back at him in surprise. She took his hand. His fingers clenched around hers almost urgently. She avoided Key's eyes. "Does anyone else know we're coming?" she asked. She was pleased that her voice sounded even. She felt as though her stomach was turning somersaults.

Key's expression went blank. "No. I didn't tell anyone. They're at dinner. We can get through the back without anyone noticing us."

"Okay. Good."

Grey frowned as they entered the long hallway. The overhead lights were off. Small red track lights illuminated their path toward the gated off area of the mall. "What is this place?" His voice was low and toneless, but Petra suspected he was nervous. An almost imperceptible tremor passed through his hand to hers.

"It's the compound where we live." Petra met Key's gaze. "Grey doesn't remember anything."

Key's brilliant blue eyes widened for a split second. Then he nodded. "Right. I understand. Come on, Grey. We'll get you fixed up."

"Thanks." They stepped out of the hall into a small vestibule. On one side, a metal gate closed off areas of the mall that had been destroyed in the looting and the fires. On the other side, a hallway led toward the shop spaces that the older kids had taken as their private rooms.

Grey didn't say anything as Key and Petra led him to the shop she used as a bedroom. She gently shook off Grey's hand to unlock the padlock on the gate. Not all the older kids or even the younger kids who shared their bedrooms on the main floor locked up their rooms. Petra, though, liked her privacy. She yanked open the heavy metal gate and pushed aside the thick emerald green curtain that hid the inside of the room from any outside observers.

Key hoisted Grey inside. Petra gestured toward the large, round bed in the center of the room. A silvery grey counterpane lay haphazardly upon it, as though she'd tossed it hastily off when she'd awakened. She had. She strode forward and pushed it aside. "Just put him down there," she ordered.

Grey sat heavily on the bed and looked around at Petra's room with an expression of unconcealed surprise. It had once been an electronic store, but it had been completely looted before she'd gotten to it. It was a huge room, though, and it served her purpose nicely. It was the first place that had felt like home since she'd been a small girl and her parents had been killed in the war.

Her computers covered an entire side of the room. Large, flat screen monitors lined the wall. The floor on the other side of the room was littered with tossed aside clothes, hand-held video games and shoes. She kicked them out of the way a little sheepishly; she hadn't expected to host a prince in her bedroom or she would have cleaned up.

"What is this place?" Grey asked again as Key bent over him to examine his wounds.

Petra paced in front of the bed. Her fingers itched. She wanted to sit down at her computers and--well, she didn't know what she wanted to do. She needed to think about what was going on, about Prince Dante and Grey and the way his sad, scared eyes made her stomach turn over. A computer probably wasn't going to be much help there.

"I told you," she said in a slightly sharp voice. "It's the compound."

"I mean, what is it?"

"Oh." She glanced at Key, but he ignored her pointedly. "It used to be a shopping mall. After the war, it was looted and half of it was burnt out. People took most of what wasn't bolted down and burned the rest--that gated off area we passed is where most of the damaged happened. It's not safe for the littler kids to wander around back there, so we keep it closed off. Most of the rest of the place is okay, though. There were still some beds and some furniture left over that was too big to carry out. There were even some food supplies and storage that no one found."

"And we all live here?"

Petra gestured around. "Sure. It's one of the nicest places in the city. We have everything we need here. Electricity, running water, Internet, plenty to eat, and a safe place to hide from Scarlet's people and the outlanders."

"They don't know about it?"

Petra shrugged. "If they do, they don't seem to care. They don't bother us here. They aren't interested in a bunch of lost kids."

Grey blinked. "Lost kids?"

Key glanced up at Petra. He looked as though he didn't approve of her telling the prince about their hideout. She wondered if he suspected Grey was faking. For a split second, she wondered if he might be right. The prince's eyes were so innocent, and they peered up at her with such frank, guileless trust, she almost felt guilty about what she was doing to him.

"Everyone who lives here has lost their family to the war or King Scarlet and his people," she explained in a low voice.

"Lost how?"

"Some died in the fighting during and after the war. Others were accused of treason by the Nobles and imprisoned or executed."

Grey's brow furrowed. "I don't understand."

"We'll explain everything to you once you've been cleaned up and gotten some rest," Key told him in a surprisingly gentle voice. He seemed to have decided the prince was harmless for the moment. He hated Dante and Scarlet as much as Petra, but he wouldn't refuse to help anyone if they needed him; it wasn't in his nature. "You look like you've been through hell. Do you know what happened?"

Grey shook his head, but Petra answered for him. "He doesn't remember any of it."

"That's probably for the better. It's worse than I expected. I need to get some supplies." Key rose and jerked his head at Petra. "Petra?" She followed him toward the door. He spoke in a quiet voice, but Grey didn't even seem to be trying to overhear. "What are you planning to do with him?"

He might not be trying to overhear them, but that didn't mean he couldn't. "He can stay in here until he feels better. I've got plenty of room for two." She stared pointedly into Key's eyes. He sighed.

"Are you sure about this?"

"It'll be fine. I can sleep on the bean bag chair or something."

"That is not what I meant."

Petra lifted her chin. "I'm sure."

When he was gone, Grey held out his hand to Petra. She perched on the bed beside him. "I can go to my own room, if I'll make you uncomfortable."

She wasn't sure how to answer this. She took his hand. He clenched his fingers around hers. "It's okay. I would prefer to keep an eye on you until you are feeling better."

He smiled. It was such a nice smile. Her breath caught in her throat. "I want to stay with you, Petra."

She felt her cheeks heat. She ducked her head to hide her blush behind her long, pale blonde hair. Grey lifted a hand to brush it aside. She looked at him in surprise. He didn't say anything, but his expression sent her heart racing. For a strange moment, she remembered the cold, austere face she'd seen on television days ago. He didn't look anything like that now. He made her very nervous.

Key swept back into the room, startling her. She shot to her feet as though he'd caught them doing something they shouldn't. Grey looked at her bemusedly, but he didn't ask any questions. He leaned back on the thick, plump pillows and kept quiet as Key bent over him.

Key didn't say anything, either, and his expression was perfectly neutral. Petra had known him long enough to know he was not happy about this. His shoulders were tense. She didn't look forward to hearing what he had to say about the prince, but when he understood what she intended to do, he'd get over it.

Maybe.

She paced as Key patched up the prince's wounds. They were bad. She was actually surprised he was still conscious, but he gritted his teeth against the pain. She suspected he had a few cracked ribs. His ankle might have been broken. He looked as though he'd put up a fight. His knuckles were bruised as if he'd gotten in a hit or two of his own. He didn't make a peep. When Key cleaned the blood and grime from his face, it was swollen and bruised. She almost hadn't even noticed. She'd been too wrapped up in his expressive eyes and his unnerving good looks.

Now she paused and eyed him narrowly. He met her gaze. She couldn't hold his eyes. She turned away from him. She pushed her hands through her hair. She could still feel his stare as it followed her from one side of the room to the other. She seriously wondered for the first time who had attacked him in the alley. Outlanders, disgruntled citizens, the boyfriend of some girl he hit on at the bar...

Prince Dante had a lot of enemies. He was one of the most hated people in Razor City. Anyone could have come upon him in the alley, recognized him and taken advantage of the opportunity. It wouldn't be the first time one of the King's people had been taken alone and unaware. The prince, though, usually traveled with at least a couple bodyguards. Where had they been?

"I think that's as good as we're going to get," Key said finally.

Petra spun back toward the bed. Grey looked better. His faced was cleaned and his wounds were bandaged. He smiled weakly at Key. "Thanks for fixing me up."

Key patted his shoulder a little awkwardly. He looked up at Petra. She perched on the edge of the bed. Grey reached for her hand. He looked as though he wanted to say something to her. He didn't. She brushed his dark hair from his eyes without thinking. "You should get some sleep."

He groaned. "I don't know if I can sleep. It hurts."

Petra glanced at Key. He was frowning slightly, but he nodded and dove into the first aid kit beside the bed. He handed Grey a couple pills. "Take these. They'll help with the pain and help you sleep."

Grey hesitated, but Petra nodded encouragingly. "It's okay, Grey. You can trust Key. He wouldn't let you take anything that would hurt you. You should get some sleep."

This seemed good enough for him. He tossed the pills into his mouth and swallowed them. He leaned back on the pillows. "Thanks, Key." His eyes rolled back to Petra. "I'm lucky you found me, Petra."

Her eyes cut to Key, but she nodded. "Yeah. Lucky."

"Did you know where I would be?" Grey's voice sounded a little dreamy, but his eyes were still alert.

She looked at Key again, but he didn't offer any help. She'd chosen to lie to the prince. It was her show. "No. But you knew I was working a job at the King's Ransom. You must have come back to find me after you were attacked."

"By outlanders," he murmured. His eyes were starting to droop a little now.

Key's mouth tightened. He glanced at Petra. "Yeah," she said. "By outlanders."

"Where did I go tonight?"

Petra shook her head. "I don't know. You didn't tell me where you were going."

He could barely keep his eyes open. "Oh."

She pulled the silver counterpane up to his chin. "Maybe you'll remember more when you wake up."

He was asleep before he'd finished nodding. Key stepped forward and seized Petra's arm. He dragged her all the way out of the room and into his own. It was much neater than hers. "What the hell are you thinking?" he hissed.

Petra yanked free of him and crossed her arms over her chest. "I found him beaten up in the alley outside the club. He had no memory. What else should I have done? Turn him into one of the King's men?"

Key frowned. "You have no idea what happened to him?"

"No. I just found him like this. He was alone. I don't know what happened to his bodyguards."

Key sighed. "So the King might not even know he's missing yet."

"Right. And when he figures it out..."

"What are you planning to do with him, Petra?" His voice suggested he suspected whatever she planned was a bad idea.

"He's the prince, Key! We have leverage now."

"Leverage?"

"Over the King. We could use him...maybe with him we can get Ren back. And the others."

He frowned. "How do you think that will work?"

"When they discover he is missing, we can trade him."

"That's crazy, Petra. It's too risky. We can't do something like that. Scarlet's people would kill us all."

"Not if they can't find us. We'd have to be careful, but we could work it out. We can't let this opportunity pass, Key."

He sighed. "We should talk to the inner circle about this."

She frowned. "How long do you think we have until he regains his memory?"

"No idea. It could be minutes. It could be never. I'm not a doctor. Do you plan to just lie to him until then?"

"Yeah, that's pretty much exactly what I planned. We need to keep him here until we have our opening to use him."

He stared at her for a moment as though he hardly recognized her. "Petra, this is...I don't even know what this is."

"It's all we've got, Key! If we play this right, we could get our friends and family back."

"Yes, and if we mess it up, this entire compound and everyone in it is in danger."

Petra lifted her chin. "Then we won't mess it up."

* * *

Meanwhile, in dreamland...

He was small. He knew he was small because Elia was small, and he stood at exactly the same height. Elia was a pirate. He was a pirate, too. They wore red bandanas and black eye patches, and they brandished their swords at each other in an epic battle to the death. He was having fun. He always had fun playing with Elia.

He jabbed his sword at Elia, who giggled and smacked it away with his own sword. They clanked like metal, and they gleamed in the sun. They weren't sharp, but they were real swords. They hurt when they hit each other. They weren't supposed to hit each other with them, but they did anyway. There was a bruise on his arm. Elia's leg looked purplish, but they were having fun and real pirates got hurt.

They were in his backyard. It was sunny and warm. The grass was soft and green. A man came over the rise of the hill. He saw the man over Elia's shoulder. He wasn't scared. His father's friends came sometimes and played with them. They brought him toys and masks and hats to play with.

The man was carrying a gun. Pirates used guns sometimes, but he really wanted a cannon. The man raised his gun. Elia didn't see the man or his gun. He didn't know what was happening, but for the first time, he felt a shiver of fear. There was shouting in the distance. Men in red suits came running over the hill toward the man with the gun.

They were too late. He'd never heard a noise so loud. It was like an explosion. If cannons sounded like that, maybe he didn't want one. He covered his ears, but it was too late. He fell to the ground. There was another explosion. He trembled. What had happened to him? He didn't feel as if anything had happened to him.

He opened his eyes. The men in red suits stood over the man with the gun. A large, red puddle pooled around the man's body. He looked around. Elia. Elia was laying in a puddle, too. He rushed toward his friend. What was this game?

Elia wasn't playing a game. Red spread over Elia's white shirt.

"Elia?" His voice was small and scared.

Elia's tiny fingers clutched feebly in the air. "Daddy..."

"Elia?" He didn't understand what was happening. Elia didn't move or speak, but his eyes were open. He prodded at him, but nothing happened. Elia didn't sit up or laugh as though he'd played a masterful trick.

There was more shouting. He looked up. His vision blurred with tears. He couldn't see his father's face, but he knew his voice. He knew he was there. Elia's father screamed and fell to the ground beside him. He tried to prod him awake, too, but it didn't work. Elia's father clutched him to his chest and sobbed.

The scene spiraled wildly, as though he was spinning quickly round and round. He couldn't see his father. He couldn't see Elia's father. He could only see Elia, who seemed fixed in space, lying silent and still in a pool of thick, crimson blood....

* * *

Grey shot up in bed. Ice cold sweat dripped from his brow and soaked the sheets. He gasped. "Petra?" For a moment, his vision blurred and he couldn't see anything in the pitch black room. "Petra!"

A tiny light sparked in the darkness. He heard her move before he saw her. Her pale face appeared above him. Her long, blonde hair brushed his cheek. "What's the matter, Grey?" Her voice was soft and gentle. The moment he heard it, he relaxed. He reached for her.

"Petra."

She wrapped her fingers around his. His hands were slick with sweat. "It's okay. It was a dream. Did you have a nightmare?"

He sighed. "I saw a little boy. He was shot. I was there. I saw him die."

He could barely see her face in the dim light, but he thought he saw her brow furrow.

"Was it a memory?"

She stared at him. "I don't know." She smoothed his moist dark hair back from his forehead. "Go back to sleep."

"Will you stay with me?"

She sighed, but she did not move away from him. "I'll be right here."

He nodded and leaned back on the pillows. His eyes were already closing. For a moment, Petra was still. He tucked her hand against his cheek.

His breath was slow and even. She tried to tug her hand away, but even in sleep, he didn't let her go. She sighed. For several long moments, she waited. He didn't release her. Finally, she curled up beside him. He was warm and his chest rose and fell with such a calm, steady rhythm, she was asleep in mere moments. She didn't dream of blood or war or Scarlet's men converging upon her in a dark alley. All she saw was grey.

CHAPTER FOUR

The next day, in the compound on the edge of Razor City...

"Petra!" Lux barked. "You did what?"

"She's kidnapped Prince Dante," Key said matter-of-factly, frowning at Petra across the round table in his bedroom around which they all sat. It was the older kid's typical meeting place. One of the chairs was conspicuously empty. No one mentioned Ren, but they didn't have to. If he'd still been there, they wouldn't even be having the conversation.

Petra lifted a shoulder. "Not kidnapped, as such. I found him in an alley. He was beaten up and he had no memory. He came with me on his own. What else was I supposed to do?"

"Not bring him here!" Lux replied, surprising her. "Are you crazy? The security of the entire compound is compromised!"

"No one has seen him," Petra said defensively. "No one saw me take him or bring him here. We're safe enough."

"Until he recovers his memories and remembers who he is and calls his dad," Jesse said, pushing his hands through his ginger blonde hair. He rose to pace the length of the room.

"That won't happen," Petra told him. "I have his cell phone."

"You honestly think that's enough to stop him?" Beth asked gently. She sat in the seat beside Petra, but she didn't seem as supportive as her position suggested.

"Petra, this is crazy," Lux repeated. "What are you planning to do?"

Petra lifted her chin and met Lux's gaze squarely. "All of us have people in one of the King's prisons. All of us want our families back. King Scarlet will want his son back, and when he does, maybe we can make a trade for our people."

For a moment, all six of them stared at her. They didn't all look angry. Lux didn't look as though the argument swayed her much, but Jesse turned to peer thoughtfully at Petra. Key sighed in a long-suffering sort of way that suggested he would follow Petra, even if he thought she was completely out of her mind; he'd made it perfectly clear that he did. Rip's face brightened. Beth still looked uncertain. As usual, Ellis' expression was perfectly unreadable.

"That's not such a bad idea," Rip put in.

"What? What are you talking about?" Key snapped. "It's a terrible idea!"

"What else have we got?"

Petra nodded. "Scarlet runs this city. He rolls over everyone who gets in his way. This is the first chance we've ever had. It's the first chance anyone has ever had."

"Yeah, but what are we going to do?" Lux demanded. "Keep him prisoner? Where is he?"

"He's in my room. He's sleeping. Key and I are keeping him...sedated."

"What?" Lux snapped incredulously.

"He's on painkillers. He's been badly injured. He isn't trying to get away yet. He still doesn't know who he is."

"He really doesn't know he's Prince Dante?" Beth asked.

Petra glanced at her. "He doesn't know anything. He thinks he's one of us."

"For how long?" Jesse asked.

"No idea."

They all sighed. Lux scowled. "How do we know the people who attacked him aren't going to come back for him?"

"We weren't followed. No one knows he's here. If we can keep it that way for just long enough..." When Petra looked up at them all, her dark eyes looked a little crazy. They all looked at each other uneasily. "The King hasn't reported him missing yet. For all we know, Grey--Dante does this all the time: disappear for days and not come home. I'm not sure how long we have before Scarlet notices he's gone. Or how long before Dante remembers Grey doesn't exist and he doesn't belong here."

"That doesn't sound like a plan, Petra," Lux said, scowling. "It just sounds insane."

Petra rose to pace the room. "The world is insane! Everything around us is insane. I want Ren back. I want everyone back. And if the King wants his son back, we can trade him."

"It's not going to be that easy," Key told her.

"How do we even know the King isn't the one who set him up?" Lux demanded. "Where were his bodyguards? How did he end up alone in the alley

52

like that?"

"Why would Scarlet do that? Why would he set up his own son?"

"Why does he do anything he does? We don't know him. Maybe he was trying to teach him a lesson. Maybe that's why he's still alive. We've all heard all sorts of things about Dante. He's a nightmare. He's as bad as his father. Maybe he's worse because he doesn't even have a reason to be a prick. He doesn't have a city to rule. As bad as Scarlet is, he has a reason for the things he does."

"Are you saying it's okay?" Jesse barked.

Lux shook her long, black braids. "No. I'm just saying he started out good. He just lost sight of what he was doing. He probably still thinks what he's doing is right. Maybe he didn't like what his son was becoming and decided to show him the consequences of his actions. Dante doesn't do what he does because he's trying to keep the city together. He does it because he likes the power."

Petra frowned. Something about this didn't sit right. The boy she knew wasn't the sort of person who liked power. Grey was as gentle and sweet as a child. She felt a strange surge of irritation at this.

She opened her mouth, but Key was the one who spoke. "I don't know if Dante was really like that or if it was all just rumors, but...he doesn't seem much like that now. He's docile. He trusts Petra and me."

Petra nodded slowly. "I think we could convince him..."

"What?" Lux asked. "To fight against his father?"

"Maybe not fight against him. But maybe we can convince him that what his father is doing isn't right. He wanted to rush out into the street and save some girl from the Marshals. He's...nice. He's a good person, I think, on the inside."

"So, what? You think a bump on his head changed his personality?"

"I think maybe he's...back to who he was when he was innocent. I think he wants to do what's right. He's lost the part of himself that's been corrupted."

Key sighed. "But we've only known him a couple hours. We can't know what he'll ultimately do."

Petra nodded reluctantly. "I think we can influence him. Enough to keep him on our side for now."

"This is so dangerous, Petra," Beth murmured. "It just leaves so much to chance."

"I know, but we don't have any other choice."

"This is not how civilized people behave."

"This is not a civilized world!"

"When the King reports him missing, every bounty hunter in the city will be gunning for him," Jesse said. "They don't follow rules. They will break down every door in the city, including this one."

"We'll hide him. We'll be prepared."

"How can we prepare for that? Just having him here puts us all in danger."

"But letting him go would be worse! When are we going to have another chance to get our families back? To make things right?"

"There is no making things right!" Lux snarled. "This city is ruined. It's destroyed and corrupt."

"That means we have to be just as bad, then. We do what we have to do."

Lux sighed. "How far are you really prepared to take this, Petra?"

Petra lifted her chin. She wasn't as confident as she sounded when she replied, "As far as I have to."

No one spoke for a long moment. They all looked at each other uneasily. Finally, they looked at Key. They always looked at Key. He sighed. "Petra acted rashly, and I don't think she thought this through all the way. But she has a point. If any one of you saw the prince in the same situation, would you have done any different? Dante's the only leverage we have against Scarlet. Scarlet rules this city. He has all the power. Now we finally have a little power of our own. Maybe we can get our people back this way. And if we can't..."

Lux sighed. "If we can't...if we can't, maybe we all die or the people we love die."

"Or maybe we can hit Scarlet where it hurts him the most." Beth's eyes were as cold as ice. Petra was forcibly reminded that she was one of the Uprising. There were things about her best friend even Petra wasn't sure she wanted to know. "Maybe we can break him down a little like he breaks us all down."

Petra's eyes narrowed. "We aren't going to do anything to Grey."

Key lifted his eyebrows. "We might not have a choice, Petra. We will try to do what we can not to, but you brought him here. You might have to face the consequences. If it gets too hot, we might have to take drastic measures."

Her stomach roiled. For the first time, Ellis spoke. "I think it might work."

They all turned to look at him in surprise. "What?" Jesse demanded.

Ellis didn't speak much. When he did say something, they all listened. "We might be able to make it work for us. Petra didn't necessarily do right by bringing him here, but we can't let him go. We can't let the opportunity pass us by. Now that we have him, we just have to find the right way to use him to our advantage." He looked as Petra with mild, amber colored eyes. "Maybe we can convince him to see things our way."

"It will be difficult," Key answered for her. Petra glanced at him. "But he seems pliable right now."

"Now," Lux repeated. "Now! What about when he regains his memory?"

Petra spun to her. "We'll have to do it quickly then." She frowned around at them. "I don't suppose I have to remind you all to keep this a secret. We don't want anyone to know he's here. Not even our closest friends." She met Beth's green eyes. Her friend inclined her head almost imperceptibly. "If they aren't in the inner circle, they don't need to know about it."

"Come on," Lux said. "Don't be stupid. None of us are going to be crazy enough to tell anyone. It could sign all our death warrants."

"Right now, keep him quiet," Ellis told Petra. "If he starts to regain his memory, keep him sedated. Do what you have to. All we can do right now is figure out how we're going to make this work without getting anyone killed."

Beth rose. "I'll monitor the news, see if anyone has reported him missing."

Lux followed her. "I'm going to check the perimeter in case anyone is lurking around looking for him. We might already be compromised."

Petra crossed her arms over her chest. "We aren't."

"I want to see for myself. You and Key can take care of Dante."

Jesse threw up his hands. "Yeah. Because the rest of us don't want anything to do with this."

"Fine." Petra frowned at him. "I'll figure it out on my own, then. Consider yourselves off the hook."

"I don't think it will matter," Lux said grimly. "If anyone finds him here, it won't matter who knew he was here and who didn't. We'll all be dead."

* * *

Meanwhile, in the darkness...

A young boy's face as he died. Blood pooled around him. Blood formed on his lips as he called his father's name...

Grey shot up in bed. Petra was already awake, watching him sleep as though his steady, rhythmic breath might answer the questions swirling in her mind. His sudden movement startled her. She looked at him in surprise as he fell back down on the pillows beside her. She rose up on an elbow to look at him. Her long, blonde hair tickled his cheek. He brushed it aside gently and breathed a heavy sigh of relief.

"Another dream?" Her voice was only a whisper.

He didn't reply. He wrapped his arms around her and hugged her against him. He didn't know who they had been to each other before his attack. Now, she was all he had. She knew it. She tried not to think too closely about what would happen when he regained his memory. She tried not to think too closely about what she was doing. She tried to ignore the peculiar roiling in her belly.

His voice was soft and hoarse in the darkness. "I don't know what it is. I don't know why I keep seeing it. Is it a memory?"

She considered this a long moment. "It could be. Maybe it's just a nightmare."

She felt him tremble slightly. "It feels so real. It feels like it happened."

"Who do you see? Who are the people in your dream?"

He shook his head. His dark, shoulder-length hair tickled her cheek. "I don't know. I can't really see them. I just see the boy." She sighed. She leaned her cheek against his shoulder. He brushed her hair from her shoulders and rested his cheek on the top of her head. She'd started to nod off when he spoke again. "How did I get here?"

"What?" She lifted her head. "I brought you here."

"No. I mean the first time. How did I end up living here with all of you?"

She looked up into his face. She could barely see the sculpted line of his jaw in the darkness. She thought about this. For a brief, crazy moment she considered telling him the truth, telling him everything and hoping for the best. She didn't. Instead, she lied.

"Your parents were accused of treason by one of the Nobles."

He was silent a moment. "Which one?"

"I...I don't know. You never said. You tried to get them back. You tried to convince the King they were innocent, but it never does any good."

"Are they still there? In prison?"

She didn't say anything for a moment. "No. I'm sorry. They were executed."

His breath caught. Suddenly, she wished she could take it back, but it was too late. His hands clenched on her arms. Her pulse leapt. "How did I find you?"

"I found you." She smiled, but her eyes stung. "Just the same as last time. You were wandering the city alone, in a fog. You were angry. It's the way we find most of the people who come here."

"You take us all in?"

"When we can. The lost kids. They have nowhere else to go. We have food, shelter and comfort for them. We're all they have."

His voice was strange. "You're all I have."

She lifted her head to look at him. "Yes."

Through the gloom, she could see his stormy eyes flash. He looked better than he had when she'd first brought him here. His bruises were still fresh, but they didn't seem to give him as much pain. Without thinking, she lifted a hand to stroke her fingers over his sculpted cheekbone. He caught her hand. He kissed her fingertips. She shivered.

"Were we together?"

"What?" Her voice sounded dreamy.

"Were we a couple?" She looked up at him in surprise. He folded her hand into his. "I feel all these things when I look at you. Things I haven't felt before."

Petra's breath caught. "How do you know you haven't felt them? You don't remember anything. You wouldn't even know if you had."

His laugh surprised her. "I don't think that's true. I think I would know if I'd felt this way. I think it would feel familiar. Other things feel familiar."

This made her slightly uneasy. "Like what?"

"Coffee."

She laughed. "Does it feel familiar when you look at me?"

"No. I feel something else."

She lifted her head to look at him. "Like what?"

"Strange. Tingly. Warm."

Her heart leapt, but her stomach churned uncomfortably. "I..."

"Do you feel that way when you look at me?"

She should tell him no. She'd kidnapped him. She was manipulating him and lying to him, and he was falling for her. She shouldn't make it worse. She did. "I...yes. Sometimes."

"But we weren't together," he guessed.

"No. We weren't."

"Why not?"

"We just weren't. I suppose we might have...we might have been. We might have gotten around to it sometime."

"How about now?"

She opened and closed her mouth. She didn't know how to reply to this. There was only one answer. She didn't like the answer. Grey didn't wait to hear it. He tilted her chin up and pressed his lips against hers. She caught her breath. She should have pulled away, but she didn't. His mouth was soft and warm. His fingers traced up and down her arms. A shiver ran down her spine.

When he pulled away, she sighed. She could hear the smile in his voice when he said, "Petra? How about now?"

She leaned her head on his shoulder. Her heart thumped in her chest. It didn't matter how much she'd liked kissing him, though. They could never be together. Even if he never regained his memory, even if he stayed Grey forever, she intended to turn him in to his father to get her brother back. She couldn't turn back now. The effort to lie was almost painful. "Maybe. When you're back on your feet. If you still want to be."

"I will."

"You don't know that for sure. You're...well, you're vulnerable right now. Things might change when I'm not the only one you see."

Even in the darkness, she saw his brow furrow. "That's not why I feel this way. That's not fair. It's real."

She sighed. "I know it feels like it is."

Grey sat up abruptly. "Don't do that, Petra. I know how I feel. Don't dismiss it."

"I'm not! I just...don't want you to get too carried away before you...recover."

He made an angry noise and turned his face from her. She sighed and rose. Before she could move away from him, he caught her arm. "Don't go."

"I...Okay."

"You leave me alone all the time. Why can't I see anyone else?"

"It's safer that way. I don't want anyone to know what happened to you. I don't want to scare them."

He sighed, but he relaxed almost instantly. He didn't release her arm. "I suppose it would be confusing for them if I didn't remember any of them."

It would be confusing for them if he waltzed into the common room.

She nodded. "It would be painful for everyone."

He tugged on her hand to draw her down beside him once more. "Do you think I'll get my memory back?"

"I don't know. I don't know how it works. I'm not a doctor." She smirked. "Just a computer genius."

His face lit up suddenly. She could see it even in the gloom. She lifted an eyebrow. "Can I look?"

She blinked. "What?"

"Can I look at your computer?"

She hesitated. "What for?"

"To learn about Razor City. About life here. What I've forgotten."

She thought about this for several long moments. There was curiously little information about Prince Dante online. King Scarlet had seen to that. He kept him strictly offline and out of the limelight. Scarlet was notoriously wary of the kings and queens of neighboring cities. The cities' monarchs battled constantly, invading others to expand their own empires. Scarlet was good at preventing invasions. He was good at hiding his weaknesses from his own people and the people outside Razor City. If Petra hadn't seen him once on television, she might not have ever known Dante's face.

She might have left him alone in the alley, and he would not be here with her now. He wasn't likely to encounter his own face. He was likely to learn what his father really was. Posting information online about the King was illegal, but it did leak. The Uprising and their people still popped up, spreading propaganda and exposing his corruption. They were arrested if they were caught, and the information disappeared almost as quickly as it appeared. No matter what he did, though, there was always more.

Once or twice, Petra had been responsible for tracking down the source of the information for the Nobles. Sometimes she succeeded. Sometimes she failed. When she failed, it was usually by choice. Once or twice, she'd been responsible for the information disappearing.

And once or twice, she'd been the one to put it there.

Finally, she nodded and flipped on the lamp beside the bed. Grey held up a hand to shield his eyes from the light. She smiled at him and handed him her laptop. "Go ahead."

His mouth turned up slightly. "Is there anything on here you don't want me to see?"

She rolled her eyes. She wasn't stupid enough to leave important information on her computer; she had thumb drives for that. She smiled at him. "I have no secrets."

"I don't believe that."

She shrugged. "Go ahead. See for yourself."

He thought about this. "I think I would rather learn Scarlet's secrets. I want to know what we're up against. I want to know what he's doing out there. If he's terrorizing us and the rest of the city, maybe someone should stop him."

Petra stared at him in surprise. Then she nodded. "Maybe someone should."

He smiled and tugged her back down onto the bed beside him. Before she realized what he was doing, he caught the back of her head and pulled her in for a kiss. A jolt shot through her entire body. She pulled away and rose to her feet. He looked a little surprised. "Where are you going?"

"I'll be back soon. I'm just going to talk to the others."

He didn't look suspicious, but he looked curious. "What about?"

"The usual things."

"What are the usual things?"

She smiled. "Sometimes work, sometimes running this place, the new kids, the city."

"What work?"

She nodded toward the computers. "The stuff I do for people. Computer stuff."

He lifted an eyebrow. "Do you all work?"

"No. Some of us. I work on computers. Others do other things."

"Did I work?"

She shook her head slowly. "I don't...think so. You haven't been here long. Just...a few weeks, really. You didn't do anything I knew about."

He thought about this. "But you let me stay here anyway."

"We do what we can for the kids who need help. They have nowhere else to go. So we take care of them. We have to keep the place running and safe for everyone."

"You sacrifice a lot for this place."

"Yeah. Just about everything." She looked at him silently a moment. "I would, anyway. If I had to."

He smiled, and a lock of dark hair fell over his eyes. He looked sweet and young. Her heart fluttered a little. She felt a stab of guilt. She couldn't let this go on, but there wasn't anything she could do about it. She turned away from him and walked out of the room.

She nearly collided with the young man in the hallway outside her door. "Damnit, Shaw!" she complained.

Shaw smiled. He was the same age as she was, but he hadn't been at the compound as long. He hadn't been there very long at all. He was very good-looking with dark hair and sky blue eyes, but he had an arrogant, entitled attitude that rubbed her the wrong way. There was a shifty look in his eyes. She'd never trusted him. Most of the kids at the compound didn't trust him.

"What are you doing outside my door?" she snapped.

He lifted his chin. He looked offended by the abrupt question. "Just looking for you."

"Why?"

His brow furrowed. "I wanted to see you."

She scowled. "What do you mean you wanted to see me? Why?"

Shaw looked a little hurt by this question. Then the look was gone so quickly, she thought she must have imagined it. He narrowed his eyes. "What are you hiding in there?"

"What? What are you talking about? That's my room. I'm not hiding anything."

"Why do you have that curtain, then?"

"It's my room. It's not anyone's business but mine."

He scowled, but he didn't reply to this.

She sighed impatiently. "What do you want, Shaw?"

"Nothing. Never mind." But the look in his eyes was strange. For a moment, she thought he almost looked...nice. "I just wanted to make sure you're okay. Not working too hard or anything. You've been a little stressed lately."

She stared at him in surprise.

"Is it a job?"

She relented a little. "Yeah. It's a job."

"What kind?"

"I don't want to talk about it, Shaw."

He shrugged. "Okay. But I'll be here if you want to."

She lifted an eyebrow. "Why? When have you ever done anything without an ulterior motive? Oh. That's right. You wanted me to find you a buyer for your program."

Now he did look hurt. "Is that what you think of me? That I'm only your friend because I want something?"

"No. I'm sorry. Things have been strange. I don't want to talk about it. It's nothing to worry about."

He lifted a eyebrow. "I wasn't worried about it."

"Good. Don't." She spun away from him. He scowled after her, but she didn't turn back. She paused in front of Key's door and rapped once on the gate. "It's Petra."

The inner circle was already sitting around the table. Lux frowned at her as she walked in. "People are starting to talk. They've noticed Dante's missing. The King hasn't released any information because he's not sure what's happened to him. If he ran off, he doesn't want anyone to know about it." She rolled her eyes. "I don't think he wants anyone to think there's any discord in his own house. If he can't keep his son on a leash, he'll lose credibility."

"There's nothing on the news about it," Beth added. "But even in the outlands, people have heard."

"Not on the news," Petra repeated. "That's good."

"Why?"

"Grey's on my computer."

"What?" Key demanded. "You're letting him look online?"

She shrugged. "I thought he might like to learn what his father is really like. Maybe if he knows the truth, he'll come over to our side."

"That's risky, Petra," Beth scolded. "You shouldn't have let him."

"What do you want me to do? Tie him up?"

"It might come to that if you intend to continue this charade." Lux's voice was mild, but her dark eyes glinted. "You can't keep this up forever. He's going to figure out who he is. He's going to be upset when he finds out. It might be all we can do."

Petra sighed. "I know."

"There's not enough time to set him against his father before he regains his memory or realizes people are looking for him," Key said.

"I know."

"Not to mention the bounty hunters," Lux continued. "They're probably already looking for him, even if the public doesn't know he's missing. There will still be a reward for his return."

"I know."

"We're running out of time. We have to decide what to do, and we need to do it quickly," Beth said.

"I say we get him out of here."

"Lux! We can't just kick him to the streets in his condition," Petra growled. "It wouldn't be safe for him."

"That is not my problem! We're risking the whole compound for him."

"You said the King isn't looking for him."

"No. I said the King hasn't publicly announced he's missing. Of course he's looking for him."

"So what do we do?" Jesse demanded.

"We've already decided," Ellis replied. "What Petra did put us at risk, but we're going to face the consequences and try to make it work for us. We'll see it through."

They all turned to look at him. "Have you got a plan, then?" Rip asked.

"Not yet. I've been thinking about it. I have some ideas about how we're going to do it, but it's delicate. We can't make a mistake, or we're dead."

"We're really going to use him." Beth sighed in resignation.

Petra's stomach roiled, but Ellis nodded. "Yes. It's our only choice."

They considered this gravely. "Are we really prepared to go this far?" Jesse's voice sounded small. He was strong, and he was smart, but he wasn't cut out for this. He was in over his head.

They were all in over their heads.

"It's already gone too far," Ellis said grimly. "We don't have another option."

"Petra, you shouldn't have brought him here!" Lux repeated.

"We've already covered that, Lux," Ellis told her. "You're not helping with that."

"I'm sorry," Petra said. "But you said yourselves you would have done the same thing. We can't back down now. We need him if we're going to stop all this and bring our families back."

"Sure. Best case scenario is they release our people, we release him," Lux said. "But we know it's not going to go down like that!"

Petra sighed. "It might. It might work, and if there's a small chance it could, we have to try, don't we?"

"Ellis, what are you thinking?" Key asked. "How are we going to do this?"

"Send an anonymous email," Petra put in before Ellis could speak. She'd thought about it, too. "They release the prisoners, we'll release Dante."

"That's ridiculous," Lux argued. "They won't do it. They'll send their best people to track us, figure out where he is and kill us all."

"They'll just imprison us if we're lucky," Jesse added.

Petra rolled her eyes. "I know how to send an email without being tracked. When the prisoners are released, we'll send him home."

Lux scowled. "This isn't going to work. Also, they'll know exactly who we are when we give them the names of the prisoners we want released. They'll kill them and then come find us."

Petra shrugged. "Then we just demand they release all the prisoners who've been falsely accused."

"Petra, what fantasy world are you living in?" Beth asked gently. "What are you thinking? That is insane and it won't work."

"Just get him out of here. Before it's too late," Lux ordered.

"No." Petra rose to her feet. "I'm going to do it with or without you. I want my brother back!"

Beth grabbed her arm. Her expression was sad. "You're forgetting one thing, Petra. What if Scarlet was the one who attacked him or had someone attack him? He might want him dead. He might be waiting to discover where he is to send someone to finish the job."

Petra's stomach sank, but she shook her head. "If Scarlet wanted to kill him, he would be dead."

"Something is not right here, Petra. We don't know how he ended up in that alley. It is dangerous for him to be here."

Ellis held up his hand. "Beth is right. He is dangerous to us. We need to get him out of here as soon as we can. As long as he's here, we're putting all those kids in danger. Ransom is one option, but it might not be the only option. We could turn him in."

"What?" Petra demanded.

"The bounty hunters will be looking for him. They will expect a reward when they do. Maybe we can make a trade for him in person. We could bring him in and ask for our people as the bounty."

They all stared at him a moment. "If we do that, our faces will be all over the court," Lux said, but she sounded as though she was seriously considering it. "They might just take the prince back and kill us."

"Not necessarily. The bounty system is as corrupt as any of the others, but the King honors the bounties. If a bounty is offered for an outlaw, they pay it when they're brought in. They don't double-cross. If they did, the system would collapse. They need the bounty hunters. They won't risk it."

"Yes, but we wouldn't be asking for a typical cash reward."

"We might be able to rename the price. This isn't a typical fugitive."

Beth thought about this. "We could intimate around town we have information about the prince, find out what it's worth."

"No," Lux replied. "That could get us killed faster than showing our faces. It's too risky, and it isn't worth it. We're going to get one strike. One shot. We have to make it good."

Petra sighed. She pressed her hand to her forehead. "So we are going to do this."

Lux lifted an eyebrow. "It was your idea."

"Yes, we're going to do it," Ellis said firmly. "But we need time to plan and think about it."

"I'm not sure we have it," Beth told him. "We might have to move him. We could take him somewhere else where the rest of the kids won't be in danger."

Lux nodded. "I can do that. I have a place. I'll get it ready."

"I will talk to some of my contacts. Maybe they have some ideas what to do with him," Beth added.

Petra glared at her. "No! We can't let the rebels know we have him. If we do, they might attack us to get to him."

Beth frowned. "That's not what they do. It's not what they will want to do with him. He is too useful to them. To all of us." She sighed and looked at the others. "The truth is, we do need him if we want to change this world. It has to change. This may be our only hope. We just have to do it right."

"Well, the rebels aren't the way!"

"And kidnapping and ransom is, Petra?"

Petra sighed. She dropped her head into her hands for a moment. The truth was, she wasn't sure she could go through with it. She liked Grey. He was different than she expected. She didn't want to use him, not anymore. But there wasn't any other choice. She had started this, and she would have to take it all the way to the end.

"None of this is going to matter if he remembers who he is," Lux reminded them. "If he does, he'll figure out what we're planning to do with him. He could bring the King down on us."

"We can keep him sedated," Key said grimly. "It will at least keep him quiet until we can figure this out."

"No," Petra said. "That's not going to help anyone. He trusts me. He trusts us right now. We might still be able to work him to our side."

"There isn't enough time. We have to act quickly."

"So what do we do with him?" Jesse demanded.

Lux considered a moment. "I have some contacts inside the King's regime."

They all looked at her in surprise. "What? You have spies?" Rip asked.

"Sort of. They tell me things when they can. They don't cross the line. They're careful."

"Then what can they do?"

"Maybe they can tell us if the King is the one behind the attack. Maybe they can give us an idea how to use him to our advantage."

"It's too dangerous, Lux," Key said. "We can't risk letting someone even suspect he's here or we know where he is."

"Okay, the priority is to get him out of here where he isn't going to put the kids at risk," Beth said. "If we're going to strike, we need to be ready, and we need to get our people out of danger."

"Lux, how soon can you have the new location set?" Ellis asked in a remarkably calm voice.

"Tonight."

"Okay. Petra, you'd better stick with him. You're going to have to figure out a way to move him to the new place."

She hesitated. "I think he'll go with me, wherever I tell him to go."

If they suspected what she meant by this, they didn't say anything. "Okay, well, let's hope that's true," Lux said. "I really don't want to have to knock him out and drag him out of here." She smirked. "But I will if I have to."

Petra scowled at her. She rose and spun out of the room without replying.

Shaw was waiting outside in the hall. She nearly collided with him. "Shaw, what are you doing?"

He lifted his eyebrows. "Looking for you."

"Again? What do you want? I don't have time for this."

"Why? What are you up to in your room?"

"I told you. Work. It's not any of your business."

He scowled at her. "If it concerns the compound, it concerns me."

She scoffed. "Since when? All you ever cared about was yourself."

Shaw looked affronted. "Why are you being like this with me? Why are you being such a bitch?"

Petra glared at him. "What do you mean? When have you ever given me any reason not to be?"

His dark eyes narrowed to slits. "What's that supposed to mean?"

"It's means you've never been nice. You've never been anything but an arrogant, selfish jerk who thinks the world owes you something. You think you're better than the rest of us."

Shaw looked completely shocked at this. "That isn't true."

She stared at him a moment. She felt suddenly guilty for being so harsh. She sighed. "I'm sorry. I shouldn't have said that. You're in the same position as the rest of us."

"You're right. I am."

"I'm sorry. I've just been...distracted. I'm working a job, and it isn't as easy as I would like it to be."

He didn't look as though he believed this. "Are you sure it isn't something else?"

"I don't know what you mean."

"Is there something the rest of us should know?"

She lifted her chin coldly. "No."

"You don't have to leave me out of everything all the time, Petra. You can trust me."

She frowned. "I'm not leaving you out. I'm just busy." She pushed past him. "I have to go."

Shaw turned and scowled after her, but he didn't call her back.

CHAPTER FIVE

Meanwhile, in dreamland...

He knew the face, but he couldn't seem to place it. It was a handsome, strong face, but it was stern and cold. He saw it when Elia died. He saw it looming over them with an angry, terrible expression. Someone would pay for what had happened. He wasn't so sure it wouldn't be him...

The man is back, and he knows him suddenly. He has seen his face. King Scarlet. Scarlet is angry. Scarlet is always angry. His face isn't handsome now. It's twisted with fury. His eyes are dark and wild. He is shouting.

"I would rather see you dead!"

He doesn't know why Scarlet is angry at him. He doesn't know what he's done wrong.

"I will kill you myself!"

Scarlet rushes toward him. He shoves him, but his hands move through him as though he's not really there. Who is he yelling at?

"I will kill you!"

Grey tossed fitfully in the large, round bed. He was murmuring something, but Petra couldn't hear it. He whimpered like a small, frightened child. Petra hurried to his side. "Grey." She touched his shoulder. It was hot and moist with sweat. "Grey!"

He shot up abruptly. He shoved her away so forcefully, she nearly toppled from the bed. Then his stormy grey eyes cleared, and he caught her. He pulled her against him in a bone-crushing hug. He sighed.

"Are you okay?" She leaned back to look at him. "What was happening? Were you dreaming again?"

"Yeah." He drew her with him to lean back against the pillows.

"Tell me about it."

"I saw King Scarlet."

She lifted her head in surprise. "Was it a nightmare?"

He shook his head. "Maybe. Now I see his face in the memory of the little boy dying. He's there, and he's angry. He looks at me like it's my fault." He frowned. "Then I saw him threatening me."

"Threatening you? What did he say?"

"He said he would rather see me dead and that he will kill me himself."

Petra lifted her eyebrows. "Do you think it's a nightmare from reading all those articles about him?"

He exhaled heavily. "It could have been, I guess. But it seemed so, so real. I could hear his voice. It sounded so familiar."

She rose up to look at him seriously. His expression was so troubled, her stomach roiled uneasily. "Do you think you might be in danger from him?"

He looked completely shocked. "Am I?"

"I don't know, Grey. I don't know what happened to you that night or who was after you."

His hands tightened on her arms. "But you know me, right? You know about me."

"I don't know everything. I just know how you were when you came here." This was the first completely true thing she'd said to him. "I didn't know you long before this. I suppose there are a lot of things I don't know about you."

His brow furrowed. She lifted a hand to brush his dark hair from his forehead. He looked so young and innocent. He looked so troubled. She wished she could tell him it had only been a dream. It probably hadn't. She wished she wasn't lying to him. She wished she didn't have to do what she was going to do to him.

But it wasn't a dream, she was lying to him and she was going to ransom him off to his father. A father who might have threatened to kill him. He might even have tried.

"Go back to sleep," she murmured. "It might have just been a dream."

He clutched at her. "I don't want you to go. I don't have the dreams when you're with me."

She smiled. "I will stay with you until you fall asleep." He didn't look happy, but he didn't argue. He drew her down to rest against his side. She draped an arm over his chest.

He winced in pain. She'd almost forgotten he was still injured.

She sat up and grabbed the bottle of pills on the table beside the bed. "Take another pill. You'll feel better."

He sighed and shook his head. "I think they're keeping me from remembering anything."

"I'm not sure that's such a bad thing, Grey."

"I don't want it."

"Okay." She rose up abruptly to kiss his forehead. It felt hot.

He caught the nape of her neck and guided her mouth to his. She sighed and wrapped her arms around his neck. Kissing him would only make it worse, but she wanted to so badly. His lips moved against hers. Her stomach flipped.

He sighed deeply and leaned back down on the pillows, drawing her with him. She lifted her head to look down at him. He smiled dreamily. His eyes flickered open for the briefest moment. They looked sleepy and calm. She stroked a hand down his face. He was asleep in seconds.

She stared down at his face for a long moment. He was so gorgeous, he made her stomach hurt. Or perhaps that was just the guilt. There was a horrible, hollow feeling inside her that was only getting bigger and more horrible by the second. She rose from the bed and turned away from him.

Outside in the hall, Shaw was still lurking. She stared at him incredulously. "Seriously, Shaw, what are you doing here? Stop following me around!"

His lip curled. He crossed his arms over his narrow chest. "I'm just trying to talk to you."

"Well, then talk instead of creeping around outside my room and following me around!"

"I just want to be involved!"

"I told you, there is nothing you need to be involved in. I told you. It doesn't concern you. It isn't any of your business." She strode past him, but she paused to look back at him.. "I don't have time for this. Leave me alone, Shaw, or I will have Lux toss you into the cage."

Shaw stared at her in shock. "You wouldn't."

"Just leave me alone. I don't want to be your friend. Find your own buyer." She spun away from him and stomped back to Key's room.

Everyone but Lux was still there. Petra wondered if they were planning to remain in there until Grey had been moved or they came up with the perfect way to barter him off. They were talking quietly, but they looked up as she stormed in.

Key frowned. "What's up, Petra? You look upset."

"I am. That--Shaw is creeping around outside, following me around."

Beth laughed and rolled her eyes. "He likes you, Petra. Don't you know?"

Petra shuddered. "No! I didn't know that." She sighed. "No wonder he's following me around, I guess. Anyway, Gr--Dante had a memory."

"What?"

She sighed. "Well, it might have been a nightmare, but he thinks it might have happened."

Key leaned forward keenly. "What did he see?"

"He said Scarlet threatened him. He told him he would kill him himself."

Ellis frowned thoughtfully. "Why?"

She shook her head. "I don't know. He didn't know. There wasn't any context. Just the threat."

They all peered at each other for a moment. Ellis was the first one to speak. "If Scarlet really was the one behind the Dante's attack, this will never work. We can't risk ransoming him to someone who wants him dead. It could get everyone killed. We need to know the truth. We could lose our shot."

Key considered this. "We need him to remember what happened that night. We need to try to find out who wants to kill him."

"Now you want him to remember?"

"Yes," Ellis said. "We need to at least learn what happened in that alley."

"What about moving him?"

"Yeah, that's still going to happen," Key said. "It's even more crucial now in light of this information. The sooner he's out of here, the sooner everyone here is safe again."

Ellis' eyes were serious. "Petra, you have to help him remember."

Her stomach sank. If he remembered...she wasn't ready for him to remember. She wasn't sure what was happening between them, but if he remembered what happened, and he remembered who he was, he'd know she lied to him.

But she wanted Ren back. No matter what was happening with Grey, no matter how she was beginning to feel, Ren was more important. And Grey wasn't real. When he did remember who he was, she would lose him. He would become Prince Dante again. She was better off forgetting what she was feeling. She couldn't lose sight of everything now because a cute boy had kissed her a couple times.

She nodded sharply. "Fine. Let me know when Lux comes back. We'll move him as soon as she is ready. I'll talk to him and see what I can do."

She was relieved Shaw wasn't waiting for her in the hall. She had enough problems. Grey was out of bed pacing the room when she returned. She lifted her eyebrows in surprise. "I thought you were sleeping."

He turned to her. His face looked pale, but he was moving all right. He was getting better. "I woke up when you left. Where did you go?"

She sighed and strode toward him. He met her halfway and caught her hands in his. She looked up into his stormy grey eyes. "Grey, you need to remember what happened the night I found you."

He blinked in surprise, but he nodded. "I know. I have been trying." His brow furrowed. "You don't have any idea why anyone would attack me?"

She sighed. "Maybe, but..."

"But what? Why can't you tell me?"

She shook her head. "I'm sorry, Grey. I just need you to remember. It could be important. The people who hurt you might try to come after you again."

He looked surprised. "They might try to come here? They could hurt you, too?"

She hesitated. The worry in his eyes made her feel worse than she already did. "Yeah. They might."

Grey sighed. He clutched at his head and spun away. "I've been trying to remember. I've gotten some flashes. I think I keep...forcing myself not to remember. I've been avoiding it. It might be why I'm having the nightmares. Maybe my subconscious is trying to protect me from remembering."

Petra stepped toward him and laid a hand on his back. "I'm sorry, Grey. You have to. Tell me about the flashes. Maybe it will help."

He nodded and turned back to face her. "I remember...flashing lights. I think maybe I was drinking, so it's all a little hazy." He frowned. "Do I drink?"

Rumor was, he drank a lot. "Yeah. Sometimes, I guess."

"I think I might drink a lot. I get a lot of flashes like that but none of them make sense. I see faces but there's no context. I don't understand any of it."

"What about that night?"

"I remember the pain. The alley." His face screwed up with the effort of remembering. "I think I walked out of the place with the flashing lights. Someone attacked me from behind."

"Did you see their face?"

He shook his head almost violently. "I can't remember!"

"Okay. It's okay, Grey." She stepped forward and wrapped her arms around him. He crushed her against him. "Keep trying."

He held her away from him. "I don't want to remember this, Petra!"

"It's important! Please try. I'm sorry you have to. I wish you didn't, but it could put us all in danger if we can't figure out who did this."

He nodded and released her. He turned away and pushed his hands through his hair. For several seconds, he was silent. When she spoke again, Petra wished he didn't have to. "Someone hit me in the head from behind. I fell down. They kicked me..." He winced as he remembered and clutched almost self consciously at his side. "I did look up at him. I did see him."

Petra lifted her eyebrows. "Did you know him?"

He thought about this for a long time. "No. I don't think so. There's no familiar feeling when I see him--what I can see of him. There was blood in my eyes. I was drunk. But I don't think I've met him. I might have, though. I don't remember enough from the rest of my life to know for sure."

"Okay. How did you get away from him?"

"I had something in my pocket. I think it was a stun gun or something. I hit him with it, and I crawled away. I must have passed out. When I woke up, I saw you."

"Okay. That's good. That's something."

He turned his head to look at her. "It's not enough is it? I don't know why he attacked me. Remembering the attack without knowing why it happened isn't helpful." He let out a frustrated growl and pushed his hands through his hair again.

Petra strode forward and folded his hands in hers. Grey tugged her into his arms and hugged her tightly against him. She sighed deeply and pulled back to look up into his face. He leaned down and pressed his lips to hers. For a moment, his lips were soft and sweet against hers. Then he crushed her closer to him and deepened the kiss. He walked her backward, and they tumbled back onto the bed.

She wrapped her arms tightly around him, running her hands over the flat muscles of his back and shoulders. He looked slender, but he was stronger than he looked. Her pulse leapt. He lifted his head to look down at her. His eyes were stormy and intense. He brushed her pale blonde hair from her eyes. His breath was as ragged as hers. He leaned back down to kiss her again.

He stiffened suddenly. He tore his mouth from hers. She stared up at him in shock. He squeezed his eyes shut. "Grey? What's wrong? What's going on?"

Grey rolled off her. He lay on his back a moment. He was breathing heavily. "It's my mom, I think."

She lifted her head to look at him. "Your mom?"

"It's a woman. She died."

"What?"

"I was there. I don't know what happened to her. She's covered in blood. I'm trying to stop it, but..." He shuddered. Petra clutched his hand. He squeezed his eyes shut and pressed the heels of his hands to his eyes. "I don't want to remember this! Why are you making me remember this?"

"I'm sorry. I'm so sorry, Grey, but it's really important."

He shot out of bed so quickly, Petra started. His muscles of his back trembled slightly under his black tee-shirt. Moments ago, she was running her fingertips over those muscles. Now they hitched. He half turned his head so she could see only the line of his sculpted cheekbone. She thought she saw moisture glisten on his cheek.

His voice was low and toneless when he spoke. "I think I need to be alone."

She sighed and rose. "Okay. I'm sorry, Grey." She moved toward him and lifted her hand. She didn't touch him. She turned and left the room without saying goodbye.

She didn't notice Shaw watching from the shadows.

* * *

Petra heard voices from inside Key's room, but they weren't coming from the members of the compound's inner circle. She knocked gently on the glass door. "Yeah, come in." Key was watching the news from a thick, plush armchair. The voices she heard came from the large flat screen television mounted on the wall. He turned to her when she paused beside him. "Hey."

"Hey." She perched on the chair beside him.

"I thought you were trying to help the prince remember what happened to him."

"Yeah. We hit a little snag."

Key frowned. "What do you mean a snag?"

"I think a lot of bad things have happened to him. He needed some time alone." She didn't mention what he'd said. Key was her closest friend, but she felt responsible for Grey. She didn't think he would appreciate her spilling his secrets, even if he did trust Key right now.

"What about the night of the attack? Anything?"

"Yeah. A bit. Actually, I think he remembers most of it, but it doesn't help us much."

"Why?"

"He doesn't think he knows the person who attacked him."

Key sighed. "Do you think it might have been a hit man?"

"Yes. Probably. It was someone he's never seen."

"So it could be anyone who ordered it. Or just some vigilante who recognized him and wanted to take revenge on him or the king."

"It could be. That's not exactly a good thing, but sadly it's best case scenario." She frowned. "Do you really think it's a good idea for him to remember?"

"No, not really. Not at all. But it's not safe to have him here. We're in too deep now. We have to go through with it or let him go."

"We can't just let him go." All of a sudden, she wished they could.

"I know. So now we have to make it work. If he remembers, at least we'll know what we're dealing with. We can plan accordingly."

"Have you heard from Lux?"

"No. She hasn't reported back. I'm not sure what she's doing. She hasn't answered her cell phone."

Petra pressed her hand to her forehead. "We have to get him somewhere safe."

Key frowned. His expression was so serious, her stomach flipped a little. "Do you like him, Petra?"

She opened and closed her mouth. Then she scoffed. "What? No. That's just stupid. That's got nothing to do with anything."

He didn't look as though he believed her, but he didn't push it.

She frowned. "It just isn't safe for the rest of us to have him here. Maybe the others are right. I shouldn't have brought him here. I should have taken him somewhere else as soon as I found him. I should have thought of protecting the others."

He sighed. "You acted rashly, Petra, but you acted that way because you thought it would help Ren. I see that. He's my best friend. I would have done the same. I think. Even though it's the stupidest thing you've ever done and would be doubly stupid for me because I don't do nearly as many stupid things as you."

She snorted. "So, is there anything about him on the news yet?"

"No. The King hasn't publicized his disappearance. Either he hasn't figured out he's missing yet, or he doesn't want to let anyone to know there's a chink in his armor. But there are patrols out in the city. More than usual. And they aren't doing their usual thing. They are probably looking for him."

"Are the bounty hunters on it yet?"

"I don't know for sure, but yeah. Probably."

Petra sighed. "I think we're in over our heads."

"Yeah. We are."

"I can't stay here."

He blinked in surprised. "What? You're supposed to be watching Dante."

"I know, but...he needs some time right now. I can't stand just waiting for all this to blow up."

"What do you think you're going to do?"

"I want to go out into the city. See what I can hear." She glanced at him. "Want to go?"

He frowned. "That's not very responsible."

She laughed. "Neither was bringing him here in the first place. Maybe we can reach Lux and check out the safe house before we bring him there."

Key sighed. He looked as though he wanted to argue, but he seemed to realize there wasn't much point. He flicked his fingers at her in dismissal. "Fine. Go on, then. You're always better at drudging up information than I am. I'll...make sure the prince is comfortable." He paused and glanced at her. "What do you want me to tell him if he asks me where you are?"

"Just tell him I'm...trying to find out who hurt him and why. It's almost the truth."

He chuckled wryly. "And the only true thing you've told him so far."

She turned back at the door. "Not the only true thing."

* * *

In a compound on the edge of Razor City, things begin to go wrong...

She didn't notice Shaw behind her as she slipped past the kids in the common room. She didn't turn around or pause to see if anyone was following her. She didn't even say goodbye to the inner circle as she snuck out through the tunnel that lead out into the city. For the briefest moment, Shaw considered following her out of the compound, but he hadn't been out into the city since Eloise had found him wandering the outlands, orphaned and lost, cowering in an old, abandoned house in fear for his life.

He hadn't wanted to go back out into the city. There was too much fear and danger and death. Even now, the outlaws and the rebels and the King's Marshals waited to snatch up the first hapless, weak lost child that wandered into their path. It wasn't going to be him.

He turned back at the tunnel entrance. He peered at the kids playing in the common room. The compound's inner circle was lying to them. They were involved in something that could put them all in danger. They deserved to know what it was. He deserved to know what it was.

He hadn't heard everything, but he had heard enough.

Now was his chance. He strode quickly toward the hall of shops where the inner circle stayed, where they kept everyone else out. Even if they deserved to know what was going on. Even if they were old enough to lead the younger kids and help make the decisions that effected them.

He paused in front of Petra's room. He wasn't sure, but he thought he'd heard voices behind the thick curtains. The inner circle was talking about someone, and whoever he was, he was inside that room. Shaw wanted inside that room.

Key's gate opened abruptly. Shaw ducked around the corner. Key crossed the hall to Petra's room. He unlocked the padlock and slipped inside. Shaw hurried forward. The padlock hung open. He fished in his pocket for a small piece of paper. It was a note from Clarice. He hadn't replied. He wasn't interested in younger girls. He liked girls who weren't afraid of the outside. He liked girls who weren't afraid of anything.

He tore a corner from the paper and rolled it into a ball. He stuffed it into the lock on Petra's door. It was risky. Key wasn't stupid; he might notice the lock didn't catch. But it was worth a try. Shaw didn't have a key, and he thought Petra would notice if her lock was busted open when she arrived home.

He waited. Key wasn't inside the room for long. There was no expression on his face, but Shaw was sure he'd been talking to someone in there. He was sure he'd heard the soft hum of voices.

Who is it?

When the gate closed Key back into his room, Shaw strode forward. The padlock was closed, but Key must have been anxious to leave. It popped open easily. Shaw glanced around. If the inner circle caught him breaking into Petra's room, he would be expelled from the compound. He would be back out on the streets.

No one was nearby. He yanked open the gate and pushed aside the curtain. He poked his head inside the room.

There was someone inside. It was a young man. He was tall with dark, shoulder-length hair. He was standing in the center of the room. His shoulders were tense. He spoke before he turned. "What now?" The tone of his voice was slightly sour. Shaw wondered if he and Key had been fighting.

The young man spun around. When he saw Shaw, he looked surprised. He wasn't as surprised as Shaw. Shaw knew him instantly. He had seen him in the city. He knew his reputation.

Prince Dante.

"Oh," the prince said. His sour expression softened. He didn't look like the Dante Shaw knew. He looked different. He wasn't sure what had changed. "Sorry. Hi." He frowned. "Who are you?"

It took Shaw a moment to reply. He knew what it was that had changed in the prince. There was no cruelty or malice in his gaze. "I'm Shaw. I'm a friend of Petra's."

The prince didn't seem to like this. He frowned. "Friend?"

Was he jealous? This was interesting. "Yeah. Just a friend."

"Do we know each other?"

The question was strange. Shaw shook his head slowly. "No." He knew the answer to his next question, but he wasn't sure the prince did. "Who are you?"

"I'm Grey."

"Grey." Shaw stared at him a moment. His mouth turned up slightly at the corners. "Are you really."

* * *

Meanwhile, in the city center...

The Blade was pulsating with the loud, insidious dance beat. The music didn't drown out the low, persistent buzzing of voices in the air. Razor City's underworld was talking. Petra didn't need to listen. She knew what they were talking about. Or rather, whom they were talking about.

Prince Dante.

She glanced around the club. There were more than the usual small groups of outlaws, rebels, bounty hunters and masked dancers. None of the King's Marshals had dared enter, but there were nobles sitting alone or in groups of two or three. It seemed as though the bounty hunters, too, had come out in droves. They scattered around the room, eyeing the patrons intensely. They all wanted to be the one to find the prince. If there was a price on him, it was steep.

A huge, scarred man in a long, black duster and a battered old cowboy hat sat at the bar, sipping on a drink that looked too small for his enormous hands. There were two huge guns strapped in leather holsters on his hips. His dark blonde hair was longer than she remembered. It brushed his broad, muscular shoulders.

He was young, only a few years older than she, but his face looked as though he had been to hell and back. Petra sat beside him at the bar. He didn't glance at her. She raised her hand to attract the bartender's attention. He nodded to her.

"Tripp."

The bounty hunter at the bar turned toward Petra in surprise. He lifted a thick, dark blonde eyebrow. He looked as though he'd been in a fight recently. There was a cut over his left eye. "Petra."

The bartender handed her a drink. It was clear and crisp. It tasted tart and tangy on her tongue. She felt almost normal again. She waved her hand toward the bounty hunter. "Another round for my friend Tripp here."

"You want something, Petra?" Tripp didn't look happy to see her. He never looked happy to see her.

She lifted a shoulder. She waited for the bartender to slam a pint of beer in front of Tripp. She smiled at him. He didn't look as though this swayed him, but he didn't refuse the drink. He took a swig with a pensive look in his dark eyes.

"You looking for information?" he asked finally. He didn't glance at her. His eyes stared blankly up at the television screens above the bartender's head.

She shrugged again and sipped her drink. "I've been hearing things around town."

"Oh?" He didn't sound as though this were interesting.

"I heard the King's guys are out in the streets, patrolling hard. Looking for something."

Tripp's mouth broke into a smile. He chuckled. "Yeah. They sure are."

"What is it?"

He glanced around them as though he expected one of the Marshals to be hanging around. No one was listening to them. They were all talking about the same thing, anyway. "Not what. Who."

"Well? Who?"

He lifted an eyebrow. "Are you looking to snake another bounty, Petra?"

She laughed. "I don't think I'd give you much competition."

"Is this professional or personal?"

She considered. "Professional."

"Yeah? So is there any money in it for the person who gives you the information?"

She smiled. "There's another drink in it, and I'll promise not to snake your bounty."

He laughed. He liked Petra, even though he didn't act like it. "All right. But how about a deal."

"Yeah?"

"Fifty percent of whatever you make off it."

She considered. "Forty."

"Two more drinks, then."

"Okay."

"The word is, the King is looking for his son."

"Dante?"

"Yeah."

"He's missing?"

Tripp shrugged. "He might be. Or he might be on a bender and shacked up with some young girl."

Petra scowled into her glass. "Does he do that a lot?"

"It wouldn't be the first time. He's got a reputation."

She scowled and grunted in reply.

"Anyway, the King doesn't want anyone to know about it, but his people have leaked it. Word got around to the hunters. It always does. I don't think the King is too happy about it. He might be ashamed Dante's drunk and shacked up with some slut or worse. He doesn't want anyone to know if he ran away and breeched his loyalty."

"I get it. But isn't he worried? It is his son."

"Worried?" Tripp snorted. "I don't think Scarlet worries about anything. He's one cold guy. I've heard he and Dante aren't exactly on good terms. They argue a lot. From what I hear, Dante's a bad guy. He takes advantage of the family name to drink and womanize and terrorize everyone who gets in his way."

Petra's stomach sank, but she nodded.

"I hear Scarlet wants him to grow up and start behaving like he's going to be taking over the city one of these days."

"So he might have run away to avoid doing that."

"Maybe. There's no bounty on him yet, not officially. He doesn't want to admit he's really missing. No one's seen him or heard from him in days. So no one knows where he really is."

"So Scarlet's got men out there patrolling, keeping an eye out for him to pop up and show his face?"

"That's the general idea, but some of the hunters are looking."

"What happens if you find him and turn him in? Is there a reward in it?"

"There's always a reward for things like that. They just don't advertise it. The King likes to keep his personal business quiet. He'll have his own people investigating, but if one of us gets to Dante first, Scarlet will honor it."

Petra considered this. She felt as though her insides had turned to liquid ice. It was as bad as she'd feared. The compound was in danger as long as Tripp and the hunters wanted Grey. She had to get him out of there as soon as she could. "Any ideas yet where he might be?"

Tripp laughed. "Nah. But if I did have, I wouldn't tell you." Then he glanced at her. "We could work together. Maybe you could work your magic and figure out where he's been. Maybe we could track where he's gone."

Petra forced a smile. "I'll think about it." She slapped a bill on the counter. "Thanks for the tip."

Tripp smirked and lifted his glass to her. "Don't forget our deal."

"Yeah." She rose and spun away from him. She had her cell phone out of her pocket before she stepped into the alley outside the Blade. She punched up Lux's number.

Lux answered on the second ring. "Yeah?"

"It's Petra."

"I know who it is."

"Is the safe house ready?"

"Yeah. There were a band of outlaws outside. I had to deal with them."

"I assume the problem is solved."

"It's done. It's ready. We can move Grey when I get back."

"Okay. Good. I don't think we have any time to waste."

CHAPTER SIX

Back at the compound on the edge of town...

Petra avoided the kids skating, dancing and playing together in the common room when she arrived at the compound. Her heart thumped in her chest. She rushed to her room with a breathless urgency that took her by surprise. She gasped in relief when she saw him, as though she had expected hunters, outlaws, or Marshals to have beaten her there.

Grey shot to his feet to meet her in the middle of the room. "Petra. Where have you been?"

"Out." She paused to look at him. He looked better than he had since she'd brought him there. He had showered, and he smelled like citrus and cedar. His dark hair shone. Key must have lent him some clothes. He wore a fresh tee-shirt and jeans that looked slightly too big for him. "I met with some of my contacts in the city to find out if anyone saw or heard anything the night you were attacked."

"Did you find out anything?"

"No. No one saw anything. Not that they were willing to admit, anyway."

Grey sighed. He reached for her abruptly and wrapped her into a hug. "I was worried about you. I didn't know where you'd gone. Key didn't tell me anything." He laid his cheek against her hair. His voice was low and dark. "I think there's more to what happened to me that night than we thought. I don't think it was random at all. Whoever it was came after me for a reason."

She leaned back to meet his troubled gaze. "Yeah. I know."

His brow furrowed, and she was uncomfortably certain he was going to ask her what she meant. What he said instead startled her. "Who's Shaw?"

She blinked. "What?"

"He came in while you were out."

Petra stared at him. "He came in here? In my room?"

"He said he is a friend of yours."

She scowled. "He isn't a friend. He saw you?"

"Yeah."

"What did he say?"

"Nothing. He just told me his name. When he saw you weren't here, he left."

A shiver of icy trepidation raced down her spine.

"Is there something I should know?"

His tone was wry. For a moment, she thought he was teasing her, but he looked completely serious. She stared at him for several startled seconds before she replied. "What? Shaw? Are you kidding?" He didn't smile. "God, no. He's just...he just wants into the cool kids club."

Grey didn't smile at this. His frown deepened. "I think he wants more than that."

"Are you actually jealous?"

"Yes."

Petra shook her head. "Now is not the time for this. We have to tell someone he saw you." She spun away to pace restlessly in front of him. "We have to get you out of here as soon as we can. We need to move you before someone realizes you're here."

"What? Like who? Do you know something I don't, Petra? Why won't you tell me?"

"I don't—I don't know anything. I just know someone wanted to hurt you in that alley, and we can't take the chance they'll find out you're here. We have to get you to a safe place. If the person who attacked you comes looking for you, we're putting everyone in danger." She paused to look at him. "We have to get you out before someone else gets hurt."

"Okay. You think that might happen?"

She pushed her hands through her long, pale blonde hair. "I'm sorry. I should never have brought you here. It was stupid."

He blinked at in utter bemusement. "Petra, what are you talking about?"

Petra stepped forward and pressed her lips abruptly against his. He caught her around the waist, but she pressed her palms to his chest to push him just as abruptly away. If she started now, she might not stop, and she might do something even stupider than bringing him here—like confessing everything. "Lux will be here soon to take us to the safe house."

"Lux?"

"She's in charge of security for the compound. She's been preparing a safe place to go."

"But–"

"I'll explain everything when there is time, okay? And I hope..." She peered up into his stormy grey eyes. "I hope you'll forgive me."

"Petra–"

She ignored him. She was already fumbling out her cell phone to summon the inner circle to Key's room. She paused and turned back to look at him from the gate. Her expression was troubled. "Don't go anywhere."

"Petra, what–"

She slipped out the curtain and yanked the gate down before he could finish. He heard the padlock click into place. He sighed in frustration. No, he wasn't going anywhere.

The inner circle converged upon Key's room the same moment she arrived. Key was waiting for them. "What's up, Petra? Did you learn something?"

She looked around at them grimly. They didn't seem to like her expression. They glanced at each other uneasily. "Yes. A little, but that's not important right now. Shaw knows."

"What?" Jesse demanded.

"He went into my room while I was out. He saw Dante. He knows he's here."

"Damn it," Key cursed, pushing his hands through his dark hair.

"That nosy, entitled little bastard," Rip muttered. "I knew he couldn't be trusted."

"Yeah," Petra said darkly. "And if that wasn't enough, I talked to Tripp. Scarlet hasn't announced that the prince is missing, but he has people out all over the city investigating. Word is getting around. The bounty hunters found out, and they're trying to beat out the King's people to find him and bring him."

"There's a price on him?" Key asked, frowning.

"No. Not officially. Scarlet doesn't want anyone to know he's gone off in case he's gone rogue or is shacked up on a bender somewhere. He doesn't want the city to think he can't control his son. But the people who need to know do, and we can bet they'll do just about anything to get him back."

"Nothing has changed," Beth said firmly. "We knew this was going to happen.

We need to move him as soon as we can and take it from there." Her pretty, sweet face looked pinched and tense.

"We're doing that as soon as Lux gets here. She's secured the safe house, and she's on her way back now."

"Nothing's changed but now someone else knows. Someone we can't be sure won't use the information to hurt us," Ellis said. His young, smooth face was expressionless, but his pale eyes were narrowed thoughtfully. "What do you think he's going to do now that he knows?"

Petra shook her head. "I don't know. He's been lurking around trying to talk to me. I don't know what he's after, but if he decides to blackmail us, he could do some serious damage."

"Where is he?" Beth asked.

"I don't know. I didn't look for him. I came right here to tell you what happened."

"We need to find him," Key said. "We need to find out what he knows and what he plans to do about it. He could be dangerous, or he could just want to use the information to get something from us. We'll just have to give it to him. If he wants into the inner circle, we let him in. We have to give into whatever demands he has. At least until we have the situation under control."

Petra scowled, but she didn't argue with this. Key was right. Whatever Shaw wanted, they would have to give it to him. She didn't like to think about what that would mean for her if Beth was right about what he really wanted from Petra. Would she have to pretend she wasn't completely disgusted by him? Would she have to...She shuddered and turned back to the others. They needed to find him first. "Okay, let's spread out and find him. Whoever finds him first, bring him here and text the others."

No one argued. "Petra, you stay with Grey," Key ordered. "We have to keep him contained until this is under control. We can't risk someone else finding out about him before we're ready to move him. We'll call you if we find Shaw."

Petra sighed, but she nodded. "Yeah. Okay." She followed the others out of the room. She wanted to join them in the search for Shaw, but Key was right. She needed to stay with Grey. She had to be prepared for the moment he realized there was a really good reason he might want to escape. She had to be prepared to do whatever it took to hold onto him. He could regain his memories at any moment. And when the dam broke, she had no way of knowing how he would react.

That wasn't entirely true. She did know how he would react. She only hoped that when he did finally remember who he was....well, she didn't hold out a lot of hope that he would actually forgive her. She didn't think he would decide the feelings he'd been experiencing since he'd lost his memory were real.

She didn't think he was going to be able to look past kidnapping, lying and manipulating. When he remembered, Grey would be gone. Everything he felt and everything he thought he was would be gone with him. She'd better get used to it now.

When she slipped back into her room, Grey was on the computer. He didn't glance up as he heard the gate rattle up to admit her. He stared at the screen with narrow eyes. He'd been pushing his hands through his hair. She could tell because it was even more mussed in the back. "Grey?"

He lifted his head to look up at her with grey eyes. He wasn't seeing her. His gaze was far away, in some other time and place. "I think I remember something."

She frowned slightly. "What is it?"

Grey shot to his feet. He paced briskly in front of her, absently ruffling the back of his hair even more. "I was drunk. It's fuzzy, but I was talking to someone. I remember. I threatened him.

"What? You were threatening someone? Are you sure?"

"It's pretty blurry. I remember seeing a man I knew talking to someone in an alley. I don't know what they were doing or talking about, but it must have been something they shouldn't be. I didn't talk to them, but I remember seeing the man later somewhere else." He scrunched up his face with the effort to remember, but he finally shook his head in frustration. "I don't know where we were. It was dark. I can't make it out. I said I would turn him in if he didn't give me what I wanted."

"What did you want?"

He shrugged. "I don't know. I don't know if he gave anything to me." He looked extremely troubled by this. She suspected he was beginning to doubt himself. He was afraid of who he had been. With good reason.

Petra stared at him narrowly for several long seconds. "You don't have any idea at all who the man was?"

"No. No, I can't even see his face. I don't even know what I thought he was doing. It's like it's just spinning around. I was so drunk. I probably couldn't even see straight." He frowned. "I think I was drunk a lot."

Her pulse leapt. If Dante was blackmailing someone, perhaps it wasn't his father who'd ordered the attack, after all. It would make the trade considerably more straight-forward, but it wouldn't help them much in figuring out they were actually up against if he couldn't remember anything else. It could have been anyone he'd spoken to that night. Dante's reputation for cruelty and terrorism was wide-spread and well-known. It might have been a civilian, a Marshal, a hunter—even a Noble. It wouldn't have been the first time he'd fingered one of his father's men for treason. There were probably dozens of people out there who had good reason to want him dead.

"Maybe the person I threatened is the one who attacked me."

"I was thinking the same thing. Do you remember anything at all about him?"

He shook his head. "No. Not really. It's all a blur. I might recognize his face if I saw him, but...I can't make it out. I don't know if it was the same person as I saw the night I was attacked." He sighed deeply and dropped his head. When he looked back up at her, his expression was grim. "Petra, what kind of man am I?"

She sighed. "Grey...whatever you were...I don't know if you're that person now."

"How can that be true? The things I remember...I don't think I'm a very good person." He stared at her. "Is that why you wouldn't be with me?"

She blinked in surprise. "No. No, I..."

"I don't feel like that same person. I feel like me." Grey frowned. "But I don't even know who that is." He sat down on the edge of the bed. "If I was so bad before, can I be good now?"

She sat down beside him. "I don't know, Grey. I don't really know about stuff like that, but I believe you can. Maybe you can at least try."

He rose to pace in front of her. "I will. I will try. I don't want to go back to those memories. I don't want to be the sort of person who would threaten or blackmail someone and doesn't even know why."

"We can worry about this later. I need to get you out of here right now."

He turned to her with an air of resolve. "Okay. Yes. I don't want to put anyone else in danger."

Petra rose and pulled her cell phone from her pocket. "Lux should be here any second to take us to the safe house. Don't worry. We'll figure this out."

He strode toward her with an intensity in his eyes that made her stomach flip.

Suddenly, a scream echoed through the hallway outside. Grey and Petra spun toward the sound. "What is that?."

"Grey, stay here."

"No. I'm going with you--"

She ignored him and spun around to scoop up her laptop. She shoved it hastily into her satchel and turned back toward the door.

The gate clattered violently as Key burst into the room. He looked more frightened than Petra had ever seen him. "We have to get to the safe house now. We're under attack." For a moment, they just stared at him in shock. "Go!" he growled.

"They're searching for him, aren't they?" The color drained from Petra's face. She looked at Grey.

"Yes. Just go! Get him out of here! It's your only chance."

"Key! What is happening down there?"

"You have to go. Lux is back. She's ready to take you."

"We have to get the others out first, Key!"

"We can take care of it. You two need to go."

"No!" Grey snapped. "We can't just leave while the others are in trouble. If they are after me, I have to do something to help."

Key glared at him. "There isn't anything you can do. If you go down there, you will just make it worse. You need to leave."

"Where's Lux?" Petra demanded.

"She just came in. She's in the damn thick of things, as usual, but she's ready to take you where you need to go." He called after her as she raced toward the door. "Keep your head down. Stay off the main floor if you can."

Petra cursed and grabbed Grey's hand. There was no one in the older kid's hall, but as soon as they stepped out of the room, they could hear the screaming and shouting from the main floor. Petra's stomach sank, but there was no time to worry about what she'd brought upon them. They had to find Lux and get Grey out of the compound before anyone recognized him.

Petra led him up to the top floor where they could look down upon the common room without being seen. She wished she hadn't. The scene there was horrifying. A pack of bounty hunters raged through the compound, picking up the scattering kids or knocking them down as they stormed past, throwing open doors and gates and trampling the kids' toys and belongings underfoot. The man leading the of the hunters was tall and thin. He wore a long, black coat that covered him from neck to foot.

He didn't look like a hunter. He didn't look like a Noble. He certainly wasn't a Marshal. She paused and stared at him. She didn't recognize him, but his expression was so cold, so determined, he sent a chill down her spine. As she watched the chaos below, the screaming kids and the vicious bounty hunters, she saw the leader pick up a small boy with spiky orange hair by the collar.

His voice carried with eerie clarity. "Where is the prince?"

The boy looked terrified. He shook his head wildly. The man tossed him aside as though he were nothing more than a rag doll. The boy didn't move. Petra didn't even the boy's name. She thought he might have been a new kid, only just joined the lost kids in the old mall. Her heart hitched.

She tugged on Grey's hand. "We have to go! We have to find Lux. Come on!"

He didn't move. He was frozen in horror. "Prince?"

"Grey, we have to go!"

"We have to help them! If they want me, I should just let them take me. It's got to be better than letting this happen--"

"No! Grey, come on--"

He shook off her hand and started toward the stairs. She chased after him. He didn't make it to the main floor. Lux rushed up the stairs to meet them. She seized Grey's arm and dragged him with her toward Petra. Grey looked startled, but he didn't fight her.

"Lux!" Petra exclaimed in relief.

Lux didn't stop to chat. "Come on! Shaw must have told the hunters. We have to get him out of here now."

Grey frowned as they dragged him toward the tunnels. "This is about me. They're looking for me. The prince? What does that mean?"

Lux and Petra ignored him. "We'll explain when we get to the safe house," Petra promised. She glanced back down at the chaos below. She stopped dead in her tracks.

Key had stepped forward to meet the leader of the hunters. He was a good fighter, but he was no match for the thinner, taller man. Petra hesitated, her pulse leaping in fear. Key needed help–

"Petra!" Lux shouted.

She shook her head. "Key. He's—"

"Petra, come on!"

Grey looked between the two girls. "Petra, you can't go down there. If these people are looking for me, I should just go to them! I can stop this all."

"No!" Lux snapped. "Just come on."

"These could be the people who attacked you," Petra told him. "They might kill you if they find you. Or they will take you to King Scarlet."

Grey scowled and glanced down into the chaos. Then he stopped dead, as though something had struck him. He lifted his hand to point at the leader, who still sparred with Key below them. "Him. I think I recognize him. I think he is the one who attacked me that night."

"All the more reason to get out of here! Grey, please."

Finally, he listened. They raced through the halls toward the tunnel in the back of the compound. The hunters hadn't found the alternate entrance, and the escapees broke out into the night air without a fight.

"Beth and the others will get the kids out," Lux told them as they burst out of the burnt out part of the mall and crept along the side of the building toward the outlands.

Petra nodded and gripped Grey's hand almost painfully as they followed Lux away from the no-man's land around the mall. She was taking them further into the outlands. Petra's heart raced, but they didn't stop. They avoided the clusters of outlaws and vagrants that lingered in the streets, throwing Molotov cocktails into abandoned buildings or gathering around trash can fires under crumbling awnings.

The safe house was an abandoned warehouse in the outlands, about a mile from the compound. It was on a dark, quiet street. It was boarded up and covered in graffiti. It looked as though no one had dared enter since the war. Lux had made sure of that. She had been using it as training grounds for the compound's security force for years.

It wasn't as glamorous as the old mall, but it was comfortable enough. There was a small office upstairs, but the rest of the place was one large room with high ceilings and concrete walls. Cots and mattresses spread along the walls in neat little rows. There was a large supply of food stacked along one side of the room. The place even had running showers in the back. The stalls were makeshift, just curtains around facets that jutted out of the wall, as though they hadn't originally been there when the warehouse was built; Lux must have had them put in.

Petra dropped her laptop on one of the mattresses. Grey stood in the center of the room. He didn't move. His eyes raged and stormed. He looked angry and helpless, but there was something else, too. He looked as though something was happening behind those eyes that made Petra's insides churn uncomfortably.

"We'll be safe here. At least for now," Lux said grimly. "Until we can figure all this out."

Petra swiped a single, traitorous tear from her cheek. "Key?"

Lux shook her head. "I don't know, Petra." She sighed. "I have to get back and help guide the others here. You'll be safe."

The door burst open, and a few of Lux's security people ushered in a cluster of the kids from the compound. Some of them had bruises on their cheeks or their arms and legs. Others just looked scared and confused. They huddled together on the cots and mattresses, but they didn't talk much.

Petra felt her stomach sink into her knees. This was her fault. All of it.

Lux looked around at the kids. When she turned back to Petra, her expression was thunderous. "Get him upstairs to the office. We need to keep him hidden. They don't need to see him. We don't want anyone to know he's here." She scowled. "We don't need another Shaw, especially after all this."

Grey shook his head violently. "This is all about me. What's going on, Petra?" He frowned and stepped toward her. He didn't sound angry. He sounded hurt. "It's time you tell me what this is all about. You've been lying to me. I know you have. I want to know the truth."

She stared at him for several seconds. Her heart leapt uncomfortably into her throat. Finally, she nodded and spun toward the stairs that lead up to the private office. She didn't turn to ensure he was following her. She could feel him behind her, and he felt different than he used to. He felt cold and tense. It chilled her. Dante was there, right below the surface. It wouldn't be long before Grey realized it, too. He might already know.

Dust danced on the air in the office. An old, metal and black desk sat alone along one wall. A rickety chair sat on broken wheels behind it. The room had an air of neglect. If it had been used before the war, no one had bothered to tend to it since. Petra ignored it. She pulled the door closed with a finality that sent a chill up her spine. She didn't want to look at Grey. She wasn't sure what she would see there. When she finally did, he was staring at her. He looked different. His eyes were cold and serious.

"The prince. Prince Dante." She couldn't tell what he was thinking or feeling. He just looked like an ice statue. He looked like the real Dante now more than ever. "Those hunters were looking for me, but they were asking for the prince. I'm him, aren't I? I'm Dante."

She stared at him. Her chest ached peculiarly. If she told him now, it was over, but she couldn't keep lying to him. It was over. He already knew. She could see his life rushing back into his brain like a computer downloading information. She could almost see the pieces of memory passing across his eyes like a data stream. It was already coming back to him. Everything was falling apart.

"You told me I was Grey, but I'm not, am I? I'm Prince Dante. I'm King Scarlet's son."

She dropped her head. Her long, pale blonde hair fell over her face. She took a deep, hitching breath. It was all over. "Yes."

"I don't understand, Petra! Why would you do this? Why didn't you just tell me the truth?"

"I couldn't. You were in danger...there were people after you."

"And they found me! All of this...it's all my fault."

"No." She stepped toward him. He took a sharp step away from her. His eyes were chilling. She froze. "It's my fault, Grey."

"That isn't my name! Was anything you told me true? I know I don't live with you in the compound. I live in the King's mansion...I remember now. Now that I know, it's coming back. Did I even know you? Why did you lie to me? Tell me the truth, Petra! Why did you do this?"

She stared at him. She didn't know what to say. She didn't know how to explain without admitting the truth, without destroying everything between them. She didn't get to try. The door burst open with a clatter. They spun to face the inner circle. They looked distressed, but mostly they were furious. Key wasn't with them.

"Most of the kids are here and safe," Beth said in a low voice. Her eyes glinted in a way that worried Petra.

She was afraid, but she asked anyway. "Key?"

Beth shook her head slowly. She turned her face from Petra, but not before Petra saw a single tear streak down her pale cheek. "He's here. He made it out. But he's in bad shape. I'm not sure he's going to make it."

Petra's breath hissed out. "I want to see him."

"No!" Beth's anger took Petra by surprise. "You've done enough."

Jesse lifted a hand to point at Grey. "You brought him here. You brought this on us, Petra."

The color drained from Petra's face. She stared plaintively around at her closest friends. None of them defended her. None of them said a word. She didn't blame them. Jesse was right. She dropped her head in her hands. "I know." She glanced at Grey. He was staring at her as though he wasn't sure whether to give into his anger or pity her for her friends' admonishment. She didn't need his pity. She didn't need anyone's pity. She lifted her chin in defiance. "I was just trying to save our family and friends!"

"This was not the way!" Lux growled.

"What is the way, then? Has anyone else come up with anything better? Anything at all? There was nothing else we could have done!"

"He has to go. We have to get him out of here," Jesse said, pacing tensely across the floor. "We should turn him in. If they have him back, they'll leave us alone. They'll forget about us. We can go back to how it was."

"Don't be stupid. Shaw already told them we have him. They know it was us who took him," Ellis said reasonably. He peered at Grey with a thoughtful expression. "But if he told them we saved him from the attack. If he stands up for us—"

Grey scowled. He seemed to have understood a little too well. "You kidnapped me? Why? Did you intend to ransom me?" When they all stared silently back at him, he glared. "I'm not going to help you!"

"Then we will all die," Beth said in a low voice.

"We can kill him now," Lux put in suddenly. "We could give Scarlet his body. Say we found him dead in the outlands after an outlaw attack. They might believe it."

Petra stepped in front of Grey. "No! No one's going to do anything to him. It wouldn't do any good anyway! It would never work!"

"You lied to me, Petra." She turned to face the prince. He didn't look angry now. He just looked hurt. "You made me think I was one of you. That we were friends. All along you were lying. I trusted you!"

It was true. It was all true. But she had done it for a reason. She met his gaze. "I did what I had to do. Your father is evil. He's taken our families and our friends and locked them up for nothing! He will do anything to keep his power! Do you even know who attacked you? Do you know who he is and who sent him? How come your father didn't announce that you were missing? He might have been the one who ordered it. We might have saved your life taking you away from there."

Grey looked troubled. He might have been thinking the same thing. He spun away from her with a frustrated sigh and pushed his hands through his dark hair. "I can't trust you. I can't trust anyone. I'm better off on my own."

"You can't go out there, Grey. It isn't safe."

He turned back to her. "What do you care? You don't care about me. You don't even know me." He swept his hand toward the others. "None of you do. You only care about what I can do for you."

There was a terrible, heartbroken look in his eyes. Petra's chest ached.

Lux stepped forward and seized Petra's arm. "Let him go, Petra. It's safer for all of us if he's gone. This has gone too far. We can't force him to stay." She turned to give Grey a dangerous look. "We didn't hold you against your will. We took you in and we helped you. We protected you."

He scowled. "I'm not going to tell on you."

"But Shaw--" Jesse began.

Lux's head snapped to him. "Shaw doesn't know anything. He didn't know what we were planning. He wouldn't have been able to tell anyone. Just let him go."

"You think it will matter what they know for sure?" Jesse hissed. "If Scarlet gets it into his head we kidnapped his son, we're all dead."

"I'm not going to let that happen," Grey said firmly. "I won't tell anyone where I've been. But I can't be here anymore. I have to go. I need to remember who I am and what happened to me."

He started toward the door. Petra stepped forward and caught his arm. "Grey--"

He turned to glare at her. "That isn't my name, is it? You made it up. I'm

Dante."

"Yes." When he tried to pull his arm away, she tightened her fingers on his wrist. "Dante, please stay and think about this. Try to remember before you go. You need to know what you're getting into, at least! This is the only place you are safe."

Dante shrugged her off. He didn't turn back to look at her again. He strode out the door with an awful finality that felt like a kick in Petra's stomach.

Beth caught Petra's arm. Petra glanced at her. Her eyes blurred with tears. "It's better this way," Beth said softly. "You have to let him go. It all went wrong. We have to cut our losses before we make it any worse. He made his choice. He's on his own."

Petra took a hitching breath. "I want to see Key."

Beth looked as though she didn't want to take her, but she finally nodded. "I'll take you to him."

Key looked terrible. He lay in the midst of the injured in a small cot that was almost too small for him. He wasn't dead, but his face was purple with bruises. Eloise, a short, curvy girl with short, curly black hair, was mopping the blood gently from his face. His chest rose and fell as though even breathing was painful. Petra suspected his ribs were cracked or broken. She didn't know why the cold, vicious leader of the hunters had left him alive.

She didn't know why they'd left anyone alive. Perhaps the bounty hunters hadn't wanted the blood of so many innocent children on their hands. It was on their hands, though. Some of the kids were badly hurt, but everyone had made it out alive. This, at least, was a relief.

Eloise glanced up at Petra with a cold expression. Did she know it had been Petra's fault? "He's going to be okay, but it's going to hurt," Eloise said. "We weren't able to bring anything with us from the mall, so we don't have any pain meds."

Petra sighed. "I'll get some." She sat down beside Key and laid a hand gently on his forehead. He didn't even stir. She took a hitching breath and swiped a tear from her cheek. She couldn't look up into Beth's eyes. She knew even her best friend blamed her for all of this, and Beth had every right to.

Lux strode into the main room. She paused to look around at the devastation. Those who had not been badly injured tended to the others. The room filled with the sound of quiet sobbing. The littler kids complained bitterly about leaving their things at the mall, but they did not realize how lucky they were to be away from it.

Petra glanced up at Lux as she paused beside Key's cot. Lux's dark eyes glinted angrily, but she didn't loose her frustration on Petra. Instead, she knelt down next to them. "He going to be okay?"

Petra nodded. "I think so. He's just beat up. I need to go into town and get some meds for everyone." She hung her head. "This is all my fault, Lux. I thought I could save us, but I just hurt everyone."

Lux considered this. She laid a hand on Petra's shoulder. "You made a mistake. But everyone is going to make it. Get it together. We need all hands to make this right again. We're safe for now."

Petra sighed. "What are we going to do, Lux?"

"Nothing. We wait until it all calms down." She rose abruptly. "I'm going into town, too. I'll see what I can find out about the fallout from all of this. I'll see if I can find that little bastard Shaw and figure out who he told. Maybe it'll tell us who is behind the attack. I'll get some supplies while I'm out."

Petra was surprised. "You're still going to try to find out what happened to Dante?"

"I want to know. I want to know who was responsible for this. That guy who was leading the pack wasn't a hunter, but I don't think he was one of the King's men, either. I want to know who he is."

Petra thought about this. "Dante said he was the one who attacked him in the alley the night I found him. I don't think he knows who he is. Someone must have hired him. He thought he might have been blackmailing someone. It could have something to do with it."

"I intend to find out who is behind it. Maybe if I can find Shaw, it'll tell us something." She stared narrowly at Petra for a long moment. "I know you cared about him, Petra. I can tell."

She looked away. "I didn't even know him."

Lux laid a hand on her shoulder. It was oddly soothing. The anger drained from her dark eyes. "Maybe you did. I can see it's important to you. Are you just going to let him go out there alone and get killed? Someone is still after him. Those hunters might have been looking for a payout, but the leader...there was something about him. I think if he finds Dante, he'll finish the job. Maybe if we can help figure out who's after him, if we can help him, maybe he'll help us."

"I did it all wrong. If I hadn't lied from the beginning...this would have gone a lot differently."

"Yes. You did do it wrong, Petra. But it's too late now to think about that. Now we have to work with what we have."

Petra considered this a long moment. She looked down at Key. His lip was swollen, and bruises stood out garishly blue on his tanned face. She squeezed his hand. "We'll fix this," she whispered. "I promise, Key. We're going to figure out who did this to you. This isn't over."

CHAPTER SEVEN

Meanwhile, in the treacherous streets of Razor City...

Dante followed the winding path through the shadows and back alleys of Razor City. His heart thumped. He wished he had a weapon. In the darkness behind an old, dilapidated tenement building, he knelt and searched the debris. He didn't find a knife or a gun, but he found a large, jagged rocked amongst the torn newspapers and trash. It would have to do.

He avoided the main streets, even in the city center. Marshals in scarlet suits patrolled, hassling the citizens who passed by or standing around in small groups, chatting and laughing. Even if the Marshals weren't behind his attack and the attack on the compound, he didn't think showing his face to them was wise. He'd seen them in action. He knew what they were really like now.

He needed to remember. If he could just remember...Part of him wanted to leave it all behind. He remembered just enough to know plenty of reasons why someone would want to kill him. He remembered enough to know exactly why there were many people who wanted to see him dead. His memories, the flashes of his life—they were horrible. Blood, misery--not his own misery. He'd been perfectly happy, but he'd caused so much unhappiness. He'd hurt and tormented so many people, and they all hated him for it. He didn't really blame him. He was beginning to hate himself.

His father's face, twisted and angry...The man in black in a dark alley with his hand raised to strike a killing blow...Petra...His mother. She'd been young and beautiful and sweet...His mother lying in a pool of blood...Elia...Blood...more blood. So, so much blood. A city of blood. A city of scarlet.

The flashes were coming fast and furious now. It was as though simply finding out his own name had broken the wall in his mind that had been keeping him from knowing himself. He didn't want to remember. He didn't want to know who he had been. He wanted to go back to Petra's fairy tale. He wanted to be a lost child. He wanted to feel the way he'd felt when he was with her. He wanted to be innocent. He wanted Grey to be real. He didn't want to know the truth. He didn't want to know all the things he'd done and the people he had hurt.

Suddenly, as though wishing them away had only drawn them closer, the memories crashed over him in a terrible, disorienting rush. He cried out and clutched his head, falling against the dirty alley wall. Then it was all back. Every ugly, horrific moment.

The war, the terrible, bloody civil war that had torn the country apart...the moment the government had been destroyed and everything had gone dark until the fires started and all hell broke loose...the fighting and looting in the streets... his father tearing through the city, crushing anyone who got in his way on his rise to power...innocents shot dead in the streets...children crying over their parents' dead bodies...himself accusing innocent men of treason and enjoying their fear as they faced a firing squad in the blood-soaked courtyard outside the King's mansion...so much blood, always blood everywhere...the Uprising spreading through the people like a silent, deadly predator, evidence of their influence appearing in every corner of the city...so many nights drinking...the women, the people he had hurt and humiliated...his father shouting at him, his eyes filled with rage and shame for the corrupted, wicked young man his son had become...his father, always his father who was willing to kill him himself if he had to...

He didn't want any of it. He begged to go back. He begged to be Grey again. Grey had been innocent. He hadn't known any of the horrors and the endless tiny evils that Dante knew so well. He'd been so desperate to remember who he was, but now that he did, he would give anything to go back. At least when he'd been Grey, he hadn't known what sort of person he truly was. There weren't any of these images, these hideous nightmares that were his entire world. When he was Grey, there had been only longing and fear, and there had been Petra.

The person he was--the person Dante was--was disgusting.

The flood subsided, but the pain did not. He groaned and straightened up. He pictured Petra's face. He'd cared for her. He'd genuinely cared for her, but he knew now that he hadn't known her at all. She'd lied and manipulated him. Everything she'd told him had been to keep him quiet and contained until she could use him to get back her family and friends--the ones who had been falsely accused. The ones who shouldn't even be locked up.

He pressed his hand to his forehead. He didn't know what Petra was. He wondered if he would have done the same. Yes, he certainly would have. Dante would have done much, much worse. He had done much, much worse. Those people she'd been so desperate to save, for whom she was willing to do anything, were in prison because of him and his people.

He couldn't really blame her for trying to use him to get them back.

Tears streaked down his cheeks. He took a hitching breath.

He knew everything now. And he knew Petra was the first person—the first thing—in his life that had made him feel safe and decent and loving since he'd lost his mother to Scarlet's city of blood. Even if it had been all a lie.

* * *

Meanwhile, in the outlands...

"What do we know about Shaw?" Lux asked. She shot out a hand to press Petra back against an alley wall as two men with spiky hair passed by, laughing raucously.

Petra sighed and shook her head. "Not much. His parents were imprisoned for treason. Jayne brought him in about two months ago, said he found him hiding out in one of the burnt out houses in the outlands. He was beat up and looked like he hadn't eaten in a few days."

"Yeah, and since he got to the compound, he's been acting like we owe him something."

Petra considered. "He just wanted to be part of the inner circle."

"Yeah, well, turning Dante in wasn't the way to do it."

"I never expected he would turn on us like that. If I had known..."

"I would have booted his traitor ass right out."

Petra snorted. "Yeah, I think I would have, too. I would have taken any excuse."

"So no ideas where he might be hiding out?"

She shook her head. "No. No ideas. As far as I knew, he didn't have a friend in the world before he came to us. I don't know where he could be. Probably hiding out in the outlands again."

"He might've gotten paid enough for his information to be camped out in one of the hotels in the city center."

"We could check."

Lux snorted. "I don't think we'll have much success with that. I don't see a desk clerk giving us guest room numbers."

"Maybe your guy can get it for us."

Lux shook her head. "If he knows about the hit on the compound we might not have to."

"Why wouldn't he?"

"Because it was the hunters who hit us, not the Marshals. Don't you think the King would have sent his own people if he'd known where Dante was?"

Petra considered. "Did you find out anything about the guy who was leading them? The one who attacked Dante the first time?"

"A little. One of my contacts heard the call out for hunters, but she didn't make the hit. She doesn't go after kids."

She scowled. Petra peered out into the street. It was clear. She tilted her head, and the girls ran across to the next alley. A pile of newspapers stirred. They jumped as an old, dirty man cursed furiously at them. They ignored him. "Who is he?" Petra demanded.

"His name's Saer Dagon. No one knows that much about him. He doesn't usually work with the hunters. He works for money up front."

"He's a hit man?"

"He does jobs for the King and the Nobles. Only people who can afford to pay him. He doesn't pick up bounties. He solves problems."

"So he was sent to kill Dante."

"Maybe. I don't know. He didn't manage to do it the first time, so he might have had some other reason for going after him that night. He's good. He's the best. Even the hunters are afraid of him. They seem to think he's something inhuman. Like he's had some kind of augmentation or something. There are a lot of rumors."

"What sort of augmentation?"

"To make him faster and stronger, I guess. He was in a coma during the war, and word is some mad scientist did experiments on him. When he woke up, he killed the doctor, left him all torn up in the lab. Then he went on a rampage and killed a bunch of the King's men before they caught up to him. Scarlet didn't imprison him, though; he hired him to do his dirty work."

Petra frowned. "It sounds like a load of rubbish."

"Yeah, I thought so too. He's like a bounty hunter boogey man. Anyway, they're sure he's on some kind of drugs. He's pretty much unstoppable when he's juicing."

Petra exhaled heavily. "And he's after Dante?"

"Yeah, but like I said, he might not have been trying to kill him. The hunters seem to think that if he's sent to kill you—you're dead. You don't get a second chance."

"I think Dante took him by surprise. He remembered having a gun. He shot him."

"From the sound of it, a little gunshot isn't going to take this guy down. You saw him at the compound. He didn't look like a bullet wound was slowing him down."

Petra considered this. "If he's the one after Dante, we need to find him."

"Saer?" Lux sounded completely incredulous. "What do you think we're going to do?"

"No, not Saer. Dante. We have to make sure he knows who this guy is."

"Petra, that's nuts. What do you think we're going to do? Knock on the King's palace doors and ask to see him? What are you going to tell them—you're the girl who kidnapped him and now you want to warn him his life's in danger? Come on."

She sighed. Her chest ached. "I know it's stupid."

"Petra, we've already covered the outlands. He's made it back to the city center. He's probably back at his dad's house now. You made a mistake when you lied to him, and now he's gone. You have to let it go."

"I thought you were on my side."

"I was. I am. But now that he's back with his father, there's nothing we can do. I'm not going to let you go rushing into a bad situation because you have a crush."

Petra glared at her. "I don't have a crush."

"Whatever. Come on. We're here. Keep your guard up. This isn't the Blade. This is the outlands. This club is rough."

"The Blade isn't rough?"

"Not like this."

The entrance to the club was in an alley across the street. No one was outside. Even in the daylight, it looked sinister and dangerous. There wasn't even a name over the beaten, peeling black door. Lux rapped once with her knuckles. A tall woman with long black hair and piercings in her nose and lip that connected with a thick, metal chain opened the door. Her eyes were sharp and suspicious. When she saw Lux, she nodded and stepped aside.

"Just keep your head down and let me do the talking," Lux ordered. "This isn't your average hunter. This is one of the King's guys. If he gets caught talking to us or has any idea we had Dante, this could get ugly for all of us. He can't be trusted."

Petra nodded. The man they were meeting looked as though he was in his late twenties. He had dark hair combed back from his face. He was clean shaven and looked well-kept, as though he spent a lot of time tending to his appearance. He wasn't handsome, but he had the look of a man who lived well.

He wasn't wearing a scarlet suit. He was dressed in neat jeans and a long black coat. There was a bulge under his arm that Petra was certain was a weapon. In the outlands, he'd need one. He'd look extremely appetizing to muggers and outlaws.

He was sitting in a table in the corner. It was a quiet place. Soft music played over the speakers. Voices hummed in the dusty corners and at the long, beaten wooden bar on the far side of the room. There were only a few people in the bar this early in the day, but there was a breathless, cagey quality to the air, like the patrons might fly at each other at any moment like animals upon their prey. It was a good place to meet if you didn't want anyone to come looking for you. Most people would have the good sense to stay away.

"Hello, Lux," the Marshal greeted.

Lux inclined her head. "Raff."

Raff's eyes flicked to Petra. He didn't ask who she was. He didn't seem to care. He nodded to her and turned back to Lux. "You wanted to talk."

"Yeah. You heard anything about the prince lately?"

Raff didn't seem particularly interested in why she wanted to know. He didn't even bat an eyelash. He shook his head. "No. He still hasn't turned up."

"What?" Petra exclaimed. Lux elbowed her in the ribs, and she snapped her mouth shut.

"I'm sorry I didn't warn you the hunters were coming," Raff told Lux with a frown. "I didn't know."

"You didn't know?" Lux sounded surprised.

"No. None of us knew. We were all shocked when we heard the hunters crashed your compound. No one had even heard the tip he was there before they hit."

Lux and Petra exchanged a frown. "The King didn't know about it?"

"We don't know if he knew. We just know we didn't know. He didn't send us."

"It was Saer Dagon. He was leading the hunters."

Raff's eyebrows traveled up toward his neatly combed hair. "Saer? He was there?"

"Yeah. Any idea who would send him and why?"

"All he does is kill."

"Who does he work for?"

"You know who he works for. I've seen him around the palace. He works for the King, as far as I know. We never know what he's been hired to do until it's happened. Sometimes we don't even know then. He doesn't come out for just anything. He's the best. And he doesn't fail."

"He tried to kill the prince once," Lux told him. "He failed."

Raff stared at her for several seconds. "You have to be mistaken."

"Why?"

"If Saer went after the prince, he was sent by Scarlet."

Petra's breath caught. "Are you sure about that?"

"I've never heard of him working for anyone but the King's people. No one else can afford him. But I don't see a Noble hiring Saer behind the King's back to kill his son. Saer isn't loyal to anyone, but if someone wanted to go after the prince, they wouldn't send an assassin that's in the King's pocket. The King would find out about it. Saer would tip him the moment he offered some cash or juice. None of the Nobles would take that risk, and no one else can afford him."

Lux sat back in her seat. Her expression was blank, but Petra could see the flash in her dark eyes. "Do you know who our traitor talked to?"

"I don't know. Like I said, I never heard about the hit until afterward. The Marshals were never involved. We didn't hear a word about it until it was too late to do anything about it."

"So you think the King might want to have the prince killed?"

Lux's voice was soft, but Raff reacted as though she'd shouted it. He hissed out his breath through his teeth. "It isn't safe to make those kinds of accusations about the King."

"But you think he did!" Petra whispered.

He glared at her. Lux nudged her sharply in the ribs again. Raff scowled. "I'm not saying anything of the kind. I'm just saying that Saer works for the King. He works for other people, too."

"We have to find him," Petra hissed to Lux. "We can't let him die."

Lux glared at her incredulously, but Petra leapt to her feet before her friend could shush her again. She raced toward the door without looking back. Lux's legs were longer, and she was in better shape. She caught Petra in the alley outside. "What the hell are you doing?" she demanded.

"I have to find him!"

Lux stared at her. "And how exactly do you intend to do that?"

"He isn't in the palace. He's still out there in the streets."

"And you think we're just going to find him? He could be anywhere. We don't know anything about him! He could be hiding with a friend or some girl somewhere."

Petra felt as though she'd been hit in the stomach. Lux was right. They didn't know anything about Dante's life. They didn't know where he could be or who he would be with if he was in trouble. She shook her head. "It doesn't matter. I have to try."

Lux sighed. She reached out to catch Petra's arm as she started away. "Wait."

Petra spun angrily back to her. "What?"

"I have an idea."

"What idea?"

"I have some friends. A network around the city. They are in most of the corners. If Dante shows his face somewhere, they'll know."

Petra perked up. "You'll talk to them?"

"Yeah. I'll talk to them. I'll put them on the lookout." She pulled her cell phone out of her pocket and punched in a message. She looked up at Petra. "It's done."

Petra frowned. "Is that safe?"

"Sure. I've been using them for years. I trust them."

"We trusted Shaw, too. Grey trusted me."

Lux patted her arm. "Things went horribly wrong, Petra. Suck it up. Get over it and move on." She jerked her chin. "Come on. You should get back to the safe house and check on Key. There's nothing else you can do."

Petra hesitated. She wanted to dart out into the streets and begin knocking on every door until she found Dante and warned him about Saer and his father. That was stupid, though. Finally, she sighed and nodded in resignation. "You think they'll find him?"

"If he's out there to be found, they'll find him, Petra. But right now, Key needs you."

"Yeah, you're right." She dropped her forehead in her hands. "I hope Key's all right."

"He will be. You need to have a little faith."

"I lost my faith a long time ago, Lux."

* * *

Meanwhile, in the heart of Razor City...

The King's mansion loomed over him. For a moment, Dante's step faltered. There were men in scarlet suits stationed outside. He could step out into the light of the courtyard and command the men to take him inside to his father, to bring all of this to an end in a single, easy instant. He could become Prince Dante again. He could have it all back.

He didn't step out into the light. He crept around the side of the mansion to the servant's doors. There were no guards there. He'd used the entrance before, on nights when he'd slipped his bodyguards or spent the night somewhere he shouldn't have and didn't want his father's watchdogs to rat him out.

The entrance wasn't locked. It was never locked. Dante didn't think his father and his people even remembered the servant's entrance. No one had used it in years. In fact, he couldn't remember a time anyone had used it. There were enough guards watching the perimeter around the house to keep any ill-intentioned citizens from even wandering close enough to find the unattended entrance.

Dante wasn't a wandering citizen. He knew exactly how to sneak inside through the chinks in the guards' armor. It was dark, but he'd navigated the steep, narrow stairs many times, usually drunk. He could find his room and slip inside before anyone noticed. He could probably hide in there for days without anyone realizing he'd ever come home. He didn't know how long he'd been gone. Perhaps he could claim to have been there the entire time and simply gone unnoticed.

Yeah, right. He would have to answer to his father. He wasn't sure what he was going to tell him. He could tell him the truth. He could have Petra and the innocent kids from the compound tossed in prison without a trial. He knew exactly where they were. He knew how to find them. They had committed a crime. They had kidnapped him. They'd lied to him. Petra had committed a crime. Kidnapped him. Lied to him.

But she and her people had protected him, too. They hadn't given him to the hunters. They'd suffered terribly for it, but they hadn't given him up. He didn't know what to do. He hadn't been telling the truth when he'd promised not to turn them in, but he wasn't sure he meant to do it, either. He needed time to think. He needed time to decide who to trust. He needed time to understand what Petra and her people had meant to him in those few, blissfully ignorant days. He needed to know what they still meant to him.

He sensed movement in the dark; heard the faintest rustle of fabric. His eyes hadn't adjusted to the darkness, but he felt the air change as something moved toward him. It was big, and it was fast. It hit him squarely in the chest. Dante staggered back down several stairs, but he didn't fall. He caught the railing before he tumbled down to the stone floor below. He didn't have to see the man to know who he was. He knew.

He felt rather than saw the man in black—the man from the alley and the compound—bracing for another attack. Tension crackled in the air. He heard the faintest intake of breath. Dante reached into his pocket. He hadn't needed it in the streets. He hadn't met any outlaws or muggers in the outlands or the city center, but he still carried the jagged rock that he'd picked up amongst the rubble in case trouble found him on his way to the palace. He wasn't a match for a man who killed for a living, but he knew these stairs, and he had the home team advantage.

When his assailant rushed him again, Dante lifted the rock and struck out blindly at him. He made contact. The man in black grunted. The blow was only glancing, but it must have been startled him or stolen his breath because the assassin stopped moving.

Dante didn't waste the brief seconds he had before the man came back to his senses. He rushed forward grabbed hold of his long, black coat to shove him toward the chilly stone floor. He heard the man hit the stairs as he fell. His attacker didn't fall far; he must have caught himself on the rail. Dante heard him scrambling to regain his feet, his shoes scraping against the stone floor. He didn't say a word.

Dante ran. He could hear the man struggling to his feet behind him, but Dante was fast, and he knew the King's land better than anyone. He didn't look back. He slipped past the Marshals the way he had come and hurtled into the dark, sinister streets around the city center.

He only had one place to go. He prayed he could remember the path back to Petra's safe house. He prayed that when he got there she would take him back. He couldn't go home again, not until he knew who the man was and why he was waiting for him in his father's house. How had he known where Dante would go? How had he known he would return? Who had sent him, and how had he gotten past the Marshals. Unless...unless he had been placed there on purpose. Unless he'd been sent by King.

He couldn't focus on that now. He didn't stop running. His lungs burned, but he reached the edge of the city in mere minutes. He'd been careful to pay attention when he'd left the safe house. He'd thought he'd meant to tell his father and their people where it was, to get back at the people who had tricked him and lied to him and kept him prisoner. But perhaps...perhaps he had really known all along there might be a time when he needed somewhere to run. Perhaps he'd suspected all along he'd need a way back.

The outlands, though, were a twisted, dirty, dilapidated maze. He'd only been there once on his own, and the streets all had the same sinister look to them. He wished he'd left a trail of bread crumbs or tied a string to something. He was hopelessly out of his element here. A gang of outlaws rushed through the streets, shouting and laughing. He ducked into an alley to avoid them. He clutched the rock in his hands. It was slick with blood. He grimaced and tossed it away.

When the outlaws were gone, things got worse. He was hopelessly lost. He didn't recognize the streets around him, even if he had traversed them mere hours ago. He cursed. It was dark. He couldn't possibly find his way to the safe house now, even as the fires burned around him and illuminated the streets and shadowed the back always. He would have to find a place to camp for the night.

He was going to need another rock.

* * *

Meanwhile, in a safe house in the outlands...

"Petra!"

Key was sleeping peacefully for the first time since the attack. The pain meds seemed to be helping. Eloise had given him a lot of them. He was badly beaten up, but Eloise had patched him up right enough. He would make it. Petra lifted her hand from his brow and looked up at Lux. She rose to meet her with a frown.

"Key just got to sleep. What the hell are you shouting for?"

Lux grabbed her arm and pulled her away from Key's sick bed. "We have a hit."

"A hit?"

"We found him. One of my people spotted Dante in the outlands. It sounds like he was heading here."

Petra blinked. Then her face lit up. "Here? He's okay? Is he alone?" Then her face fell. "Or is he...is he with..."

"No. He hasn't brought his dad's people. He's alone. He's okay for now, but he's in the outlands and he's unarmed."

"We have to go find him."

Lux hesitated.

"What?"

"Petra, he might...well, he might be coming back here for a different reason. He might be leading someone here."

"You said he was alone."

"Yes, he's alone. But that doesn't mean he doesn't just appear to be alone. He could just be bait for the Marshals. We have to be careful."

"He wouldn't do that."

"Petra, he's Prince Dante. He isn't Grey. He remembers who he is now. Whether he remembers everything, he at least knows who he is. We don't know the way he's going to react to what you did. We don't know how much of either person he is right now. He could be all Dante and no Grey. You know what he's capable of."

"It doesn't matter, Lux. We have to warn him about Saer and his father. He is in danger. He should know."

"If Raff was right, he's as safe as he can be right now, as long as he's not with his father."

"Safe? He's out there in the outlands by himself. He's in enemy territory. If he's spotted by someone else, his father and Saer will be the least of his worries!"

Lux stared at her a moment. She sighed. "You do care about him, don't you?" When Petra looked away, she shook her head. "That's stupid, Petra. You know who he is."

"It doesn't matter. It doesn't change anything."

Lux shook her head sadly. "All right. I'll help you."

Petra smiled. "Where is he?"

"Come on. He's not too far."

Key was wide awake when Petra and Lux passed him. He caught Petra's arm. He didn't look at all as though he'd just downed three pain meds. He looked sharp and suspicious. He frowned. His lips were swollen and bruised, but he could still talk. "Where are you going?"

Petra glanced at Lux. "Grey is wandering the outlands."

"So?" Key frowned. "I thought you let him go."

"We did, but he's still in danger. The guy who was leading the hunters is an assassin. He was the one who attacked Grey the night I found him. And he works for the King."

"You think Scarlet really is trying to kill his own son?"

"Yes. He could be anyway. We can't take that risk. He needs to know it isn't safe for him to go home until we know for sure."

"We have spies watching him," Lux put in. "He's still in the outlands—and he's still alive—so he probably hasn't found his way out yet. He'll probably head there as soon as day breaks or he finds a way to get a hold of his father's people."

"We have to warn him before Saer gets to him and it's too late."

Key sighed. "Petra..."

"We have to help him, Key. He's a victim in this, too."

"Maybe if we actually help him this time, he'll help us," Lux added.

Petra lowered her head. "I'm sorry about what happened, Key."

He waved a hand. "I'll make it and so will everyone else. Look, Petra, if you think this will save us and Grey, you have to at least try. At least warn him. Even if he doesn't forgive us, it's the right thing to do. You can't just sit back and let him die if you have the chance to stop it."

Petra smiled. She leaned down to kiss him on the forehead. He winced a little. "Sorry. But for the first time in a long time, Key, I agree with you. I think it's time I do the right thing for once."

Lux's phone chirped. She frowned down at it. "He's on the move, Petra. He's entering rebel territory. We have to go. If we don't get him now, we'll lose him to the Uprising. You know what they'll do to him."

Petra didn't need to hear more. She spun toward the door. "Bye, Key!"

He grunted in reply, but she wasn't listening anymore.

The streets were eerily quiet. Word of the attack on the compound must had spread to the outlanders. They were keeping their heads down in case any of the hunters got it in their heads to sweep the area for rogue bounties. Petra didn't mind; they didn't have time to tangle with outlaws tonight. Lux checked her phone and grabbed Petra's arm. "Come on. He's this way."

"Is he moving?"

"Not anymore. He went inside an old house. I think he might be camping out for the night."

"That's not very safe."

"Well, from the sound of it, being the prince isn't that safe right now regardless of where you are."

They hurried through the crumbling, deserted streets. Petra's heart pounded. She was thankful there were no gangs or vandals wandering around, raising hell or waiting to accost innocent, unsuspecting children. She didn't know have any idea they were going, and Lux didn't bother to tell her. She led Petra swiftly through the alleys and main streets with the ease of someone who spent a lot of time in the outlands. Petra felt safe with Lux.

She was still anxious. She hadn't been so anxious since she'd lost Ren.

Lux shot out an arm to push Petra back against the wall of a dark alley. Despite the loaded, charged atmosphere in the air all around them, a group of rebels suddenly tore through the street beyond, whooping and hollering. It sounded as though they were celebrating. Petra didn't like the sound of it. Her pulse leapt.

She peered out around the corner to catch a glimpse of what was happening.

Lux slammed her back against the wall. "What the hell are you doing?" she hissed.

"Is he with them? Let me see."

Lux scowled. "No. Stay back. They aren't after us, but we still don't want to be seen. You never know what they will do."

"What are they so happy about? Lux!"

Lux cursed. She ducked out toward the street to peer cautiously around the corner. "They don't have him. At least I don't think they do. I don't see him."

"Are you sure?"

"No. I'm sorry. I can't tell. There are too many of them. But our guy said he's inside the house." Her cell phone chirped. She glanced down at it and cursed again. "Yeah. Forget what I just said. We lost him."

"What? I thought you said he'd stopped moving. He was supposed to be in the house. I thought he was camping for the night."

"Apparently not. He must have gone. My guy says he isn't inside anymore."

"Where did he go?"

"I don't know, Petra!"

"How did he lose him?"

"He must have gone out a different way and my guy didn't catch him. I'm sorry, Petra. He's gone."

"We have to follow those rebels and see if they've got hold him. They might have found him in the house and taken him out."

"Petra, you know we can't. If the rebels do have them, they won't kill him. He might be safe enough for now. Probably safer than at home."

Petra scowled. "How can you be sure about that?"

"That's not what the Uprising does. They aren't killers or vigilantes. They're just trying to do something to change the way things are here in Razor City. They probably intend to do exactly what we planned to do with him."

"And failed."

Lux shrugged. "Maybe they will do a better job."

"That isn't making me feel any better! I want to go after them."

"No, Petra." She looked back down at her phone. Her fingers flew over the keys as she typed a message so quickly, Petra was amazed she'd had time to say anything.

"Lux!"

"Just hold on." She held up her hand. After several seconds, her phone chirped. She looked back up at Petra and caught her arm to drag her through the alley.

Petra bared her teeth in irritation, but she didn't resist. "Where are we going? The rebels went that way."

"Just shut up and come with me."

Petra didn't argue. Lux led her through the winding alleys to a door with a buzzing neon sign overhead. The sign still illuminated the name in jagged, flickering letters: Cutthroat Tavern.

Petra didn't like the sound of that. Bars in the outlands were risky. She didn't protest when Lux pulled her inside, though. Lux wasn't the sort to give up. Whatever the reason she was bringing Petra to the sinister place, it had to do with getting Grey back.

"What are we doing here?"

Lux rolled her eyes. "Just be patient. We're meeting someone."

Petra glanced around at the patrons. They hunched over their drinks when the door opened, as though they didn't want their faces to be seen. Petra didn't care about any of them. She followed Lux toward the back of the room. There was a young man sitting in a corner booth. He looked like a typical outlander. His clothes were tattered and torn, and his beard was thick and scruffy. He was wearing a wide-brimmed hat that concealed his eyes.

He tilted his head back to look at Lux as they walked toward him. He nodded and hunched back over his beer. When she slid into the seat across from him, he tipped his hat up to meet her gaze. "I'm sorry, Lux. I didn't mean to lose him."

"You were watching Grey?" Petra demanded, leaning forward.

The young man looked at her strangely. "I was watching Prince Dante."

"Right. What was he doing? What happened to him?"

"I don't know. I caught sight of him on the edge of the city. He seemed to be avoiding the King's Marshals."

"Yeah, because they're trying to kill him. I'm just glad he listened to something we said."

"What? They are?"

Lux waved her hand dismissively. "And?" she demanded.

"I wasn't sure where he was trying to go, but he seemed to be moving in your direction. He was looking for something, anyway. I think he got lost so he went into the house to wait out the night."

"Sounds about right."

"But he left the house?"

"He didn't come out for a few minutes, so I went in to make sure he was okay, like you asked. He was gone."

"Did the rebels take him?" Petra demanded.

The spy shook his head. "I don't know. I don't think so. I didn't see the rebels. They usually make themselves known."

"But they could have been in the house when he went in. Did you see them leave?"

"I didn't see anyone leave. I'm sorry. I walked around the immediate streets, but I couldn't catch up to him again."

Petra scowled. Lux nodded and rose. "Thanks, Bano. Let me know if you see him again." She passed him something across the table. Petra didn't see what it was. She probably didn't want to know.

Lux didn't move toward the door. She paused near the bar. Petra scowled. "What are you doing?"

"Petra, you need a drink. I need a drink."

"We have to find Grey!"

Lux squeezed her arm. She frowned. "You need to stop acting like a schoolgirl with a crush. You have to start thinking like an adult. This is not a game, Petra. If he was taken by the rebels, we can't just crash in there and get him. If he wasn't, he isn't far. Another of my spies will pick him up."

Petra sighed. She dropped her head in her hands. Lux waved over the bartender. He poured two shot glasses of amber liquid. Lux pushed one toward Petra and held hers up.

"Drink it."

Petra did. It burned down her throat. She winced and pushed away the empty glass.

"Petra, if you were thinking straight, you would have realized by now that, if the rebels have Dante, Beth will find out for us."

Petra's stomach flipped. Her face broke into a grin. "Lux!"

"Get it together, girl."

Petra leapt toward the door. "I will once we've found him. Come on!"

Lux rolled her eyes. She slapped a bill down on the counter and followed Petra back out into the uncannily noiseless streets.

CHAPTER EIGHT

Later, back at the safe house in the dirty, dilapidated outlands...

The safe house was quiet when they arrived. The younger kids were already asleep in the mattresses and cots. The older kids gathered in small groups, talking in subdued tones. No one was playing or laughing. The atmosphere in the place was like the refugee camps that had popped up all over the city during the war. Petra's stomach roiled. It was all her fault.

Lux frowned around at the kids and shook her head. "Beth isn't here."

Petra scowled. "Damnit. Where is she?"

"She's probably with the Uprising. That's good. She'll be able to tell us when she gets back if the rebels have the prince."

"Call her. I want to know."

Lux rolled her eyes. "No. It's safer not to alert the rebels that we're looking for him. We never have known for sure that Beth doesn't tell them what we know. If he's still out there in the streets somewhere, we don't want to risk them finding out about it."

"Beth is trustworthy. She doesn't tell them what we tell her."

Lux lifted an eyebrow. "Don't be naïve, Petra. The Uprising considers this a war. Beth is part of it. She believes in their cause, and she does what she has to. She isn't going to keep things from her people to be loyal to children."

"If she had told them, they would have come for Grey when he was at the compound."

"Not necessarily. They might have been waiting to see what was going to happen. And they might know he's out there now in the outlands somewhere."

"I trust Beth."

"Fine. Then you can speak to her when she gets home. It should be anytime; she usually comes home before it gets too dangerous out there in the streets."

It wasn't as good as Petra had hoped, but it was as good as she was going to get. She nodded and spun away from Lux before her disappointment could get the best of her. She couldn't just sit there, safe in the old warehouse while Grey was out there alone, while everyone in the city was searching for him. While someone wanted him dead very badly. She climbed the stairs to the private office two at a time. She wasn't sure what she planned to do, but she needed a few moments alone. She needed time to think.

The light was off in the office. When she flipped it on, she realized someone was already inside. Petra jumped in surprise. It was a young man with dark, shoulder-length hair. His clothes looked dirty and torn. There was blood on them. She almost didn't recognize him until he spun to face her. She gasped. "Grey?"

He didn't say anything for a moment. He looked back at her with an expression of such profound uncertainty, such terrible defeat, her stomach lurched. There were fresh bruises on his face. She ignored the state of him. She rushed at him and threw her arms around his neck. He staggered slightly backward with the force of her weight, but he wrapped his arms around her and hugged her back with a fierceness that took her by surprise.

"I was so worried!" she told him in a rush. She didn't release him. Instead, she tightened her arms around him and buried her face in his dark hair. "I thought something had happened to you."

She pulled back suddenly to look at him. His expression was so serious, her pulse leapt. "My father--" he began. At the same moment, she said, "Your father--"

"Where have you been?" she demanded.

He sighed and stepped away from her. "Remembering. Figuring out who I was and why someone wants to kill me." He sat down on the rickety chair in front of the desk. His expression was grimmer than Petra had ever seen it. "It wasn't too hard to figure out once I remembered."

Her breath hissed out through her teeth. "Do you remember everything now?"

He hung his head. "Yeah. Most of it. Not everything, I think. Just...enough. Bits and pieces." He looked up at her with haunted eyes. "I don't want to remember the rest. It hit me like a shot. I think...I think I might have been trying to avoid remembering before." He sighed. "I really wanted to believe I was one of you, Petra."

She was surprised. "You would prefer it to being the prince?"

He snorted wryly. "Prince? Yeah. I would have preferred to have been a decent person, not who I was. I would rather have been poor and orphaned. At least you made me believe I was good."

She didn't know what to say to this. He looked different than she'd ever seen him. A terrible storm raged behind his grey eyes. She didn't know what was going on in his head. She'd almost thought she knew him once. She understood now she didn't know anything about him at all. Grey was gone. She wondered if he was still there somewhere, in the back of Dante's mind. She hoped he was.

"So what happened? I thought you went home. Why are you back here?" Her stomach flipped a little. Had he missed her? Had he wanted to see her?

"Before it all came back, I remembered my father. I remembered him threatening me. He said he would rather see me dead than see me turn into the man I had become. I didn't know it was my father then, but now I understand. I think I was trying to tell myself something then. I shouldn't have gone back there before I understood everything."

"Do you understand it now?"

He shook his head. "No. Not really, but I think I'm starting to. He wanted me to be more...like him. He wanted me to work with him and learn what he does all day. I refused. I didn't want....well, I didn't want to do anything. I just wanted to be free. I wanted to drink and gamble and..." He sighed. "I think we both know what kind of person I was, or you wouldn't have done what you did."

"Grey--"

"It's okay, Petra. You don't have to explain. I understand all too well now."

"What happened?"

"I went home to talk to my father. I don't know what I planned to do. I thought it would all make sense if I just went home. But I was attacked as soon as I arrived."

Petra lifted her eyebrows. "By your father?"

"No. I didn't see his face. He came at me in the dark, but I would have known my father if it had been home. It was the man who attacked me in the alley. The one who came looking for me at the compound. I'm sure. "

"His name is Saer."

"Saer?" He frowned as though he knew the name. "I've heard of him. I think I've heard of him."

"Do you know who he is?" Her pale eyes were intense. Grey stared back at her with an equally grim expression.

Finally, he nodded. "I know who he is."

"I'm sorry, Grey. He works for your father."

"Yeah." He closed his eyes in resignation. "I know what you're trying to say, Petra. It's okay. I had already worked it out. I don't think there was any way he could have gotten into the house past the Marshals."

"What are we going to do?"

He shook his head. "I don't know." He smiled wanly. "Any ideas?"

She sighed. "We need some kind of proof. But...I don't know what good it will do. Your father owns everyone. He owns the city. It's not like we can take it to a higher authority. He's the only game in town."

"But...if it's enough...maybe we can get enough and then we can let everyone know. We can turn the entire city against him. Even his own people. There are enough of them. If they all move against him, he will not be able to withstand it, even with his Marshals and Nobles."

She lifted her eyebrows in surprise. "But how? We'll need a lot of proof. People know what he is. It only makes them more afraid to do anything about it."

Grey looked at her seriously. "You're the one who can find anything, aren't you? Can't you come up with something that will change their minds? Something they have to do something about?"

Petra frowned. "Maybe. If he records things on his computer, there might be an electronic trail."

Grey considered this. "There could be. He does a lot of work on the computer. He's always in front of it when he isn't out in the streets doing press conferences."

"I've trued to get into his system and see his files, but I haven't been able to crack them," she admitted. "He has some very serious security."

"What if I can help?"

"What do you mean?"

"I know about him. I know a little about the system, though I didn't spend much time at all actually learning about it. Still, I might be able to give you enough information you'll be able to get in."

"It's worth a try, anyway."

He sighed and stood up. He pushed his hands through his long, dark hair. "Petra, this is dangerous. I still shouldn't be here. I'm putting you all in danger by being here. And if my father's people catch you..."

She moved toward him and clutched his hand in hers. "I know what the risk is, but I'm not letting you go again. Saer found you again. In your own home. You could have died. You're not safe there, and you really aren't safe in the streets." She tugged on his hand to pull him closer and laid a hand on his cheek. For a moment, he flinched back from her. Her breath caught, and she dropped her hand. Her stomach sank a little. Then he gripped her shoulders and pulled her closer to him. She sighed. "Grey, when you disappeared, I thought the rebels might have you. If you leave here, they could get their hands on you. And they will do much, much worse to you than I....than I planned to do."

She braced herself for his renewed outrage, but it didn't come. Instead, his brow furrowed thoughtfully. "Who is it, Petra? Who did father take away from you? They must be important if you would go so far as to kidnap me to trade for them."

"My brother. Ren. He was put away for treason."

"He was innocent, wasn't he?"

"Yes. He was innocent. Most of them are innocent."

Grey nodded. "If we do this--expose my father--I will help you get him back. I'll help you get everyone back. What's happening in this city isn't right. It shouldn't be this way. No one should make people live this way, in terror for their lives for making the wrong move or annoying the wrong person. My father...he is horrible." He looked away. His jaw worked, and he looked so unhappy, her heart lurched. "I was horrible, Petra. I understand that now. I don't blame you for what you did. I can't really even blame the people who want me dead."

She shook her head fiercely. "That isn't you now. It's not the way you are now. You understand now. You're different than you were."

He chuckled wryly. "Imagine a blow to the head fixing all my personality problems."

She didn't smile. "I wish it were that simple."

"It helped me get perspective, anyway. I know now that we have to do something about all this."

"But not at the expense of your life."

"From what I remember, before I lost my memory, before you and all of this-- thinking I was one of you--my life wasn't worth much. Even my own father didn't think it was worth anything."

Petra sighed. She wrapped her arms around his neck. She expected him to flinch away from her again, but he didn't. He pulled her into a hug and rested his cheek against her hair. "Okay. Let's do it. If there is something to find, we'll find it."

She drew away from him and sat down on the floor. She pulled her laptop toward her and flipped it open. She smirked at him.

"If someone's going to bring down King Scarlet, it's going to be us. Let's get to work."

* * *

"Petra."

She rose to look over his shoulder at the laptop screen. "What is it?"

He looked up at her. His eyes were stormy. "I think I found something interesting."

"What is it?"

"It's a list of people in the city."

"What people?"

"I'm not entirely sure. People who oppose Scarlet, maybe. Or people who have something he wants."

"Are any of them prisoners?"

"No. There is a separate list of all the prisoners." His jaw tightened. "It is so, so long. It's amazing there's room to house them all."

"Well, half the city is burnt out or abandoned. Most of the citizens died, ran or are living in communes like this one. There are probably plenty of places to keep prisoners." Her heart leapt. "Is there a list of where all the prisoners are being held?"

He shook his head. "No. I wish there was. There are probably separate lists for each of the prisons. It's not something my dad would keep track of. Someone else would care of that for him. He tries to keep his hands clean when he can."

"Damn. Not too clean, I hope. That would have been helpful. We could have just staged an attack on one place and gotten Ren out of there."

"It would not have changed anything else. It would only have put more people in danger."

She sighed. "I know. You're right. It's selfish of me to think it. It's not the way. So, this list might be a list of people he intends to imprison?"

"Maybe. Or a list of people he is watching out for. People who are probably in danger."

"Let me see."

He leaned away so she could see the screen over his shoulder. She scanned the list of names. It was long. She recognized some of them. In fact, she recognized a lot of them. "I know some of these people. They're business owners, mostly. But some of them are just regular people."

"They must have some kind of power or influence. My father needs to keep the balance of power with himself and his people. Anyone who gathers too much is usually shut down. He puts his own people into these businesses and positions. It's the way he's been slowly taking over from the beginning."

"So these are people who are not his. They're people who might join the rebels if they had a good enough reason?"

"Or they're suspected members of the Uprising. There's no way to know why any of them are on this list; there isn't even a title. I found it buried in a file without name. It was just a string of random numbers." He sighed. "These people could interest him for any reason. I wouldn't know. He never talked about any of that with me. There isn't any proof of anything with just this." He glanced at her. "You? Have you found anything to connect this with the Uprising?"

Petra shook her head. "I'm not a member of the Uprising. I don't know who is involved, so I can't be sure whether it's connected to them or not. It might just be people he considers worth watching." She frowned at the screen. "What about any indication that things are happening to the people on the list? Have any of them been imprisoned or killed or anything? If there is, it could change everything. If we could spread the word that the King is plans who is being imprisoned or who disappears ahead of time, it could compel the people who are too afraid to come forward to side with the rebels. It might convince them it's time to start protecting themselves. It would give the Uprising an advantage."

She wasn't sure this was exactly what she wanted, but right now, between the King and the Uprising, she would take the rebels. At least they didn't imprison innocent people.

Grey nodded. "People need to see this. They are in danger, whether they are guilty of treason or not. They all know what my father is, but they like to pretend it isn't going to happen to them. It doesn't matter what you do—if he wants something, he takes it."

"Being guilty has never made a difference in Razor City. Everyone is just too scared to admit it. They think it won't happen to them if they keep quiet and out of his way. It's a lie. And it isn't just the people on this list. Ren had nothing he wanted. He had nothing at all, but your father took him anyway."

Grey sighed. "I'm sorry. I don't know what he did to draw his attention. It isn't only the people who threaten the balance of power who are in danger in this city. It doesn't matter if they've done anything or not."

"People should be able to speak out against their leader. They shouldn't have to live in constant fear of being put on this list."

"That's what we're doing here, Petra. We will do everything we can to find a way to stop it. I'll look for some kind of trail indicating something is happening to these people once they've ended up on the list. It is not my father who accuses people of treason; he just decides what to do with them. It is typically the Nobles who make the recommendations."

"So there could be some communication between him and the Nobles that indicates what he actually using this list to do. He might be giving his people the names and letting them do the dirty work. Or he could be having them killed. People disappear all the time. They're never seen again to tell anyone what happened to them."

"We might be able to find enough to point to intent. We just need to show the city what he is doing and let the mob mentality take it from there."

"I think they already know." Grey's voice was grim.

"Yes, they know. But people are too afraid of doing anything about it. The idea is to get enough people to move against him and force him to make changes."

"You mean by taking him out of power?"

"It might be the only way, Grey." She looked at him seriously. "Are you prepared to go that far?"

He considered. Then he slowly shook his head. "I don't really have a choice, do I? I'm on this list now."

"Are you?"

He rolled his eyes. "Figuratively speaking." He turned back to the screen. "There might be something in his emails that can help us. He does a lot of work that way. Sometimes he doesn't leave his office for days. He doesn't go out into the city very often. When he has to talk to someone, it is not typically in person."

"Okay. Let's take a look."

They took turns sorting through Scarlet's email. It was tedious. He received so many messages a day from citizens, Nobles, Marshals and other city officials near Razor City. Most of them weren't helpful. Petra was actually surprised at how much work it took to run a city and a business. Scarlet wasn't just the leader of the city; he controlled most of the products that moved in and out of Razor City. It had been his business before the war and now he had the monopoly.

Scarlet's business had fallen under scrutiny numerous times before the war. He was rumored to be involved in organized crime and illegal business practices, but no one had never been able to prove it. When the government had fallen and the cities had dissolved into chaos, Scarlet had been the only one with the money, power and influence to take control of the city.

Now, everything was his. And it was time to take it back.

"Here are some messages from some of the Nobles," Grey said suddenly. "They are accusations of treason. Names and alleged crimes. I sort of assumed there would be something a little more official."

She leaned over his shoulder to look. "Are any of the accused on the list?"

He shook his head. "Not that I can tell. They aren't on the list now, but these are old. The names might have been on the list before. It must be updated frequently. All the names on it now are live."

"We need to see who else has that list. This must be the master. Has he sent it out to anyone?"

Grey rose. "You want to take a look?"

She sat down. It didn't take her long to find it. "Here it is."

"Who did he send it to."

"He didn't. Someone sent it to him."

"Who?"

She shook her head. "I don't know. The email address is just random numbers."

"Can you find out who it belongs to?"

"I can try." After several moments, she cursed. "It's anonymous. I can't tell

126

who it belongs to. There's no name on the account or any indication who it belongs to."

"What about the carrier?"

"It's just a general internet server. It's nothing. There is a location, though. It's Razor City."

He snorted. "Of course it is."

"But it could still help us. We don't need to know who it is to track what he's saying to the King." She narrowed her eyes and scrolled through the messages. "He sent the original list. Every few days, he sends a new name."

"Can you follow a trail through the emails to find out what happens after Scarlet gets a new name? They're probably are going on the list, but he could be sending names from the list to the Nobles one at a time."

It took several moments. Finally, she found something. "Here's one. Stan Riker. The anonymous email sent his name to Scarlet."

"Did he say anything about him?"

"No. Just the name"

Grey frowned. "Have you ever heard of him? Do you know who he is?"

"No. But about two weeks later, one of the Nobles emails Scarlet and accuses Riker of being caught with rebel papers."

"But did my dad send the name to the Noble somewhere?"

She shook her head. "No. It was just sent to the King both times."

"Could it be a list of people who are going to be accused?"

"Maybe. Who knows which comes first. Still, this proves he knows who is going to be accused before it happens. It could be the anonymous email is sending the names to the Nobles one at a time. We aren't seeing those emails."

"Can you break into the anonymous email?"

"No. I tried. It's secure. Whoever it belongs to, they know what they are doing. They know how to stay anonymous. They must have a good reason."

"Okay. But this is still good. We have a list of people who are in danger. It is only a matter of time before they go down."

"Right." Petra frowned. "Here's something interesting."

"What?"

"There's another list."

"What is it?"

"More names. They aren't the same names. They don't correspond to any of the emails. But I recognize a few of them."

"From what?"

"They died."

"How?"

"Different ways. One of them died when his house caught on fire. Another fell down the stairs. Some of them were killed by outlaws in the outlands or in some dangerous back alley."

"And they're on the other list?"

"Yeah. The list showed up and then a few of them died."

"Are they all dead?"

"No. Some of them are alive. Sometimes people end up on the list and nothing happens to them. It could be coincidence."

"Yeah, right. My father could be watching them or something. Maybe they aren't being killed or accused until they prove to be a threat of some kind."

"That makes sense. If the King was killing or imprisoning everyone without reason, he wouldn't be able to pretend he was a good leader."

Grey nodded. "It's still good. It might still be enough if we can convince people to listen. It's an obvious pattern. We could send it to the media. We could get it out to the people."

Petra shook her head. "No. It won't work. He's been implicated by the media in the past. It didn't do any good. Nothing changed. He owns all of them."

"Then we have to go to the people he doesn't own. I know there are rebels in the outlands. The Uprising is real."

"Yeah. They haven't mobilized yet, but I know they're planning to attack soon."

"Do you know anything about them?"

"No. I didn't want to know. Despite what people think, the compound isn't affiliated with them."

"Do you know anyone who is involved with them? Can you get to them?"

She was silent a long moment. "Yes. I think I can. I know someone who works with them. We'll have to be careful, though. With you involved...I don't know how they are going to react."

"Then we'll have to prepare them. Do you trust the rebel you know?"

"Yes. I trust her completely."

He frowned. "Then why haven't you become involved with the Uprising?"

"I didn't want to get involved. I just want my brother back."

"And now?"

"Now...things are different. If we're going to do this, we have to take it all the way. I can't go back to the way it was. Even if I could, I wouldn't want to."

Grey nodded. "Will you set up a meeting with the Uprising."

"Are you sure?"

"Yes."

It didn't sound like a good idea, but eventually she nodded. "Okay. I'll do it."

* * *

Beth stared down at the pile of papers with narrow eyes. She didn't say anything for several seconds. Her expression was unreadable. She rifled through them again. Finally, she looked up at Petra.

"Well?" Petra demanded.

"Petra...I think this is the first real proof we've ever had that Scarlet is setting his people up. Everyone knows he's doing it, but no one's ever been able to get anything on him before. Even knowing hasn't been enough. These are real names. These are real people. Maybe this will finally get people to move against him. This could bring many people to our side."

"Will it help your people be ready to take him on?"

"What we need are more numbers. Too many people won't join or are scared, but now...they can finally see they are in real danger. We might finally be able to do something about this, Petra." She looked at her sharply. "But are you sure?"

"Do we really have any other choice?"

"No. Not really."

Petra grimaced. "Is it really safe for Dante to meet them?"

"They won't do anything to him if that's what you mean. Not with Lux around, anyway. Even the Uprising is afraid of her. He'll be able to walk away, even if the meeting doesn't go like he wants it to."

"So you'll set it up?"

Beth nodded. "I'll set it up. Bring these documents. They'll help." She pulled out her cell phone and punched up a number. The voice on the other end answered so quickly, Petra didn't think the phone had had time to ring. "We need to meet. I have some information you will want to see." She glanced up at Petra as she listened to the person on the other end. She didn't even say good bye to them. She snapped her phone shut and nodded at Petra. "They'll meet us."

"Where?"

"In the outlands. At a bar. It's where we always meet when we bring someone new. It's a safe place." She narrowed her eyes thoughtfully. "I don't think Dante should come. Just you."

"He won't like that."

"We don't have a choice. I think it's safer to keep him here for now."

Petra sighed, but she didn't argue. She would rather not place Grey in the line of the Uprising's fire, even if he was determined to be involved. "I'll try to convince him. He won't like it, but I don't think it's a good idea for him to be traipsing around the outlands with the rebels just yet, either. I'll find a way to make him understand."

He was lying silently on a cot staring up a the ceiling when she poked her head into the office. He hadn't left the tiny room since he'd snuck back into the safe house, and only the inner circle knew he'd returned. The rest of the kids had never even known he'd ever been there. No one had argued about giving up the only private room to the prince. In fact, they'd insisted. They didn't need another Shaw, especially now.

Grey shot to his feet to meet her. "Well? What happened? Will they meet with us?"

"Yes, they want to meet. But we're meeting one of Beth's contacts first, not the leader. And Beth thinks it's best if you stay here for now."

He scowled. She braced herself for a fight. "This is my fight, too, Petra. I want to be involved in this."

"I know that. But it's not safe for you to leave here, not yet. If someone in the

130

outlands spots you, we'll be in for trouble. And we can't be sure the rebels won't try to double cross us if they think they can use you to get what they want. You need to stay here until I can be sure it's safe for you to meet with them."

His scowl deepened. "What do you expect me to do, then?"

"Sort through more paperwork, I guess. We might be able to get more on him. We could convince more people to mobilize. It's not people who want to take Scarlet down they need; they have enough of them. They need people who are willing to do something. To fight. Beth thinks the information we've found will help push them to act. The Uprising needs more numbers to stage a rebellion if it isn't going to be crushed before it ever begins."

Grey sighed. "All right, but I don't like the idea of you going without me. I won't be able to protect you if something goes wrong."

She smiled in amusement. "I'll be perfectly safe. We've been doing things like this since we were hardly big enough to look over a bar. I'll be with Beth. I trust her. She would not send me into a dangerous situation. I'll bring Lux, too. She's a good bodyguard. No one messes with her."

He didn't look happy, but he pulled her into a tight hug. "Okay. Just be safe. If it starts to look dangerous, I want you to run. Don't try to salvage it. I won't let you get into trouble for me."

She smiled. "I've done pretty well so far keeping myself alive."

"You're still young."

She rolled her eyes. "I'll be fine. We'll give them the list and let them take it from there. They will know what to do with it. Maybe we can learn more about what they are planning to do. This probably won't change it; it will just get them to move more quickly."

"Just be careful."

"I will. I'll see you again soon."

He pressed his lips to hers. He didn't move away for a long moment. Her heart thumped wildly in her chest, and she hoped she'd make it back to him in one piece. Despite her confident words, she wasn't entirely sure Beth was right about her people. She could be walking into a death trap. He didn't need to know that. When he pulled away, she smiled up at him.

His expression was deadly serious. "You'd better make it out of there, Petra. I did not come back here just to send you out to get killed for my sake."

She smirked. "No. If I remember right, you came back because you didn't have anywhere else to go."

"Yes. That's pretty much exactly the reason. I feel a whole lot better about all this now. Thanks for pointing it out."

CHAPTER NINE

Beth was waiting for her at the foot of the stairs. She was wearing her green fatigue jacket. She looked completely cool, but something in her expression made Petra's pulse leap. "There's something going on between you and the prince, isn't there?"

Petra hesitated. Her best friend knew her well. She hadn't been able to hide anything from her since they had met five years ago. "I'm not sure what it is," she admitted.

Beth looked skeptical. "You're not sure?"

Petra shrugged. She glanced around them to ensure no one was listening. "It's crazy, Beth. I think I like him."

Beth lifted an eyebrow. "Yes, I can tell. And he likes you?"

"Yeah. I think he does, but it's a little more complicated than that."

"Why?"

"Because he's the prince, and we are hoping to stage a revolt against his father, likely killing him in the process. I don't know how that's going to go for us."

Beth nodded. She threaded her arms through Petra's and led her out of the safe house into the streets. She didn't move with any urgency or fear. She seemed perfectly comfortable wandering the outlands. She did it everyday. The outlaws probably knew she was one of the Uprising; even the outlaws avoided them. "Yes, you're right. It's complicated. Even if he is on our side."

"He is!"

"You need to think about it, Petra. If he isn't on our side, he could be planning to warn his father what we're up to. It might be a trick. All of this. He could be trying to weasel out the whereabouts of the Uprising for his father."

Petra's shackles rose. "I don't think that's true. Do you really believe that?"

Beth shrugged. "It could be. I mean, we don't know anything about him but what he's done. His reputation does not exactly foster trust. Besides, we kidnapped him and lied to him. You think he just forgave us for that? Then he just comes back and wants us to help him take down his father? It seems a little...

off."

Petra lifted her chin stubbornly. "I believe he's telling the truth. He helped us find this information."

Beth nodded. "Yes, he did. And it will hurt his father more than the Uprising. If you believe him, I trust your judgment. I always have. But it will not be so easy to convince the rebels."

"What about the documentation? It's proof."

"It's good. It will be a good offering to begin a conversation. And if he is on our side, he will have to be part of the fight against his father. He might have to kill Scarlet himself or see him die. It would be hard for anyone. He might think he's ready for it and realize too late he isn't. It could ruin everything."

"I know. I'm hoping somehow we can keep him out of the actual fighting. At least where his father is concerned."

Beth lifted an eyebrow. "Good luck. I don't think that will be easy. It's too late not to take it all the way now. He'll be running his entire life if we don't stop his father."

"Do you think the rebels will help us? Will they be ready to mobilize?"

Beth hesitated. "I'm not sure."

"What?" Petra looked at her in surprise. "You think they might not?"

"This information will help us get more numbers for the cause..."

Petra didn't like her tone of voice. "Aren't they ready?"

She sighed. "I can't really talk about it, Petra. I don't have all the information. I'm not a member of the inner circle. I just help gather supplies. I help where I can with random stuff."

Petra didn't think she was telling the whole truth. She didn't ask any questions, though. She only hoped what she and Grey had found would be what they needed to make their move. It was their only hope.

Beth didn't say anything else as they wove through the streets in the outlands toward the bar where they would meet Beth's contact. It looked the same outside as any other outland bar she'd been to in the last few days. It was old and crumbling, and the sign was shattered so she couldn't see what it had once been named. An air of danger hung in the atmosphere around it. Beth didn't go inside. She walked past the door into the alley around the side of the building.

There was a man standing in the alley waiting for them, as motionless as a statue. He wore a black sweatshirt with the hood pulled up over his hair. He came to life when he heard the crunch of their boots in the debris littering the ground. He turned to them. He was younger than Petra expected. He looked no older than she or Beth. He inclined his head in greeting. Petra didn't recognize him. She had never seen him anywhere in town.

"Pablo," Beth greeted, inclining her head.

He didn't look like a Pablo. He was pale and thin. His pale blue eyes flicked to Petra. "Have you brought a new recruit?"

Petra glanced at Beth. It was her show now. Beth shook her head. "No. We have information."

"Okay."

Petra leaned closer to Beth to speak in a low voice. "You trust him not to tell anyone about Grey?"

Beth nodded. "He will not. I will speak for him. I trust him as well as I trust you."

This was good enough for Petra.

"Tell me what you know," Pablo ordered. "I will bring it back to our leader."

"You aren't the leader?" Petra blurted.

Pablo and Beth smiled at this, and Petra wondered if they were making fun of her. "No. I am his second. He is not prepared to meet with you. I will hear your information and bring it back to him."

Petra sighed. Beth nodded to her encouragingly. "Go on, Petra. You may tell him everything."

She took a deep breath, and her stomach flipped a little. She had been trying to keep Grey from the rebels since she'd found him, and now she was letting them know exactly where he was. She hoped Beth was right. "A few days ago, I found Prince Dante in an alley outside the King's Random. Someone had attacked him and left him for dead. He was badly beaten up. I brought him back to the compound and took him in."

Pablo lifted his eyebrows. "I have heard he is missing. Dante is with you?"

"Yes. He's learned that there might be a plot against him at the palace."

"The King?"

"Maybe. He might be trying to have him killed. He has been attacked by the same man twice, and it seems as though it's not going to stop until he's dead."

"What man?"

"Saer Dagon."

"The King's hit man."

"Yes."

"How did he manage to survive him twice? I don't know Saer, but I have heard of him. I understand once he is set after someone, he doesn't fail. They are as good as dead."

"Apparently Dante is very resourceful, and he has a strong will to live," Beth put in.

"But he is still the prince."

"Yes, but since he learned of the plot against him, he is prepared to join the rebels."

"Prince Dante wants to join the Uprising?" Pablo sounded almost amused.

"Yes. He believes it is the only course of action left. He cannot remain in hiding forever. Someone has to do something about the King and what's happening in this city. Who better than the one closest to the King?"

Pablo frowned. "But what does he want us to do about it?"

"Move against Scarlet. The Uprising has been building an army. You are preparing for war. It is time to move."

Pablo's expression did not change. "We are not prepared to do that."

Petra scowled. "But you have been training and preparing."

"Yes. And we are still training and preparing. We are not yet ready to launch an attack."

She felt her stomach sink in disappointment. Beth stepped forward. She drew a thick envelope from her jacket, inside which she'd slipped Petra's and Grey's evidence. "Pablo, we have information that could help us."

Pablo took the envelope. He pulled out the papers and scanned them cursorily. He did not look impressed. "What is it?"

"It's a list of people we think Scarlet is targeting for imprisonment or death."

This seemed to interest Pablo. He turned his attention back to the papers.

"There is a series of emails between the King and an anonymous address. The King receives emails from the anonymous address with a single or multiple names. Subsequently, a Noble will accuse the names of treason or some other trumped up crime," Petra explained.

Pablo frowned thoughtfully. "What is the significance?"

"I believe someone is feeding the King names of people who might pose a threat and the names are going to the Nobles, who come up with a reason to get rid of them. It suggests the disappearances and false accusations are not random; the King is directing all of it. Him or whomever this email belongs to, who works for him."

"Or whom he works for. For all we know, there is some mysterious force driving all this and the King is just a figure head."

"No. Dante would know. Scarlet runs the show. He would never be someone else's pawn."

"You didn't find out who the anonymous email belongs to?"

"No, but does it matter? This proves there is a plan behind all this. And the people on the list will want to know they are probably next in line to be sent away or killed. They can't just sit by and let it happen. They will have to join you."

"It might matter. Not for your purpose, but if someone is out there picking people in the city to be taken out, it would be nice to know who they are. They could be among us even now. It could be Dante."

"It isn't Dante. If it was, why give the information to the Uprising? It certainly wouldn't give the King any advantage."

"I don't know. There is a lot we don't understand about the King's motivations. Or Dante's."

Petra scowled, but there was no point arguing. "There is another list. The people on this list have died mysteriously."

"All of them?"

"No. Some of them are still alive. Which does sort of suggest they won't be for long, doesn't it?"

Pablo lifted his eyes to her. "How did you get this?"

"Dante helped me break into the King's system."

"We've been trying to get this sort of information for a very long time."

"We could use it to get more numbers, Pablo," Beth said. "We could use it to warn the people who are in danger. It could bring more people to us. If they know something is going to happen to them, they may want to join the fight."

Pablo looked at Petra. "The prince is going to help us?"

"Yes. He will be able to help coordinate a strike. He knows about the guards and all the King's holdings. He knows who we will have to fight."

After a long, thoughtful moment, he nodded. "I will take this to our leader. We will see what he has to say about it."

Petra stepped toward him. "That isn't good enough! I need an answer. We can't keep hiding him. There are people who are looking for him."

"That is not my problem. You are the ones who took him in."

Petra looked at Beth, but her friend didn't say anything.

Pablo nodded to them. "I will take this to our leader. Beth, I will contact you." He spun away from them and strode away without saying another word.

Petra spun to Beth. Her eyes flashed. "I thought you said he would help us!"

"It doesn't mean he won't, Petra. He isn't our leader. He's his second. He will share our information. If our leader wants to meet with us, he will contact me."

She sighed. "Grey isn't going to like this."

Beth looked at her strangely. "You still call him Grey? Not Dante?"

Petra shrugged. "It suits him. He's not the same man as Prince Dante was."

"Are you sure about that?"

She considered. "I'm sure."

"I hope you're right." Beth's expression was grim. "If you're wrong, we could lose everything."

* * *

Later, in a safe house in the increasingly restive outlands...

"I don't understand what's wrong," Grey said. He rose to pace restlessly across the threadbare grey carpet in the small office. He pushed his hands through his hair. "It's been two days. We're running out of time. What's taking so long?"

Petra sighed. "I don't know. Maybe it isn't enough."

"How can it not be enough? We don't have anything else! We've looked. This is the best we've got."

"I know." She stood to stand in front of him. He didn't look like he wanted to stop, but he paused in mid-step and looked down at her with a frustrated expression. "It will have to be enough. Maybe they're just trying to decide what to do with the information."

"Or maybe they're planning to double-cross us."

"I don't think so. If they were, they would have done it by now."

"If they don't hurry up and make a decision, they might not get the chance." His jaw flexed angrily. "My father or his people could find this place at any time and then we'll lose any chance we have."

She frowned. "Lux is looking out for the King's people. And she has spies all over the city listening for any sign they've found you."

"We might have to start thinking about an alternative plan, Petra. It isn't looking too promising with the Uprising at this point. We might have to think of something else."

Petra opened her mouth to respond, but she snapped her mouth shut as the door flew open. Beth burst inside without bothering to knock on the door. Petra and Grey spun to her in surprise. "Beth. What's happened?" Petra demanded.

"The Uprising has agreed to talk to you," Beth told them. She scrutinized Grey as though she wasn't sure what to think of him. "Our leader would like to meet Dante."

Grey nodded. "Take me to him. I'm ready." He squared his shoulders, and his stormy eyes glinted. "When is it happening?"

"Now."

"You're taking us to the base?"

Beth smiled. "No. I'm sorry. He still doesn't trust you."

"But we gave him valuable information."

"And now he's willing to listen. We'll meet in the outlands. In a neutral zone."

"Is anywhere neutral in the outlands?" Petra muttered.

"Yes. The rebels have their territory; the outlaws have theirs. They do not fight each other." She jerked her head toward the door. "Come on. I'll take you both there."

She led them through the outlands with a swift, confident step. Grey wore a dark hoodie over his hair to conceal his identity, but there didn't seem to be a lot of point. Beth knew what she was doing. They didn't meet anyone along the way.

The meeting place was a warehouse similar to the one in which they were living, but the entire outside perimeter was thick and lush with verdant gardens. Root vegetables and trees covered in plump fruit practically concealed the small, squat grey stone building. Petra looked around them in surprise, but Beth didn't say pause to explain the unexpected bounty. She strode purposely toward a door on the side of the building.

Petra felt Grey's fingers close around hers. She turned her head to give him a small, encouraging smile, though her insides felt tight and cold. Beth rapped once on the door. A young boy pulled it open. His hair looked mussed, and he had a bruise under his left eye. He nodded to Beth and stepped aside to let them in.

Inside there were cots lining the walls, but the center of the room was taken up by a large mat. Weapons were scattered all around as though they'd been recently dropped. It looked like a training facility. It was probably how the young boy had gotten his bruise. At least, Petra hoped it was.

The young boy left them alone in the center of the room. Beth didn't speak to Petra or Grey. She waited silently. They followed her lead. After several seconds, they heard footsteps above. They turned to the tall man with shortly cropped hair that descended the stairs and strode toward them with a confident gait. As he neared them, Petra's muscles coiled. She felt as though she had been kicked in the stomach.

Grey stared at him in shock. Beth didn't seem at all moved by his appearance. Petra didn't understand why. She recognized him instantly. She took a step toward him in utter fury. Beth shot out an arm to hold her back.

"You!" Petra spat. "You're the rebel leader?"

Cage Spears inclined his head. He did not look troubled by her reaction to him. He looked as tranquil and self-possessed as the last time she had seen him at the Blade club. She shoved Beth's arm away and started forward again.

Grey caught her arm and tugged her back.

"I am," Cage replied coolly.

"You're the one who accused my brother! You sent him to prison!"

"I regret that, Petra. Your brother saw something he should not have seen.

140

It was not my ideal choice, but I did not have any other. I did not want it to happen."

"You are one of us," Petra said. "How could you?"

"The Uprising is important. It is more important than one man."

"Not to me!"

"Don't be a fool. There is nothing more important than stopping Scarlet and taking back the city. When we do, we will all be free and no one will be imprisoned again. Your brother's incarceration is not forever. It will end soon, and I am sorry, but I had to sacrifice one for the good of many. For the good of the Uprising that will save our city."

Petra's eyes glittered with angry tears. Beth took her arm and pulled her away from Grey and Cage. Petra spun on her with a glare. "You knew. You knew all along it was him. You've been part of this the whole time."

Beth's voice was low. "I'm sorry. I couldn't tell you, Petra. You wouldn't have understood."

"I can't believe you...I can't believe you lied to me. Couldn't you just tell Ren the truth? You know he would not have told on him! You could have let him walk away!"

"That wasn't an option. I'm sorry."

Petra spun away from her. Grey glanced at her. His eyes were stormy, but he did not move to comfort her. She didn't meet his eyes. She didn't want him to see her tears. She didn't want him to see the hatred in her eyes. It wouldn't help their cause. No matter who the leader was, no matter what he had done, they still needed him.

Grey turned back to Cage. His eyes narrowed. "It was you. You're the one I tried to blackmail, aren't you?"

"Ah. I see you remember that."

"Barely."

"I hear you've changed. I hear things are different." Cage's voice was calm, but his eyes were cold. "But I know you, Dante. I am not so sure. Why should we trust everything we have worked for to you?"

"Things have changed." Grey's voice sounded confident now. "I have changed. Before I lived under the wing of my father, enjoying his power. Now I see what the city is really like. I see what he has done to it. I thought he was a man who wanted to help bring the city back under control. I think it started out that way, the power corrupted him. He enjoyed it too much to give it back once he had it. I enjoyed the power too much to give it back. But I don't want any of it at the expense of people's lives, and at the expense of letting these people live in terror under the thumb of a dangerous dictator. Things cannot keep on this way. We can't let the city live like this anymore. I don't have the power to fight my father myself. I need help. I need an army. You have an army."

"But what do you expect to do when the army attacks? What do you think will happen to the city then?" Cage demanded.

"It will be chaos again," Grey said. "We need someone who cares about the people. Someone who wants to help and not selfishly enjoy the power and control. We need a government. We need people who can run this city together, to control the outlaws and draw the outlands and the city center together. We need representatives in the different sectors. We need everyone to come together and make laws and rules together so no one has too much power and so this will never happen again."

Cage lifted his eyebrows. "You have thought about this a lot."

"Yes. I find I have nothing but time to think these days."

"It is rather idealistic."

"But it is not impossible if the city is in the right hands. If the King's power is thrown, we will be able to bring in people who are wise. And people who care."

"And who will be the one to choose those people?"

"Everyone. Everyone should be able to choose."

"It wouldn't be that way right away. It would have to start with a serious shift of power into the hands of a small group or one person. We would have to displace the King's regime and put in a new one."

"You have thought about it, too."

"Of course I have." For a moment, Cage's eyes blazed. "Do you think we are just training people to fight and kill the King's men? Do you think we plan to leave the city in anarchy? It would be as bad or even worse than it is now. At least now there is a police for that keeps the peace. They work for the King, but if they weren't under his orders, they could actually do good work. The Marshals are almost as useless, but they are the last vestiges of our old government. They could lead the police force to work for the people again."

"What about the bounty hunters?" Petra demanded.

"They could be used for good, too. They could be used to round up the Kings regime. We would form a tribunal. We would put people on trial for their crimes, not just toss them away with your father as judge, jury and executioner. At first it would be chaos. We will need more police than we have now. We will need to be prepared to fight the city, not only the King's people. They will be easy enough to defeat. But we have to be prepared to control the city when he is gone."

"We have a list," Grey said. "We have a list of people who the King has targeted. They can join us. They can help."

"Maybe. Or maybe they will simply run. Maybe it is what you should do, Dante. You are not safe in the city. There are many people out to get you, and if it is true the King is one of them, there is nowhere for you to go. You are the most wanted man in the city."

Grey scowled. "I cannot run! I have to do something about this. I have to help make things right. I have spent too much time allowing the corruption and the killing to go on."

"Why not talk to your father? Maybe you can sway him to see your side of things."

Grey scoffed. "You know that isn't even an option. Even if he isn't trying to kill me, he will do anything to keep his power. We have to take him out."

"Are you prepared to do that?"

"I will do what I have to. This has to stop. It doesn't matter who I am or who I was. All that matters are the people. Giving them back their lives. No one should have to live in fear anymore. We can take the palace; imprison the King and the Nobles. Whoever refuses to be absorbed by our regime will be put away with them. Once they are gone, we can begin to plan and rebuild. If we can strike quietly and quickly enough, with enough people, we can take over the city before anyone notices the strike has even happened. We will have a new regime without any chaos."

"And how do you propose to do that?"

"If I knew, I would not need you! I am prepared to offer myself. I am prepared to fight on your side and give information that will help you. I know all about my father. I have information about his operation. If we work together, we can plan and we can strike."

Cage's face was perfectly unreadable. He looked as cold as ice. Finally, he inclined his head. "We will get back to you."

Grey blinked at him in surprise. "What?"

"We will let you know if we are interested in working with you." He turned around to stride away.

"Hey!" Grey snapped. "I came here thinking you would help us!"

"Why should I help you, Dante? You have never given me any reason."

Grey sighed. "You're right. You are right about that. All right. I will help you, then. The palace is guarded all day by the King's men."

Cage rolled his eyes. "Of course I know that already. I am a member of the King's court."

"But there is a servant's entrance on the west side of the building. It is generally unlocked and unguarded. You would have to enter a few at a time, but if you are quick, you will be able to get inside before anyone even notices. If you intend to sneak in an army, you won't be able to do it through the front door, even if you are a member of the court. You can strike quietly and take out the King's inner circle before anyone notices."

Cage seemed to be thinking about this.

"I have a list of the locations of the prisons." Petra hadn't realized he had this. It was handwritten. She wondered if he'd known it all along. Grey handed it to Cage. "I don't know who is in what prison, but you can stage a strike on them all at once. You could suppress the King's people and have more numbers at the same time. All the King's holdings are on that list. You can hit everything at once, and no one will see it coming or be the wiser until you have control of the city. Then you can do what you have to to rebuild."

Cage stared down at the list. He nodded, but his expression didn't change. He turned and strode back toward the stairs without another word to them. Grey sighed, but he turned toward Petra. She didn't look as though she wanted to go. She glared at Cage.

"Petra. It's time to go," he told her in a low voice.

"But—"

"No, Petra," Beth put in. "It is time to go."

"He—Ren—"

"I know. But we can't do anything about that right now," Grey said. "We have to go before they change their minds and decide to kill me instead."

She glared over her shoulder at Cage, but she allowed Grey to lead her away.

"Cage will get back to us soon," Beth promised.

Grey nodded. "Will you tell us what he decides?"

Beth hesitated. "I will tell you whatever he wishes me to tell you."

* * *

Later, at the safe house...

Petra was on pins and needles. The rest of the inner circle were as tense as she was. They sat around a table in the tiny conference room beside Grey's office room. The doors and windows had been broken long ago, and shards of glass still littered the floor.

"You brought him back here?" Jesse demanded. "Are you crazy?"

Petra sat between Key and Lux. They stared back at Jesse as a united front. "He is with us now," Lux said firmly. "He is trying to get together with the rebel leader to stage an attack on the King."

"But having him here is dangerous! The hunters found out about him once already. I don't think I need to remind anyone here how that went down."

"Yes, the hunters did find him once, but that was because we were careless enough to let Shaw see him," Key said in a low voice. He still looked bruised, but he was beginning to look almost normal. He moved around nearly as well as he had before the attack. Petra was relieved; she had enough to worry about without worrying about Key just now.

"Shaw doesn't know about this place," Petra added. "No one knows about this place. We have sentries and guards watching the perimeter to make sure no one sneaks up on us again."

It didn't persuade anyone. "This is risky," Ellis said.

"Yes, but living in Razor City is risky. You know we can't let things keep on this way. We have to do something about Scarlet. We have to get our families back and stop all this once and for all."

"Nothing has changed since the war. It's always been like this," Jesse said. "Since when did you turn into the revolutionary, Petra? Do you actually think you can do something about it?"

"It hasn't been like this since the war," Key argued. "We let Scarlet take over because he was the most powerful. He was the only one who could bring the city back together. But he became corrupt. And now he has to be stopped."

"He doesn't have enough men to stop us all," Petra put in. "We can fight him."

"If we take out the King, the rest of the men will fall," Lux said.

"Do you think it will be that easy?" Ellis asked. "He is one man, but this is an empire you are trying to topple. His people will step in. They will just take over and perpetuate the corruption. Nothing will change."

"That is why we need the rebel army," Lux told him. "We need to take out the heart and the rest of the empire."

"Grey knows how to do it. He said we had to strike all at once. We can take all the King's holdings at once, suppress his army, and then the rebels will take control."

"I'm not so sure I want them to be in control, either," Rip said grimly.

"They are still better than Scarlet. Anything is better than him."

"And what about Dante?" Ellis asked. "Do you think he will remain loyal to our side? Until days ago, he was one of them."

"He's changed."

"Why. Because of a bump on the head?" Jesse growled.

"Because he found out his father is trying to kill him. He is part of this now. He wants what we want. You should have seen him with the rebel leader. He wants to see change in this city. He has ideas, and they're good. He is serious. He is with us."

"Petra, this is a mistake," Jesse told her. "We need to get him out of here. We can't hide him anymore."

"No!" Petra and Lux said at the same time. "This is the only place he is safe," Petra added.

"But the rest of us are in danger."

Lux frowned. "He is the key to the rebellion. If he is with the Uprising--if he is with us--we stand a chance."

"This isn't what we set out to do," Ellis said. "We just wanted a safe place for all of us to live."

"Things have changed, Ellis! It isn't safe. There is no safe place in this city anymore."

146

"Because you brought him here," Jesse said angrily.

"That isn't fair," Lux said. "Petra did what she thought was right. She saved his life. It isn't her fault the city is in trouble."

"No. It's his."

"No, it isn't!" Petra snapped. "It wouldn't matter now if he was with us or not. The ball is rolling. Things are moving. The rebels have a list of people who are being targeted for imprisonment and death by King Scarlet. The Uprising can mobilize them to fight. If they follow Grey's plan, if they strike at all the locations at once, they could suppress the King's forces before anyone is the wiser. Before anyone has time to fight."

"We're just kids," Rip argued.

"Not anymore. We haven't been kids since the war. And we can't keep letting this happen. We have to do something. Grey is the one who wants to do something. He wants to make it happen. He's the one who knows what to do. Would you rather live in a city like this forever where we live constantly in fear and are missing our loved ones who have been falsely accused? Or would you like to at least give change a chance?"

"We have a chance now," Lux added. "And Dante is that chance."

They were silent for a long moment. "We can't know that we can trust him," Ellis said finally. "And we could be risking everything to keep him here. He could be working for the King, trying to get the location of the rebel base and its leader for his father. Have you thought of that? The rebels are already in danger. He knows their leader now."

"They made that choice. Cage chose to meet him. He knew the risk."

"He might have already gone off and told his father everything."

"He wouldn't do that!" Petra argued.

"How do you know? You don't know anything about him. This whole thing could be a trick."

"I don't believe that."

"But how can you be sure? You knew nothing about him until days ago when he claimed to have been attacked."

"No. I believe what happened to him is true. I think he was telling the truth. He has changed. If he were trying to shut everyone down and spying on the rebels, the Uprising would already be in trouble, and we would have been raided by now. We have already been raided once before, and they didn't wait for anything."

"Yes, but that was because of Shaw."

"And he doesn't know where this place is. He's still just out there in the outlands or the city. He can't tell anyone. We haven't had any trouble since he left. Dante is the real thing."

"I'm not so sure," Ellis said grimly. "We want him out of here before he can cause any more damage. We've already lost our home because of him."

Petra lifted her chin. "If he's going, I'm going."

Key scowled. "Petra, no."

Jesse looked around. "We'll vote, then. We can't stop you from leaving with him. Everyone in favor of getting Dante out of here, raise their hand."

Rip, Ellis and Jesse raised their hands. Lux rolled her eyes. "You can't call a vote. Beth isn't here. And if she was, she would vote with us. It's off the table. He stays. If he is a spy, we need to keep our eyes on him so we can be sure he isn't running off to his father."

"Unless he has a means of contacting him inside," Ellis said darkly.

"No," Petra said sharply. "He doesn't."

"How can you know that, Petra? You can't watch him every second. You aren't watching him now. He could be talking to Scarlet as we're in here arguing over it. We are in danger as long as he is still here."

"Then we have to do something!"

"Like what?"

"We can join the rebels," Beth said from the doorway.

They all looked up at her in surprise. The compound--the lost kids--had never taken a side in this war. They had always remained on the outside, stayed out of the fight. Talking about Dante and Petra joining the war was one thing, but the others had never wanted to be part of it. They just wanted to get by. But things were different now; they could feel it. Something had changed, and they would never be able to go back the way it was.

Petra shot to her feet. "Has Cage given his decision."

Beth shook her head and took a seat beside Key. "No. Not yet. I'm sorry." She looked at the others. "We can all join the Uprising and stop all this once and for all. It's time to choose a side."

"We stay out of it," Ellis said. "We have always stayed out of it."

"That is no longer an option. Things have reached the breaking point. The Uprising can keep us all safe. The King's men haven't discovered their locations yet, and they have a safe house if it is needed. They are aware of the situation now. They will be preparing to hide their children and those who cannot fight. They would take in the younger kids and protect them."

They all considered this. "The outlands are dangerous for kids," Petra reminded them.

"We are safe inside this house. That's what a safe house is for."

"No. It is not safe for us anywhere in the outlands, not without an army to protect us," Key told him. "We aren't safe anywhere in Razor City."

"We have an army."

"It's not big or good enough. Some of us can stay here, but we should get the little kids out."

Ellis and Jesse glanced at each other. "That is actually not a bad idea," Ellis conceded. "Are they prepared to take them in?"

"Yes," Beth replied positively.

Ellis finally nodded. "We should give them a choice. Some of the kids won't like it. We have to let them know the danger they are in and let them make their own decision. We have been responsible for them all this time. Even in the present situation, we can't let them get hurt because of us, but we also cannot force them to choose a side. We should not force anyone who doesn't want to go."

"Fine. We will give them the choice," Petra said impatiently.

"The Uprising will protect them even if they choose not to join the fight," Beth said. "They will agree to take them in and allow them to remain neutral. Not everyone who they keep is part of the war."

"We should do it soon," Lux said. "As soon as we can."

Beth nodded. "I will talk to my people. We can plan how to evacuate the ones who want to go."

"Do it now," Lux said.

"I will gather the kids and talk to them," Key said. "We will let them know we have to move and where they are going."

"Okay," Beth rose from her seat in the circle."I will let the leaders know we are coming. They will take anyone." She looked at Petra. "Within reason. We don't want to take anyone who will cause a security breech. We can trust the people here. The ones we know."

Petra understood. She lifted her chin defiantly. Grey wasn't welcome. Chances are, neither was she. It didn't matter. She wasn't going anywhere Grey wasn't.

"I will go with you, Beth," Lux said. "We can coordinate the evacuation with our guards." She looked at the others. "It is time to get involved. It is time to do something. But the rest of you have a choice. It is up to you to decide how far you want to take this. If you aren't prepared to join the rebels, you can do what you want."

"We have been together all this time," Ellis said. "We have made our decisions and lived our lives together all these years. We are together now." He looked at Jesse and Rip. "Does anyone want to back out?"

Jesse sighed, but he glanced at Rip. Rip shrugged. "I'm good," he said.

Finally, Jesse nodded. He didn't look happy. "Okay, I'm in, too. At the very least we can buy some time and make sure the littler ones are safe."

"They won't have to join the army, Jesse. You won't have to join the army. But the Uprising will protect you," Beth told him. "You could help in other ways. They could use your skills."

This perked Jesse up a bit. "Most people could use my skills."

Petra rose to follow the others out. "I will talk to Grey and let him know what is happening."

Beth turned to her. "You know you can't bring him there."

Petra nodded. "I know."

Key looked at her seriously. "Petra, come with us."

"No. I can't leave Grey. I'll stay here with him. We will work with the Uprising here and try to come up with something to do while we're waiting to find out if the rebels are willing to work with us and make a plan. When they are ready to move, we'll be ready."

Beth stepped forward to hug her. "I will speak to you soon."

She smiled wanly. "Yeah."

"Take care of yourself."

"You, too."

Petra glanced at Key. He scowled at her. "Do you think it's safe for you to stay here alone with him?"

She shrugged. "What's going to happen without you that wouldn't happen with you here? All he wants now is to help stop his father."

Key sighed. "I know he can help. But I'm not sure he is the best one to align yourself with right now."

"He is the best one, Key. He is the reason we are in this. He has a plan. He wants to attack the palace, the holdings and the prisons all at once. He knows all the locations. With him and Cage, we have a chance. If the Uprising follows Grey's plan, it could work. We might be able to get Ren and the others out. It could all finally be over. Scarlet will lose his hold on the city."

Key sighed, but he stepped forward to hug her tightly. "We will do what we can to convince Cage. I trust you, Petra. I think you know what you're doing. At the very least, I've seen you get out of some pretty bad scrapes. In the meantime, though, at least we'll be protecting the kids in case--in case Grey isn't as he seems. The King's people won't know where to find us."

Petra squared her shoulders. "If Grey is a spy, I will be the one to face the consequences. Not any of you or any of them."

"Will you tell him what we're doing?"

She sighed. "No, not if you all agree it would be best not to. Even if I did tell him, he doesn't know the location of the Uprising safe house. They would not be in danger."

Beth nodded. "She's right. We did not meet with Dante at the safe house. The location we used was disposable. It was not one of ours. Cage is not foolish enough to let Prince Dante see where we are keeping our people. We do protect ourselves. No one knows what the prince is really after right now, and the King has been wanting to crush the rebels from the beginning. He knows they are his biggest threat. He might have finally found the way--through his son." She touched Petra's arm. "I know you trust him. Just be careful."

"I will. I do trust him."

"Okay. We will be back with you soon."

Grey paced the small room like a caged jungle animal, muttering softly to himself. When he heard her slip inside the room, his head snapped up. He turned to look at her with a tempestuous frown. "I am not a spy."

She blinked at him in surprise. "Were you listening?"

"Not to all of it. Just some of it. I'm not a spy, Petra." He strode toward her and gripped her hands. "Everything I told you has been the truth!"

"I know that. I believe you, Grey. But not everyone does."

He nodded decisively. The he released her abruptly and turned away. "I need to leave."

"What? You can't! All we've been doing here has been to protect you."

"No. It has been to stop all this. The corruption and murder and false imprisonment. Everything my father has been up to. But before that it was about keeping your people safe, and they aren't safe as long as I am here." He looked at her seriously. "I have to go."

"I won't let you."

"Petra, I'm not going to put you in danger."

"We have a plan. We have an alternative plan--"

He held up his hand. "Don't tell me! I don't want to know. Whatever your people are planning, they need to do it without me hearing about it. I don't want there to be any question about whether I'm passing information to my father. I will do whatever I can to prove it, but don't tell me."

She sighed, but she didn't argue. "All right."

"I want your people to be safe. I don't want anyone else to be hurt because of me and my father. If the rebels won't help us, I have to do it on my own."

"What? You can't take on an entire army by yourself!"

"I might be able to get to my father...get in and seize power by force."

She stared at him. "What? You intend to kill your father and take over the city?"

"I might not have to kill him. I might be able to sneak in and catch him by surprise. Maybe I can lock him up somewhere. If he was out of commission and I was back, I would be the obvious successor."

She shook her head. "No, Grey, it's too risky. You can't. If Scarlet is the one trying to kill you, Saer could be waiting for you."

152

"I beat him twice already when I wasn't expecting him. Now that I am, I think I can handle him."

She scowled. "Grey, this isn't the way."

"What other way is there? Wait? Wait for Cage to decide he's ready to mobilize? That would be ideal if the rebels go ahead with the strike, but we don't have time to wait for them. Time is running out before my father begins to suspect I have joined their side or they find me. We have to act now. We can't wait." He gripped her shoulders. "Your people will be safe. You will be safe. I don't matter."

"You do matter!"

"I matter right now only in that I might be the only one who can get into the palace and take out the King to seize power. His courtiers won't have a choice but to follow me. I will see to that. I can place myself in charge. And when I am in charge, I can stop all this. I can change everything."

"No, Grey, it's too dangerous. It's too risky. What if the people won't agree to it? What if they won't follow you? They could kill you."

"No. They won't have a choice. I will be in a position to help the rebels take all the holdings and bring change. Then they will know."

"But they might take you out. And it is power, Grey. How can you be sure it won't corrupt you just like it did your father?"

"Because it's happened to me once. I know how to give it back now. I will only take it in order to give it back to the people."

"Power corrupts. Grey, it has corrupted you in the past. How can you be sure you'll be able to let it go?"

He looked hurt. "You don't trust me?"

She sighed. She stepped forward and clenched his fingers in hers. She looked into his eyes. She did trust him. "I do. I think you mean what you say. I think you have a good heart and your intentions are good. But I think your father's intentions were good once, too. In the beginning."

Grey shook his head. "I won't keep hold of the city long enough to let myself become my father." He wrapped her into a fierce hug. "And I will have you. Won't I?" He leaned back to look at her. "Won't I, Petra? Will you stay with me and make sure I will not let this ruin me like it did my father?"

She melted into him. She wrapped her arms tightly around his waist. "I will.

Of course I will. So let me go with you."

He shook his head. "No. I can't let you. I'm sorry. You have to stay here where I know you will be safe. Or go with the rebels for now. Anywhere they won't be able to get to you."

"But—"

"I can't let you, Petra."

"Then stay here. Don't go. Not until we can sort this all out."

"What is there to sort out? I'm going to have to wing it no matter what."

"Please, Grey, don't. We're not ready yet. I'm not ready for you to go."

He leaned down and kissed her. For several moments, she leaned into him and let herself forget everything. As long as he was here and he was all right, everything would be okay. As long as he didn't go off to try to take the city from his father by force, everything would be fine. In that small moment, she didn't care about rebels or Kings or the war that she was trying to start. She just wanted to be with him.

She tightened her arms around his neck. If she just held on, he might not leave. "Just don't go," she whispered in his ear.

"I won't." He tilted her chin up to kiss her again. "Not anytime soon."

He walked her backward so they fell back onto the bed. He leaned over her. She stared up at him with pale, troubled eyes. "Do you promise?"

Grey hesitated. Finally, he replied, "I promise."

Petra smiled and pulled him down to kiss her. It was a long time before she stopped kissing him. For several moments, it was as though the city had stopped moving, as though the Uprising and the King had ceased to exist. She could almost believe they were two people who loved each other; two people who didn't have anything to fear.

He lifted his head to look down at her. "I won't let anything bad happen to you, Petra."

She smiled and drew a finger down his cheek. "I don't want anything bad to happen to you, either."

"But Cage is right, Petra. Sometimes you have to sacrifice one for the good of many."

She clutched his arms. "I'm not willing to let you go. I'm not willing to sacrifice you, Grey. You promised. You promised you won't go until we can plan this. I want to know what is going to happen."

"Okay." There was something in his eyes. She wasn't sure what it was. She wanted to trust him. She wasn't sure she should. "I promise."

"Do you really promise?"

"Yes." He looked determined now. He smiled and cupped her cheek in his hand. "I won't go. Not until we know what we're going to do."

She smiled and curled against his side. He wrapped his arms around her. She sighed contentedly and closed her eyes.

He waited. In mere moments, her breathing grew deep, slow and steady. He leaned down to whisper in her ear. "Petra?"

She didn't answer.

Grey slipped carefully out from under her her arm. She didn't stir. She hadn't slept well in several days. She probably wouldn't wake up until he was long gone. He leaned down and kissed her forehead. "I'm sorry, Petra. Goodbye."

CHAPTER TEN

Later, at the safe house where everything has fallen apart...

Petra awoke with a start. The room was eerily silent. She couldn't hear him breathing. She'd grown used to the sound of his breathing. It had been with her every night for the last few days. She hadn't even known how much she needed to hear it.

Now it was gone.

"Grey?" There was no sign of him in the room. "Grey!" She shot to her feet. His things were gone. He hadn't had much, but he had taken it all with him. He wasn't coming back.

She threw on her clothes and rushed down the stairs. Everyone was already up from their bed and moving around, tossing the few belongings they'd brought with them into bags. Petra looked around for Beth. Her friend noticed her almost at the same time. They strode quickly toward each other to meet in middle of the room. It was peculiarly quiet despite the activity.

"We're ready. We're moving the kids," Beth told her.

"Where's Grey?"

Beth blinked. "What? He's not with you?"

"No! He's gone."

"What do you mean 'gone'?"

"He left."

"How do you know?"

"He was here, and I fell asleep—now he's gone." Petra gripped her best friend's arm. "He said he was going to go home. He was going to try to take out Scarlet by himself and seize the palace."

"Petra, we're moving everyone, and we have to go. How long has he been gone?"

She shook her head. "I don't know. I've only been asleep a couple hours."

Beth's expression was grim. "It might have been enough time. There might already be an army coming." She spun toward the main room. "Everybody out! Now! There's no time to spare! Take what you need and follow Lux!" She clapped her hands together. "Now!"

"He isn't bringing anyone here!" Petra argued.

Beth looked serious. "You don't know that, Petra. He is still the prince, and if he knew we were planning to move--"

"He didn't. He didn't know. I didn't tell him anything. He didn't want to know."

"That doesn't mean he didn't overhear! At least he doesn't know where the base is. We're secure right now. No one is watching. Yet. But we have to leave now. Come on, Petra."

Petra yanked her arm away. "No! I have to find him. He can't just go in there on his own. He'll be killed!"

"He knows what he's doing or he wouldn't have gone. Or...or he's been with his father all along, in which case he is perfectly safe."

"He isn't with his father! He isn't, Beth. And he is walking right into his death!"

"We can't worry about that right now. We have to worry about our own people. Petra, are you with us or not?"

Petra sighed. "No..."

"Petra, you can't go to the palace to look for him. He's gone. Even if he isn't still on his father's side, the best you can do is wait and hope he'll make it out all right. There's nothing you can do right now. We have to go to the rebels."

Petra scowled, but she didn't refuse. Beth grabbed her arm to drag her with the others toward the door. She swiped a tear from her cheek. There wasn't time to cry over him now.

"You will see him again, Petra," Beth promised.

"I hope so. I really do, Beth, but I'm afraid I never will."

* * *

Meanwhile, at King Scarlet's gilded palace...

Grey crept carefully through the courtyard. The guards outside the palace leaned on their guns or the walls bordering the opulent, stone building, looking bored and sleepy. They didn't notice him. They talked quietly to each other. Their voices were subdued, as though the atmosphere at the palace had taken a downward turn since the prince had disappeared. Every now and again, one of them laughed but the sound seemed to fade lifelessly into the charged air. Grey slipped around the side of the building and pulled open the servant's entrance door. He didn't walk inside. He flashed a light toward the steep, narrow stairs. He lifted the gun in his hand.

If Saer was there, Grey was prepared to deal with him. Saer wasn't there. No one was there. The stairs were silent and empty.

His heart thumped wildly in his chest as though it could hardly bear to see him through this new ordeal. It was the only way. He still had no idea what he was going to do. He didn't kid himself the empty stairwell meant it was safe for him in the palace. He wasn't safe anywhere, especially not here. No one would be safe until he could stop his father and take back the city.

He crept through the darkened halls. It was late. The palace was asleep. If he could make it to his room, he could have time to think. He just needed to time figure out what he was going to do. He needed time to be ready to do it.

There were guards in the corridor outside his bedroom. He hadn't once wondered what had happened to his two ubiquitous bodyguards. Sean and Errol were still outside his door, as though they expected him to emerge any moment, on his way to a night out in the city.

He halted hastily and tried to duck back down the other way before they saw him, but Errol spotted him. "It's Dante." He sounded shocked. His voice rang out as though he'd shouted.

Grey wasn't quick enough to escape them. Sean seized his arm. His expression was triumphant. It didn't bode well for the prince; he remembered enough to know he had not endeared himself to his bodyguards. "Your father will be very happy to see you, Dante."

His heart fluttered. He could have aimed his gun at the bodyguards, but they would raise the alarm before he got a shot off, and he didn't think he had it in him to pull the trigger. He hadn't wanted them to know he was in the palace so quickly. Now they did. He would have to adjust. He was relieved, at least, that they didn't pat him down. If they took away his gun, he would have no way to protect himself or carry out his plan--whatever it turned out to be.

They steered him firmly toward his father's office. They had never manhandled him before. He hadn't realized how strong they both were. He had been lucky before to have remained on their good sides. Or, at least, he had remained under their protection. They didn't seem interested in protecting him now. His father must have commanded Grey be brought before him the moment they caught sight of him.

Sean rapped on the door. Scarlet's voice sounded gruff. "Enter."

"Sir, the prince."

Scarlet shot to his feet as Sean propelled Dante into the room. He didn't smile, but his handsome, angular face lit up. "Dante." He strode forward and folded Dante into a tight bear hug.

Grey hugged him back warily. He didn't know what was happening.

"I was so worried." Scarlet leaned back to hold him out at arm's length.

"I'm sorry, Dad."

"Where have you been?"

"The outlands."

"What?"

He didn't realize he would say it until he did, and then he couldn't take it back. "I was kidnapped."

Scarlet blinked in surprise. "Kidnapped? My god, Dante."

For a moment, he didn't say anything else. Dante's heart thudded as he struggled to think of what to say next.

Finally, his father asked, "Who did it?"

He had anticipated this question, of course, but he still hadn't come up with an answer. His mind raced. "Some outlaws. They caught up with me outside a bar. They beat me up and took me to the outlands."

Scarlet stepped forward and took Dante's chin in his hand. He looked closely at his face. "You do look as though you have been recently injured." He frowned. "Are you suggesting they let you go?"

"No. They didn't. I escaped."

Scarlet scowled. "How?"

Grey shook his head. "It's hazy. I was drugged. Some of the bounty hunters crashed the base and destroyed it. I was able to escape in the chaos."

"But how long ago was this?"

He wasn't entirely certain his father believed him. He soldiered on anyway.

"A few days. I managed to get away, but I was in bad shape. I had to avoid being seen. I knew if anyone recognized me, I would be in worse trouble."

Scarlet frowned as he thought about this. He sighed and flickered his hand across his forehead. "I am sorry this has happened to you, son. I did not mean for any of this to happen. If I had known, I would have stopped it."

He sounded sincere. Grey had never seen him look so concerned—*not since the day Elia died.* The thought rose unbidden into his mind. He pushed it away. He hadn't expected this sort of reception from his father. He wasn't sure what he had expected, but it hadn't been...affection. He needed time to think about it. Could move against his father—could he do whatever he had to do to take over control of the city if he wasn't the one who had sent Saer after him? Could he betray a man who had never betrayed him? He still loved his father, would always love his father, no matter what he was.

But, then, Dante's tenacious assassin worked for Scarlet, and Scarlet was very good at keeping up appearances.

"I am so glad you are all right. I am relieved you made it home safely."

"I'm sorry I worried you, Dad."

Scarlet stepped forward and hugged him again. "You are home now." He leaned back to look at Grey sternly. Grey's stomach flipped. He knew that look. He had seen it in his dreams and in flashes of memory. "Can you tell me anything about the people who held you?"

Grey sighed. "No. Not really. I was beaten up pretty badly. And I was drugged. I didn't see any faces."

"Were they rebels?"

"No. I don't think so. They were outlaws. They planned to hold me for ransom. I heard them talking about it."

"Why didn't they?"

"I don't know what they were waiting for. Perhaps they were waiting for the right time. I did not know their plan. I just heard bits and pieces. They kept me in a room with no windows."

Scarlet's brow furrowed. "What about when you escaped? Do you remember where you were?"

Grey shook his head. "No. Just somewhere the outlands. The streets all look the same. It's chaos out there. I just remember some old, burnt out houses all

160

around me."

"You were in a house?"

"Yeah. In the basement. I crawled up the stairs and out the backdoor while they were fighting the hunters. I was lost for days. I slept in some empty houses on the way back to the city center. I spent most of the days trying to avoid the bands of outlaws. I finally made it to the edge of town. After that, I found my way home."

"Why didn't you present yourself to the guards?"

Grey sighed. "I was scared. I didn't know who was in on it."

Scarlet scowled. "You think one of my people was in on it?" He looked so furious, Grey was almost frightened of him.

"I-I'm not sure. I didn't know. Maybe. Someone knew where to find me that night."

"Interesting. Did you see anyone you know?"

He shook his head. "No. I was drinking."

"You are always drinking."

"Not anymore, Dad. I want to change. What's happened has changed me. It was terrible to be in that basement. I want to forget it and--become better."

Scarlet considered him. "I am happy to hear it. I am glad you have finally seen things my way. A prince cannot go about acting like a spoiled schoolboy on a bender. You are expected to be a man of dignity. It is the only way you can take the reigns when I am gone or ready to retire. Does this mean you are prepared to begin working on my side? You are prepared to take an interest in matters of the city?"

Grey lifted his chin. "Yes, Dad."

"Excellent. We will begin in the morning. Until then, go on to your room. I will send the medic to look you over. I want to make sure you are well."

"I am well. I don't need a medic."

"Do what your father says. I need to know you will do so from now on and that you will be on my side. Not defying me and making a spectacle of yourself."

Grey lowered his head. "Yes, Dad."

Scarlet strode to the door and opened it wide. He gestured Sean and Errol, who waited in the corridor like motionless sentries. "Gentleman, see my son to his room. And guard him."

Grey looked at him in surprise. "Dad?"

"I am inclined to trust you have decided to join me, but I intend to verify it. I can't have you falling back into your old patterns now that you are home."

He nodded, but his stomach roiled. "Of course, Dad. Good night."

"Good night, son. See you in the morning."

* * *

Meanwhile, at the clandestine Uprising base in the outlands...

The room Petra shared with Beth was small. The two of them barely had enough space for their two cots and the few personal items they had brought with them. The Uprising's compound was impressive, despite the minimal accommodations. It was an enormous farm house so close to the outer edge of Razor City, even the outlaws rarely ventured so far away from the city center.

The farm was fully functional. The rebels sustained themselves on the crops and cattle. Everyone worked the land. They seemed happy. Petra was almost surprised they wanted to take over Razor City at all; they had everything they could possibly need here, on their base.

In the back of the house was an extensive training ground for the army. The leaders and inner circle of the rebellion had a large private meeting room that looked as though it had once been a lavish dining room. It was the nicest vigilante operation she had ever seen.

According to Beth, the farm had once belonged to one of the rebels. It was so far from the city center, its owner had managed to hold onto it even after the war. Despite how comfortable it was, Petra didn't like it as much as the old mall. She'd loved the mall. All the lost kids had loved the mall. It had been everything they could have wanted, and it was fun all the time. She'd been happy there. They had all been happy.

Until she had brought Prince Dante there. Then it had all fallen apart.

But, no. It had fallen apart before that. It had fallen apart when her brother had been taken and imprisoned. It had fallen apart when the first innocent person had been taken and tossed away as though their life meant nothing. She couldn't go back to the way it was, not ever. Even if the rebellion succeeded and Ren was freed, they could never go back.

If they were lucky, what they had to go back to would be better.

And it might all be up to Prince Dante. Her breath hitched. She hoped he was all right, wherever he was. She hadn't heard from him or heard anything of his reappearance on the news. The Uprising had not allowed her to leave the compound to check on him. She couldn't have done much anyway; she couldn't march upon the palace and demand to see him. It could put both their lives at risk. It could ruin everything.

She wanted to talk to Cage. He might have information about Dante, about what had happened when he'd returned home. He was still a Noble, even if he was the leader of the rebellion. His position had not yet been compromised. Cage, though, was staying away from the mall kids. He wouldn't speak to any of them,. He seemed particularly keen to avoid her. She didn't really blame him.

No one spoke much to her aside from Beth, and that was only to wish her good night. Even Key was staying away. Perhaps he was angrier than he'd let on about the mistakes she'd made and the trouble she'd brought down upon them. Perhaps he had simply become so absorbed in life with the Uprising, he hardly had time for her anymore.

She missed him. She wished he would come back. She felt more alone and more frightened than she ever had. She felt out of control. She didn't like leaving the fate of her people and the city in the hands of others, especially people she was fairly certain she couldn't trust. She hadn't wanted anything to do with any of it.

Not until Grey had come along. And then everything had changed.

She paced the tiny room. She opened her laptop, but there wasn't any news. It was as though the world stood still while she was in the farmhouse on the edge of town. Scarlet and his people were silent. Dante was silent. Even the people around her were silent. It seemed oddly appropriate.

She had tried to access the King's email again, to find any news of Grey or even what the palace had learned about the Uprising, but Scarlet's passwords had been changed. It was troubling, but she tried not to think too closely about what that meant. Perhaps the King's information security had noticed the breech.

Or perhaps Grey had warned him that someone was looking in on him. Perhaps it had been part of the King's and his son's plan all along.

She felt ill, but she couldn't stop trusting Grey now. If she did, everything would fall apart. She might fall apart. Grey was her very last hope.

She hoped he was all right.

There was a knock on her door. She was so startled, she almost screamed.

Instead, she yelped and turned toward the door. She really needed to relax.

Beth opened the door without waiting for her to reply. It was her room, too. Petra didn't know why she'd knocked, unless she'd intended to frighten her. She pressed her hand to her chest. "Hey," she gasped.

Beth looked serious. "Anything from Grey?"

"No. Nothing. I haven't heard anything new from the palace. The media is quiet. There's nothing at all going on."

"Or if there is, it's nothing that we know about. What about your contacts around town?"

Petra shook her head. "I'm almost too afraid to talk to them. I'm not sure what they would know, and I don't want them somehow putting anything together." She sighed. "I'm so worried, Beth."

"I know." She squared her shoulders. "Cage has made a decision."

"What? Why didn't you say so before?"

"He wants to see you.."

Petra's heart leapt. Her stomach roiled. She hadn't eaten in days. She was glad. She doubted she'd be able to hold it down.

Beth tilted her head. "Come with me."

Cage was waiting in the enormous, lavish meeting room. He wasn't alone. Pablo and a few rebels whose names she didn't know were with him. They sat around the large table in the center of the room. Lux, Key and Ellis were with them. Petra lifted her eyebrows. So they had joined them, after all.

They all looked up at her as she entered, but they didn't say anything. Their expressions were unreadable. Beth directed her to a chair at the foot of the table, directly across from Cage. The Uprising leader eyed her silently for a long moment.

Finally, he spoke in his cold, calm voice. "Petra, we have decided to move on the palace."

"What?"

"It's time."

"I thought you weren't ready!"

"We are ready. We have been ready for a very long time."

"You lied to us!"

"We were protecting ourselves. The prince's information helped us, but we have always known that we would strike and when it would happen. We will hit all the King's holdings at once. We will strike at all points. We have already mobilized the teams."

Petra rose. "You're hitting all the holdings, including the prisons?"

"Yes."

"You have enough people for that?"

"You have no idea how wide our influence spreads. The King will never see it coming. While the other teams are striking, we will attack the palace."

"But...but Grey's in there!"

"Yes, and he seems to be back under his father's wing."

"What? What are you talking about?"

"I have been in the palace. He is under lock and key."

Petra's breath caught. "Is he all right?"

Cage ignored this. "He is at his father's side at all times. Scarlet is teaching him the family business."

"You've seen him."

"I have seen him, but he has not seen me. For what it is worth, he has not revealed my identity to his father."

"So he is not a spy! He is innocent. He is trying to work from the inside. If we strike, he might be killed!"

"We have to take that risk. He went back on his own. We can't jeopardize our only chance because he might be caught in the crossfire."

She narrowed her eyes at him. "Right. You don't care about that, do you?"

He didn't not seem bothered by her remarks. "I am sorry about your brother. I am sorry about all the people who have been caught up in this fight, who were innocent. My family, too, was accused of treason, but they weren't lucky enough to be imprisoned. They were executed. I have spent years working my way through the King's ranks to become a trusted Noble and get inside. I still hadn't gotten the information we needed to plan our strike. We needed locations, the people he's working with. We needed to know what Dante gave us. And now we are finally ready. He gave himself to this cause. We have to use what he has given us now, before it is too late."

Petra scowled. "You don't have to be part of this, Petra," Beth told her. "You don't have to be involved in the strike. You can stay here."

"No. No! If Grey is in there, I'm going. And I will try to get him out before he gets hurt."

"Fine," Cage said. "As long as you do not get in our way, you may do as you like, but if you get in the way—if anyone gets in the way—they will fall with the King. We are not playing games here. There is no time for love, compassion or mercy. We go in, we bring them down, and we take the palace."

She frowned. "What about Ren?"

"We aren't sure where he's being kept," Beth answered. "But when we liberate the prisoners, we will bring them to safety. He will be all right."

Petra stuck out her chin. "Okay. Fine. I am ready when you are. I just want to move. I want to make something happen. When are we doing it?"

Cage's expression did not change. He was as impassive as ever. "We move right now."

CHAPTER ELEVEN

Meanwhile, in a room in the King's palace that had now become a prison...

Grey paced the length of his room. It was larger than the rooms he'd been sleeping in for the last several days, but it felt like a prison. He couldn't catch his breath. He felt as though the walls were closing in. He'd been under house arrest since he'd returned from the outlands.

But he was safe. At least, he felt safe. There hadn't been any attacks since he'd returned. He didn't know if his father had called off his attack dog or if he'd been mistaken all along. Maybe his compliance had been what Scarlet had wanted all along. Maybe now that he had fallen into Scarlet's plan for his life, his father had seen no further need to send his hit man after him. Either way, he hadn't seen or heard anything from Saer.

He hadn't seen or heard anything about anything. The palace was quiet. The city was quiet. There hadn't been a peep from the rebels. He wondered where Petra was. He hoped she was safe. He couldn't reach her. He'd never even gotten her number.

His friends in the palace guards and the Marshals--well, they weren't friends, exactly. They were people who he had bullied or threatened into giving him information in the past. They didn't know he'd never follow through now. They still passed him information, but they didn't have any now. Even the bounty hunters were minding their own business. They hadn't brought anyone to the palace in several days. He hadn't asked if Petra or her people had been captured. He didn't want anyone to wonder why he'd asked. He didn't want them to know her name. Once they had her name, they would have her.

Now that Dante had been found, Razor City was peaceful and serene. As peaceful and serene as a city suspended in fear and misery could be.

He knew Cage was all right. The King hadn't cottoned onto his hand in the Uprising yet. If he had, Grey would have known. When a Noble went down, everyone knew about it, even if they were on the bottom of the hierarchy. Most people in Razor City were on the bottom of the hierarchy. It helped to show even the ones on top fell when they stood against Scarlet. And they always fell even harder.

Dante waited. If the Uprising intended to move on the palace, they hadn't shown any signs yet. But they would. Eventually. He wished he knew when. If he hadn't snuck out and returned to the palace, he would know what was happening. He wished he hadn't acted rashly, but he'd had to know if Scarlet was behind Saer's attacks.

He still didn't know.

His stomach growled insistently. He'd been too sick with worry to notice before now. His room wasn't locked. He wasn't to leave the house, but he could still move freely around the palace. He hadn't eaten much in days. He was losing weight. His expensive, carefully tailored clothes hung on him like rags. He should get something to eat.

He peeked out of his room. His body guards were there, in the hall. Sean stepped in front of the door. "Where are you going, Dante?"

He didn't remember a time when he hadn't lied to them. It felt strange telling the truth. "I'm going to the kitchen to get something to eat."

Sean and Errol glanced at each other. They eyed him suspiciously. His hair was mussed and he wore the same jeans and tee shirt he'd worn the past two days. He wasn't dressed to go out. He wasn't even wearing shoes. They nodded. Apparently, they appreciated the break. "Fifteen minutes."

"Okay. Bring you some cookies or something."

They were the only people he passed in the halls of the palace. It was strangely quiet. The silence felt charged and dangerous. The hairs on the back of his neck stood up. His heart thumped. The palace felt wrong. Where were the guards? Where were the Nobles wandering in and out to meet with his father even late into the evening? Where were the servant girls bustling around the house, cleaning up after the day's business meetings and luncheons?

Petra's face flashed in his mind. He hoped she was all right. In the kitchen, he forgot about getting something to eat. Something was happening. He felt it in his bones, but he didn't know what it was. His bodyguards obviously didn't suspect anything. Perhaps he was simply going stir crazy. Perhaps his worry and fear and anxiety was getting the better of him.

The kitchen was quiet. The pots and pans from the evening's meal had been cleaned and put away. The cook had gone home for the night. If he had prepared the morning's breakfast, it was put away. It looked as though no one had used the room in days. He knew they had. Claire had brought a tray of food to him earlier in the day, but he'd only picked at it.

He moved out of the room and peeked down the stairs to the servant's entrance. It was dark and silent. At the foot of the stairs, the door was sealed shut. He didn't think it was locked. It was never locked. No one had come in. If they had, he would know. At least, he was sure he would notice if the Uprising was here.

His stomach growled again. He turned back to the kitchen. He'd make a sandwich or something. He thought he could remember how to do that, though he couldn't remember the last time he'd made anything for himself. He wondered if Sean and Errol really wanted those cookies. Even if they didn't, no one said no to cookies. He rummaged through the fridge and slapped together a turkey sandwich. He didn't bother with condiments or dressing. He stuffed the bread and meat in his mouth without thinking about what he was eating.

There were cookies in the pantry. He grabbed a stack still sealed in cellophane. His fifteen minutes were nearly up. Sean and Errol would come looking for him. At least he'd have something to show for it. Maybe the cookies could be a peace offering. He probably owed them something, anyway. He'd been the worst charge anyone could have asked for.

He wondered for the first time what they'd done to get put on prince duty. It was probably something really bad.

He started up the stone stairs in the kitchen toward the upper levels, toward his room on the third floor. They were as silent as the rest of the house. Most of the staff didn't use them, but Claire did. He almost hoped to meet her there. He wasn't sure what he wanted to say. Sorry, maybe. Perhaps he wanted to tell her it would be over soon. She wouldn't be a slave for much longer. She wouldn't have to fear that her parents would be executed. Perhaps he just wanted to tell her that he'd changed.

She probably wouldn't believe him. She probably wouldn't even listen. She'd stand there and stare at him with those huge, terrified eyes, but his words would fall on deaf ears. He wished he hadn't spent so much time frightening her. He wished he could take back all the terrible things he'd done. It would have taken a lifetime to make up for them.

He'd have his work cut out for him. He needed a good head start. Claire wasn't on the stairs, though. Wherever she was, he thought she was probably avoiding him. He hadn't called her to his room since he'd returned, and she hadn't come on her own. If she was the one cleaning his room, she did it while he was with his father. He'd never even seen her.

After a moment, he realized he wasn't alone on the stairs. There was hardly a noise, but he felt the air changed. He thought he could feel someone breathing.

He spun around.

Saer rushed toward him from the foot of the stairs. Grey was so startled, he forgot the gun stuffed into his waistband. He never went anywhere without it these days. He was amazed no one had noticed it. Saer reached him before he had a chance to realize what was happening. He gripped the front of Grey's tee shirt and spun him around. For a moment, Grey was suspended in the air above the stairs. He felt his feet leave the ground.

When Saer let him go, he reached for the lapels of Saer's long, brown duster. The assassin's cold, pale eyes widened. Grey didn't let go. He yanked hard on Saer's coat. Saer fell forward while Grey fell backward. The assassin flailed in the air to catch the railing, but he couldn't get a grip on it. With all of his strength, Grey spun him in midair.

They landed at the foot of the stairs. It hurt, but Grey hadn't landed on the hard, stone floor. He'd landed on Saer. He looked down. The assassin's eyes were closed. He didn't open them or stir. Grey didn't wait to check his pulse. He probably wasn't dead. He didn't seem like the type of man who was so easy to kill. He would probably live forever, doing the King's bidding until the King was gone. Maybe after that, he would retire somewhere quiet.

Grey scrambled to his feet and up several stairs. When he was out of Saer's reach, he leaned a hand against the wall and gasped for breath. His heart pounded. The stack of cookies had burst open. They lay in a pile of crumbs around Saer's head. For a moment, Grey felt horribly disappointed. He'd only meant to be nice. Now he would have to explain to his bodyguards that he'd failed to bring them his peace offering because his father had sent someone to kill him.

He couldn't stay in the palace. He needed to leave. He would probably never see the guards again. If they knew what he was planning, they would stop him.

He turned back toward the foot of the stairs. The servants' door was close enough. Saer wasn't moving. He still had the gun. He could just shoot him now, and it would all be over. He would never come after him again. He yanked his gun out and lifted it. He took a deep, steadying breath.

He lowered his arm. He couldn't shoot an unconscious man in cold blood. He didn't think the old Dante could have done it, either. Perhaps he was nothing more than a coward.

Behind him, on the floor above, a door burst open and banged against the wall. Grey spun. He expected to see Sean or Errol or even Claire, coming to see what the commotion was about. It wasn't any of them.

It was Warin Scanlan, his father's right hand man.

Warin stared between Grey and the silent man at the foot of the stairs. For several seconds, he goggled silently. "What happened?" he demanded finally.

Grey fell back against the wall. "He tried to kill me. I defended myself."

Warin cursed. "He failed again? What sort of unstoppable killer is he?"

His words took several seconds to sink in. "What?"

The older man didn't say anything. His face twisted, and he rushed down the stairs toward Grey.

Grey staggered back a few steps and raised his gun. Warin stopped dead on the stairs. His eyes glinted angrily. He glared at Grey as though he wished he could lunged toward him and shove him down the stairs.

"What the hell is going on?" Grey demanded. "Did my father send Saer to kill me?"

"Put the gun away, Dante." His voice was low and cold.

"You knew he sent him?"

"I don't know what you're talking about. Put the gun away. You're acting crazy."

"I'm not the one who's crazy! You tell me what is going on, or I will shoot you!"

Warin laughed bitterly. "You won't shoot me. You're not a killer. You're just a spoiled child."

"I will shoot you! Saer tried to kill me three times, and you know something about it." Grey cocked the gun. His hand didn't even waver. "If you don't start telling me the truth, I will do it."

Warin held up his hands. "Okay. Okay."

"Was it my father who hired him?"

"Yes."

Grey stared at him for several seconds. There was something in his eyes. Suddenly, he knew. "You're lying. It wasn't my dad, was it? But you knew about it. You came here expecting to find me dead. You wanted to find me dead. It was you. You hired Saer. You planned to kill me to--what? To take over the city? To be the next in line?"

Warin glared at him. "I have no interest in your father's power." He lifted his chin. "What are you going to do? Shoot me? Go on, then. My life is worth nothing anymore. Not since my son died."

Grey blinked in surprise. "What? Your son?" And then he remembered. He'd been remembering all this time. He just hadn't understood what he'd seen. "Elia. He died...I was there."

"It was supposed to be you! It was supposed to be you who died that day. They were after you, not Elia. They wanted to hurt your father, but they made a mistake and took my son instead."

Grey shook his head. "So you hired Saer to kill me--to pay me back?"

Warin sighed. "Not you. You're just a child, just a spoiled brat. You don't mean anything to me. You're a disgrace. But he still loves you. You're his son."

"My father. You wanted to pay him back for Elia. It wasn't his fault! He didn't pull the trigger. He isn't the one who killed him."

"But if not for him, if not for you, my boy would still be alive."

"You're crazy."

"I have nothing to lose now. Just shoot me, Dante. Let me be at peace. Finally, I can be with Elia again."

"No. I'm not going to shoot you." But he didn't lower his gun. "That's not the sort of man I am."

Warin laughed humorlessly. "What sort of man do you think you are, Dante? Do you even know? Do you think because you got a bump on the head and have decided to be a good boy for your father that you're suddenly decent? You're still his son. You're still corrupt and vicious. I've seen the way you behave. You're nothing but a mean, spoiled bully."

"No. No! Not anymore. I've changed."

"Please. You think nineteen years of being a spoiled brat goes away in a week? It doesn't. You're still the man you always were, and you will become your father someday. You will hurt and kill and imprison those who oppose you. You will let innocent children die to protect your own interests. You are just like him. Elia was a good boy. He was sweet and innocent. He never hurt anyone. He didn't deserve to die. You do!"

"No," Grey said in a soft voice. "He didn't deserve to die. I'm sorry he's dead.

I'm sorry it was meant for me. But I am not like my father. I want the corruption and the imprisonments and executions to stop."

Warin barked with laughter. "You think it will be so easy? You think you can just convince your father to stop"

"No. I think there are others who will convince him."

"Oh. You have an army now? What were you doing while you were away? Did you fall in with the Uprising while you were in the outlands? Or were you just in hiding?"

Grey lifted his chin. "I'm not in hiding anymore."

"No, now you can fall right back under your father's wing."

"You don't know anything about me!"

"Oh, no, Dante. It is you who know nothing. I know everything about you. I have been watching you for a long time, and you are not near as good a man as my son would have become. Just kill me." He lifted his arms at his sides. "Do it and seal your fate. Do what you are meant to do. Become Ezra. Become a monster and murderer."

"No. I will have you arrested instead."

Warin laughed again. "You will have to kill me. I won't go." He crouched suddenly as though preparing to strike.

Grey braced himself and steadied his gun. He didn't want to pull the trigger. He would if he had to.

There was a crash somewhere in the palace. And then someone shouted. Grey started and turned his head. In the moment he looked away from him, Warin rushed at him. Grey spun back toward him.

He pulled the trigger. Warin clutched at his chest in shock. For a moment, Grey was certain he saw his lips curl into a smile. He didn't wait to see him fall. He pushed past him and raced up the stairs.

His father was innocent. He hadn't been trying to kill him, anyway. It changed everything.

And it was too late. The Uprising was here.

He pounded up the stairs toward his father's office on the forth floor. If he could reach him, maybe he could save his life. The rebels hadn't made it to the main floors yet. They must have streamed silently in through the servants' entrance and up into the entrance hall. He could hear them below. He could hear shouting and gunfire.

They'd struck just exactly as he'd suggested.

His heart felt as though it might leap from his chest. He wondered if Petra was there with the rebels. He knew her well enough by now. She would be. And she would be coming for him. He missed her. He ached to see her, to ensure she was all right, but he needed to make it to his father first. He didn't stop.

Petra could take care of herself. She was the one on the winning side.

His father's office door was closed. He'd never dared to enter without knocking before. Now he burst in. The door banged violently against the wall. Scarlet shot to his feet behind his desk. His expression was thunderous. "Dante? What are you doing bursting in here like this?"

"Dad, the rebels are attacking the palace!"

Scarlet frowned in confusion. "What?"

"We have to get you into hiding. They're coming for you."

His father scoffed. "They won't get past my people. This is the safest room in the house."

"Do you have a panic room?"

"A panic room?" He sounded completely disdainful.

"You don't have a panic room? Are you crazy?"

"Son, this palace is a fortress. How could they even get in? They won't get past the gates."

"They already have! They came in through the servants' entrance on the west side."

"What? How did they know about that? I thought it was sealed up."

Grey shook his head. "It isn't."

"How do you know?"

"I use it all the time. I..." He took a deep breath and met his father's eyes. "I told them about it"

Scarlet's face turned purple with rage. "What? You what? You're a rebel?"

He lifted his chin. "I am."

"But why? I thought you had finally decided to join me, to take what is rightfully yours."

"I don't want it! This isn't right. We can't keep controlling the city and the people this way."

Scarlet slapped a hand on the surface of his desk. "You are my son! How could you do this?"

"I'm sorry, Dad. I thought you were trying to kill me."

Scarlet blinked in surprise. "So you sided with them? With the Uprising? To get back at me? To take me down?"

"I am trying to save your life!"

"By bringing them here, into our home?" Scarlet stepped forward to face him. He didn't reach out to strike him, but his expression was so furious, Grey thought he might. "I will not lose my empire, Dante. If you are with the Uprising, you are my enemy."

"Dad, we have to get out of here--"

Scarlet reached into his jacket before Grey realized what he was doing. He drew out a long barreled pistol. He aimed it at Grey's head. Grey raised his own gun.

For a moment, they didn't say anything. They didn't move. They stared at each other.

Petra burst into the room. "Grey!"

Both men looked at her in shock. "Petra!" Grey said finally.

Scarlet's lip curled. "And is this one of the rebels? Of course it is."

He swiveled and aimed the gun at Petra. She had one, too. That was three too many in the room, by Grey's estimation. He dove in front of her and lifted his hands. "Father, no!"

Scarlet did not fire. His eyes narrowed as he looked at his son. "You're protecting her?"

"Yes. You will have to shoot me if you want to get to her, and you won't be able to before I kill you."

Petra didn't have time for this. "Grey, the rebels are here. They're attacking. What are you planning to do? Who's side are you on now? You have to choose."

Grey didn't look at her. His eyes locked with his father's. "He isn't the one who was trying to kill me. It was Warin."

"Who--"

"What?" Scarlet demanded. "Warin was trying to kill you?"

"He hired Saer Dagon."

Scarlet scoffed. "But that's ridiculous."

"No. It isn't. He was trying paying you have back for Elia."

"Elia..." Scarlet's eyes slid away. "I have not thought of the boy in years."

"Grey! The rebels are here!" Petra reminded him. "They're taking out the guards. They're following your plan."

"You planned this?" Scarlet asked.

Grey did not waver. "I gave them information. Now I have to try to get you out of here alive."

"My own son is a traitor!"

"The Uprising is powerful," Petra told him over Grey's shoulder. Her eyes narrowed. "Their army is big, and your people are falling. All your holdings are being attacked as we speak. None of your people will make it out unless they are absorbed by us. Your reign is over. All you have left is a chance to live, if you even have that."

Scarlet glared at her. "Don't tell me what to do! No one tells me what to do!" He aimed his gun between them as though he couldn't decide who he wanted to shoot first.

"Father, it's over." Grey's voice was low and almost gentle. "Please. Let me save your life."

There was shouting on the floors below. It was getting closer. They were nearly upon them.

"It's the rebels," Petra said. "They're coming, Grey."

Grey looked at his father. His eyes glinted tempestuously. "This is your last chance, Dad! Please. I don't know what they will do if they catch you. I don't want you to die. You are still my father. I love you."

"You are no son of mine! You betrayed me! You brought the Uprising down upon me. You took down my entire empire!" He didn't lower his gun. He swung it toward Grey's face.

Grey's shoulders trembled, but he didn't waver or lower his own gun. He didn't want to shoot his father, but he had gotten them into this. If he had to, he would take it all the way. He'd always known it might come to this. He was relieved, at least, that it was him and not someone else. At least he would show his father mercy.

"Petra, Grey, send out the King!" Cage's voice came from the hall outside the door. It sounded firm. It sounded triumphant.

"Grey?" Scarlet repeated. He looked at his son with narrow eyes. "Who the hell is Grey?"

He lifted his chin. "I am."

"You are? What is this?"

"Grey?" Petra demanded, glancing behind her at the door. "What do we do?"

"If we send him out, they will execute him, Petra. He's my father."

"Grey, we will come in," Cage told them. "Send him out or we will come get him."

"He means it, Grey. What are you going to do?"

"We can't send him out!"

"Let them in," Scarlet said coldly. "Let them in, and I will kill them all."

"Don't be a fool!" Grey hissed. "You will die! I don't want to lose you."

"I'll go out to them," Petra said. "I will tell them there is another way. We can do what you planned. We can lock him up, lock him away and keep him out of it. I can talk to Cage. He may agree."

Grey shook his head. "I will go."

"No! You're the one holding out on them. I don't want them getting into their head they'll kill you, too." She backed up slowly, but Scarlet did not try to fire at her. He stared down the barrel of Grey's gun. She opened the door and stepped out into the hall.

"Where is the King, Petra?" Cage demanded.

Behind him, the Uprising gathered in the hall. They weren't carrying a noose, but they looked like a lynch mob all the same.

"You don't have to kill him, Cage. You can just imprison him."

Cage lifted an eyebrow, but his expression didn't change. "He murdered hundreds of people. He murdered our loved ones. And you want to let him live?"

"We don't have to do it this way."

"Get out of the way, Petra." He caught her arm and propelled her toward the group of rebels in the hall.

She tried to start forward, but she felt hands on her arms. Beth held onto her. She looked as though she'd been hit in the face, and her blonde hair was unraveling from her braid. Nevertheless, she looked excited. They had won. Whatever happened to the King now, the Uprising had won.

"Don't, Petra," she said firmly. "You can't stop it. Don't get yourself killed for that bastard."

"But Grey--!" Petra struggled, but there were more hands on her, holding her back.

Cage drew his pistol and stepped into the King's office. Grey spun and jumped in front of his father. "You don't have to kill him, Cage! It doesn't have to be like this. You don't have to start it all by killing him. You can be merciful."

"Like him?" Cage growled, glaring toward Scarlet.

Scarlet didn't look afraid. He looked furious. "You will have to kill me. If not, I will find a way to destroy you all. Including you, Grey."

"Step aside, Grey," Cage ordered.

He stood his ground. "You can't start a new era like this! With murder in cold blood! It isn't right! It will just be the same all over again. We can make him stand trial for his crimes. We cannot just execute him! We can have him judged by the people."

"If you do not step aside, I will consider you to be on his side and act accordingly."

Petra broke free from the rebels holding her arms. "Petra!" Beth shouted, but Petra was too fast. She raced into the office.

"Grey!"

They didn't glance at her. Cage leveled his gun at Grey. The prince didn't move. Petra dove for him, but she was too late. The gun exploded. The noise was deafening. Grey barreled into her. They both fell to the ground.

"Grey!"

But he wasn't bleeding. Beside him, Scarlet dropped to his knees, clutching at

178

his side. Blood poured over his hand.

"Dad!" Grey crawled to him. He cradled his father's head in his lap. "What did you do?"

Scarlet's dark eyes rolled up to him. "You're still my son." His voice was raspy. Petra wasn't sure he was going to make it. "You would have died for me."

Grey's breath hitched. "I love you, Dad. I'm sorry."

Petra looked up at Cage. "You didn't have to do that!"

Cage lowered his gun and lifted his chin. He looked cold and remorseless. "It is the end of King Scarlet. I had to make it stick."

She glared at him and knelt down beside Grey and his father. The wound was bad. Scarlet was bleeding heavily. The color drained from his face. She bent down to examine the wound. She'd seen worse. He might make it, if they could stop the bleeding in time.

She rose to face Cage. "You have your rebellion. You've won. Let him live."

Cage looked down at Scarlet and his son. For a moment, he looked as though he intended to raise his gun and finish them off.

Petra stepped forward and caught his arm. "Cage, please. You can't shoot him while he's down. It's wrong." He didn't say anything. Her fingers tightened on his arm. "He can't do anything this way. He's finished. Killing him won't solve anything. He will never be able to hurt anyone again. Don't start our new life this way. Do the right thing."

Cage stared at her. Finally, he nodded. He turned his head and barked toward the doorway. "Get a medic in here!"

"We have a hospital wing," Grey said urgently. "Unless it's been destroyed."

"No," Cage replied. He looked calmer now. Petra sighed in relief. "We didn't kill anyone innocent. Just the guards who refused to be absorbed. Those who joined us were spared. We did not kill anyone we didn't need to. It is not the way."

"Except the King," Petra whispered.

Cage didn't reply, he turned and strode out of the room. He paused in front of his people. The gathered outside the door and on the floors below. They waited. He faced them and lifted his arms.

"King Scarlet has fallen!" he shouted.

The cheering was nearly deafening. It didn't stop for a very long time.

Grey closed his eyes. Scarlet didn't stir. His breath was shallow and ragged. His eyes were squeezed shut against the pain. Silent tears streaked down Grey's pale cheeks.

Petra knelt by his side. She wrapped her arms around his shoulders. "I'm so sorry, Grey."

He shook his head. He clutched his father's hand. "I'm lucky he's still alive."

"He'll be all right. We'll make sure of it."

Grey looked up at her. There was something in his stormy eyes. It might have been relief. "It's over, Petra."

She smiled sadly and squeezed his shoulders. "No. It isn't over. Not yet."

CHAPTER TWELVE

Later, in a conference room that had once belonged to a King...

The party was still raging in the floors below. It might not ever stop. The falsely accused were still flooding out of the prisons, and the rest of the King's regime were hiding out or being rounded up by the jubilant rebels. The prisons were filling back up as quickly as they were emptied with the King's most violent and hated Nobles. The rest of the King's guards, Marshals and Nobles too insignificant to warrant Cage's personal attention, would accept the new regime gracefully, or they would face the same fate.

The Uprising had taken the city so quickly, no one outside the King's inner circle had even known it was happening until it was over. King Scarlet's Razor City had fallen with hardly a fight. The news spread like wildfire through the streets. The stunned citizens had just begun to understand what lay ahead of them.

It was freedom. At least, Petra hoped it was.

The first meeting of Razor City's new regime was underway.

Grey wasn't there. He was still with his father in the hospital wing. The Uprising was still discussing the Scarlets' fate. Petra sat around the oval conference table with Jesse, Rip, Lux and Ellis. She felt as though they were facing off against Cage, Pablo, Beth and Uprising on the other side.

"He helped us," Lux said. "Dante told us how to strike. He gave us the information we needed to win. If not for him, we would never have been able to pull this off."

"But he came back to the palace," Pablo argued. "He was working with his father. He had rejoined his side."

"No!" Petra growled. She rose to her feet. Her eyes blazed. "He came back here because Cage wouldn't give him an answer. You wouldn't let him know if you would help him. He didn't think he had a choice. He thought he had to do it himself. He planned to come here and take out Scarlet by himself in secret and take over the city."

"Yes," Pablo replied, scowling. "And then he would have been King. And he would have been the same as his father."

"He is one of us! He was not spying or he would have told Scarlet what we'd planned. He would have told him where the safe house was. We would never have been able to get through the gates without him. He meant what he said. He wants change. And if not for him, we wouldn't have it now."

Cage didn't say anything. He only listened.

"You have what you wanted. And Grey helped. We will not let you lock him up with his father. He isn't the enemy."

Pablo's reply was cut short. There was knock on the door. Beth rose to open it. For a moment, she didn't move. Then she stepped aside. She was smiling.

Key strode into the room. He was smiling, too. Petra hadn't seen him smile like that in so long, she hadn't even remembered his face could look like that, as though a light had gone on somewhere and the world was a safe, wonderful place. Key wasn't alone. Beside him, a tall, thin man with long, pale dishevelled blonde hair stepped into the conference room. His pale blue eyes sought Petra immediately.

"Ren!" She raced toward him and vaulted into his arms. She hugged him for several seconds, as though she might never let go. He felt thinner than he ever had; where he had once been solid and strong, he felt weak and breakable. Petra didn't care. He was back, and that was what mattered now. When she pulled back to look at him, tears streamed down her cheeks. Her brother looked tired, too. There were dark circles under his eyes. He was still handsome, though, and he didn't look as though he'd been badly hurt. She'd never been so happy to see anyone. "I missed you. I've been doing everything to get you out."

Ren laughed. "I didn't think you'd take down the entire city to do it, but I shouldn't have expected any less from you."

Petra smiled. "Well, you know me."

Beth stepped forward to hug Ren. Petra released him and stepped back to let her. The way Beth looked at him surprised Petra. The way Ren looked back at Beth surprised her more. She'd always thought it was Key that Beth loved. Maybe she'd been wrong.

Petra felt a stab of resentment toward her friend. How could Beth have let him be taken like that when she knew Cage had only done it to save his own skin? Perhaps it had been harder on Beth than Petra had realized. Petra had always thought she had been the one to sacrifice, to lose the people she loved to the King and his city. She'd never even considered what Beth had given to take down Scarlet.

182

She pushed the thoughts away. It didn't matter. It was over now.

Beth's voice was low, as though she didn't trust herself to speak normally. "Are you all right?"

Ren grinned. "Yeah. I'm okay."

Cage rose to face Ren. There was no expression on his face. Ren looked back at him. Petra couldn't tell what Ren was thinking as he looked at the man who had been responsible for the last few months, for the misery and pain he'd experienced. She'd always been able to tell what Ren was thinking in the past. She had known him as well as she had known himself. His time away had changed him.

"I'm sorry, Ren," Cage told him. "I am sorry that it came to what it did. I am sorry you suffered."

Ren eyed him a moment. Then he nodded shortly. He did not look as though he meant to forgive Cage anytime soon. Nevertheless, if he was contemplating revenge, it was not a sensible time to act upon it now.

"It was for the good of the Uprising," Cage added.

Ren considered this. "I understand your reasons, Cage. You don't have to explain it to me."

Cage nodded. His face was as unreadable as always. If he truly regretted what he'd done to Ren, it didn't show in his eyes.

Petra suspected he did. He was a ruthless man, but his reasons had been just in the end. He had, after all, led the people of Razor City to freedom. Perhaps he would have given anything to the cause; perhaps he had no qualms. Or perhaps every tiny sacrifice had felt like another knife in the gut. She would likely never know.

"We're just trying to decide what to do now," Beth told Ren. "Now the King and his people are out."

At that moment, Grey strode into the room. He looked pale and drawn. They all turned to look at him. No one said anything for several seconds. Key must have had the time to warn Ren of the more shocking changes in the city; her brother didn't look surprised to see Petra stride forward and take Grey's hand. His expression was utterly blank.

"Grey, this is my brother, Ren," she told him.

After a long, charged silence, Ren held out a hand for Grey to shake. Grey looked down at it in surprise. He looked as though he wasn't quite sure whether to trust the polite gesture. He looked as though he was not entirely sure he wasn't about to be shot on the spot by the leaders of the rebel army. Finally, he reached forward and shook Ren's hand. They nodded tensely to each other.

"I'm glad you're free," Grey told him. His voice was hoarse, and his eyes looked red. Petra wanted to ask about his father, but she didn't think it was the appropriate time or place.

"Thanks to you, I hear," Ren replied. "If not for you, the Uprising would not have known the locations of the prisons and Scarlet's other holdings."

Grey looked down. He didn't want credit for it. "Things had to change," he said quietly. "My father had to be stopped."

"How is he?" Beth asked. The others stiffened slightly, as though this were a touchy subject. Most of them probably wished he was dead.

"He'll live. He'll never walk normally again, if ever. But he will live. He has given up control of the city."

"He didn't have any choice in that," Pablo reminded him. "His people are done."

Grey nodded silently.

"So what now?" Ren asked, looking around at them.

"We pick up the pieces," Grey replied. "We begin anew."

They all looked at Cage. He was silent.

"What do we do, Cage?" Beth asked. "You are our leader."

Cage sighed. He leaned back in his chair. They waited. Finally, he said simply, "No."

"What?" Pablo demanded.

"No. I don't want to be the leader." His expression was as blank as ever. "I led the Uprising because there was no one else who was willing to do it. I don't want to rule. I don't want to lead. I have gotten what I want. Now I just want to be free."

Grey scowled. "But those people out there, celebrating right now, they need someone to guide them now. They need to know where they are going. What happens next. They need to have a reason to reunite now and work together to build a new future for the city."

They all looked at Grey. They considered him for a long moment. Then they looked at Cage.

"You have a vision for this city, Grey," Cage said. "You want to see the people rule themselves. You want to see the sectors come together and have a voice. And you have the people who can help you do that here in this room and out there in the streets. But until then, the city need someone strong, someone who can use his influence and power. Someone who is connected to the old regime but rose above it for something better. The city needs you."

Grey hesitated. He looked at Petra uncertainly. "I'm not sure I'm ready for that."

"You were ready when you thought you had no choice. When you had no help," she reminded him. "You were prepared to take out the entire regime yourself and start fresh."

"I have seen you grow up, Dante." Cage said. "I have seen what you are capable of. You have changed. Perhaps you have always had it in you. Your father had a vision once, too, and I believed in it. There was no one to keep him from becoming what he did. You have lots of people who can help you. You are the one who can take this city where it needs to go. You are the one who can lead us into that vision of yours."

"I..." Grey frowned. "Do you think they would even accept me?"

"This city was lost without a leader before. This was how your father was able to take control. They need someone to guide them. They need the person who was powerful enough to stop Scarlet."

"But what about someone they can trust?"

"Do you think it matters? Do you think one of the King's Nobles will be any more desirable than the prince? Do you think any of the rest of us would be better? We are no one to them. Without you, the Uprising could not have taken the city. They would not be free now. They will look at you as the person who stopped King Scarlet and the terrible things he's done."

"I have to think about it."

"There is no time. Someone needs to go out and address the people. Someone needs to let them know there is nothing more to fear and that it is time to band together. That person needs to be you."

Grey looked at Petra. For a moment, it was as though they were alone in the room. "What do I do?"

She smiled at him. She didn't know the answer. She didn't think she could decide for him. She didn't even know if Cage was right.

"What if I...what if I become like my father? What if I let the power corrupt me like he did? What if I won't let it go when it's time to give it back?"

She squeezed his hand. "I'll help you."

"We will all be here," Lux told him. "To advise you. To watch and keep you in line." She smirked. "We'll make sure you are a good leader. We won't let you get away with becoming anything like your father. You've seen what we can do."

Grey clutched his head in his hands. He shook his head. "I'm just a kid."

"Then it's time to become a man," Cage replied cooly.

"Shouldn't we vote on this or something? Just moments ago you were trying to decide whether or not to throw me in prison."

Cage looked around at the assemblage. "Is anyone opposed to this?"

They all glanced at each other. Pablo didn't look convinced, but he didn't speak up. No one spoke up.

"I'll take that as a no."

Grey sighed. He looked at Petra. "Will you go with me?"

She smiled. "Sure."

Cage stood. "It's time. We have to address the people. Get ready."

Grey looked almost ill. "I think I'm as ready as I will ever be."

* * *

The media swarmed the palace. Citizens flooded the streets around them, anxiously awaiting the appearance of the mysterious rebel leader. The rumors of his identity had spread through the city, but only those inside the palace knew the truth. They would never know that it hadn't been Prince Dante all along. They would never know that he felt as though is insides had turned to ice and his heart might leap right out of his chest. If he was lucky, they wouldn't notice how his knees shook.

He hesitated on the steps outside the palace. The podium from which his father addressed the press seemed so far away, as though through the gauntlet of cameras and microphones and shouting, cheering people who would as soon fall upon him and rip him to shreds as defer to his leadership.

He sighed heavily. Then he squared his shoulders. He strode forward with his head held high. When he turned toward the congregation, a charged and tense silence fell. He took a deep breath. They all waited for him to speak. Cameras snapped in his face. Microphones shot up toward him.

It was time. It was his only chance. He'd better make it good.

"People of Razor City, you have nothing left to fear." He looked around at them. Their faces were rapt and expectant. "My father, King Scarlet, is no longer in control of the city."

It took several moments for the crowd to process this information. Though the news had already spread, it was as though his announcement had sealed all their fates. A low murmur passed through the crowd. Many of the people still looked hostile. They waited for more.

"Your family and friends are on their way home to you now. All the prisoners who were falsely accused of treason have been released."

There was a sudden burst of noise from the crowd. The murmuring grew into a crescendo. Then the cheering began. It was deafening. Grey waited until it had quieted down.

"The King's guards and Marshals have been disbanded. The police no longer work for him. You are safe, and you are free."

He could hear the cheering as though it came from every part of the city. Every home, business and corner of the city seemed to be listening. And they were all rejoicing.

He lifted his hands. Silence fell again.

"From now on, things are going to be different. It will take time. My father's rule was bloody and it was cruel. But Razor City will no longer be a place where people have to live in fear for their lives and their loved ones. The police and the Marshals will work for the people. They will protect them. The outlaws will no longer run rampant in the outlands. The city will become safe for everyone, and everyone will have a voice.

"I do not stand before you today to announce my rule of Razor City. I stand before you today to let you know that I will help you all rule yourselves. The people will have the chance to make their own choices. Together, we will make this city a place where we can all be safe and live together without fear of violence or a leader who would take your liberty to increase his own power.

"We have our work cut out for us. But if we all work together, we can fix what's gone wrong in this city. We can take it back and make it whatever we want it to be. We can make it great. You might think you know me, but you don't. But you will. My name is Grey. And I will take you all into the future."

* * *

Later, at the sparkling new Razor City Hall...

Grey stood in front of the mirror in his father's old office. It felt odd using the room. It felt odd without his father there, sitting behind his desk, conducting audiences and commanding the city as though the tall, leather desk chair were his throne room. His father wasn't there anymore, and now it was Grey who sat behind the desk. It was Grey who led the city.

He still didn't know how to tie a tie properly. He struggled with the knot. He cursed softly under his breath and spun away from the mirror. He punched a button on his desk. "Petra!"

She might have been waiting right outside the door. She was there in seconds. When she saw him, she pressed her hand to her mouth to stifle a laugh. He frowned at her. "Do you need help?"

"Yes."

She smiled and strode toward him. "Hold still." He didn't know how she'd learned to tie a tie. When she did it, it looked easy. When she'd done, she spun him back to the mirror to admire his reflection. She smoothed his long, dark hair back from his face. "Are you nervous?"

"Yes."

Her pale blue eyes twinkled. She didn't look nervous at all. She looked cool and confident in a simple black dress. Her long, pale blonde hair was twisted at the back of her neck. She looked grown up. "You'll be fine. You always do great at these things."

He took a deep breath to steady his nerves. He smiled a little wanly. "That's a matter of opinion, I think."

"Oh, come on. Have a little faith in yourself. Everyone loves you." She smiled and patted the tie on his chest. "You look great."

He stepped closer to her. He leaned down to press his lips to hers. "So do you." There was a knock on the door. It was soft and hesitant. Grey sighed and pulled away from Petra. "Yes. Come in."

Claire strode into the room. She wasn't wearing her maid's uniform. Instead she wore a trim, black suit. She hadn't worn the uniform since he'd liberated her and offered her a position as his assistant. She hadn't wanted to take it at first, but she'd agreed in the end. She was remarkably good at it. He wasn't sure the city would have survived without her. "Sir?"

He turned toward her and lifted an eyebrow. "Claire."

She ducked her head. "Sorry, sir--Grey."

He nodded. "What is it?"

"Mr. Cage is here to see you."

Grey looked at Petra and sighed. "Here we go." He smiled at Claire. "Thanks, Claire. Send him in."

"Of course, s-Grey." She gave him a tiny bow and spun out of the room.

Petra rolled her eyes. "I don't know what you did to that girl, but I hope you make up for it one of these days. She'd be a lot better at her job if she wasn't so terrified of her boss."

Grey frowned. "I'm working on it. I think we're making progress. She doesn't squeak in fear anymore when I walk into a room, anyway."

"Boy. Dante sounds like kind of a jerk."

"He was."

"Then I'm glad he's gone."

"You aren't the only one."

Cage didn't bother to knock. He strode into the office. He looked as cool and serene as ever. He bobbed his head at Petra and looked at Grey. "Are you ready?"

"As ready as I'll ever be."

"Your tie is crooked."

Grey gave Petra a disapproving look. She smirked and reached to straighten it. "It was straight before," she told him in a low voice.

"The city prosecutor will be there. She wants to talk about the trial."

He nodded. "I know."

"Will you be all right?"

"Yes. I have to be. I knew this day would come."

"You must show a strong face at this meeting, especially during this time. You have to stay firm and accept what the people decide. It will affect the election."

Grey sighed. "I know." He lifted an eyebrow. "I don't suppose you're planning to run against me?"

Cage snorted so softly, he barely made a sound. "You needn't worry about that. I still don't want to lead the city." He stared silently at him for a long moment. "Are you sure you still do?"

"No."

Cage smiled. "Good. It's how it should be. You've done good things, Grey. You are seeing your vision for this city realized. You are the right man for the job."

"But there are others, too, who would do good work. People with more experience and more wisdom than me. They might do better."

"Well, it isn't up to you. It's up to the people."

Petra checked her watch. "Guys, it's time."

The oval table in the conference room was already nearly full. When Grey, Cage and Petra strode into the room, the assemblage stood. Grey lifted his hands in greeting and directed them to sit. He felt foolish when they rose to greet him. It didn't seem quite right. He wondered if his father had enjoyed it. He probably had.

"Welcome, everyone, to the first Razor City Council meeting. I see we have the representatives from all the sectors here, as well as the chief of police, the city prosecutor and the head of the city Marshal service. I'm glad you all could make it."

He sat in the seat at the head of the table between Petra and Cage. He looked around at the gathering. He took a deep breath to steady his nerves. "I know you all have many questions and concerns, and I hope to address them all today. You'll see the itinerary for the meeting has already been set. If there's anything we've missed, please hold it until the end and we will take your questions and address your issues."

They were all looking at him. They didn't say anything. Grey glanced at Petra. She didn't smile or nod at him, but there was something encouraging in her eyes. He felt better.

"If everyone is ready, we'll take the first issue." He glanced down at the itinerary on his desk. Claire had done a good job with it. "The representative from Sector 5, you have the floor."

190

A tall, powerful looking woman in a black suit stood. She had short, dark hair and pale skin, but she reminded Petra a little of Lux. Perhaps it was the hard, non-nonsense look in her dark eyes. She looked strong and fierce. She probably had to be; Sector 5 was the outlands.

"Thank you, Grey. Anna Bane, Representative Sector 5. The outlands are still being overrun by the outlaws. Our patrols are systematically gathering and arresting the wanted fugitives, but they aren't keen on the new regime entering their territory. Some of the Marshals who have been caught out alone in the streets have disappeared."

Grey frowned. "That's troubling." He turned to the tall, thickly muscled man on the other side of the table. "Mr. Wolf, do you have any thoughts on this?"

The Marshal inclined his head. "We need more resources in that area. Greater police presence and more patrols. We have lost three men. Two of them have returned, but we are still missing one. We fear the worst."

"The outlaws are still running wild, despite the regime change," Anna Bane added. "I propose we approve a systematic search of all the dwellings in the sector for fugitives."

This caused a stir among the representatives. Grey frowned. "This is against city policy. It's a violation of our people's liberties."

Anna frowned. "This isn't the old United States, Grey. There is no Constitution anymore to prevent us from fighting the rampant crime that is still flourishing in our city."

Grey shook his head. "That is not the way I intend to run this city. I'm sorry, Anna."

"In some cases, the fugitives are wanted based on the old regime's laws," Cage put in. "We would be robbing innocent people who'd done nothing wrong of their freedom to live their lives in peace and privacy."

"There is no peace in the outlands," Anna replied.

"Then we will assign more resources to your sector, Anna," Grey told her. "We can shuffle some of the unneeded patrols in the less populated and less concerning areas of the city. We will do the very best we can, but we can't lose sight of what we are trying to do here. We're trying to prevent creating a new regime in which we can declare martial law and rob our people of their basic freedoms. Mr. Wolf, can you assure me that no Marshals will be patrolling one their own? I don't want to lose any more men."

Wolf inclined his head. "Nor do we. We will reevaluate our patrols and assign them accordingly.

"In regard to the fugitives, do we have a plan to address the issue of those who should be pardoned?"

Police Chief Younger raised his hand to speak. "Our people are working on it. We have removed several dozen people from the most wanted list based on their alleged crimes, but it is difficult to sort through all the records. We hope to have the list updated soon."

Grey nodded. "What about the bounty hunters?" Randall Wiley, the representative from Sector 2 asked. "Can't they help in the outlands? The bounty hunter system has always been effective in reducing the outlaw population. They are willing to go where the patrols are not."

"They often operate outside the confines of the law," Chief Younger said, frowning. "We are still experiencing an influx of hunters entering uninvited to drag out fugitives."

Grey considered this. "I am inclined to allow the bounty hunters to continue their work. Most of them follow the code, and they are effective in bringing in fugitives."

Anna lifted her chin. "I am willing to allow the bounty hunters in to clean up my sector."

"They're still busy rounding up the Nobles who are in hiding," Petra put in. "I don't think they're interested in small fish right now."

"And they have done very well in bringing in the remnants of the old regime," Chief Younger said. "We have assigned a task force to deal with the Nobles and Scarlet's supporters. They are a full time job on their own."

"So, what am I to do in Sector 5?" Anna demanded.

"We will get you more people to patrol your streets. We will move as many as we can," Grey told her. "A stronger presence in the streets might prevent opportunity street crimes. As long as the outlaws remain in their homes, we are unable to invade their privacy. On the other hand, if they remain in their homes, they are less likely to be committing crimes."

Anna didn't look entirely satisfied with this, but she finally nodded. Petra looked at her. "I know someone who might be able to help you. Our compound's head of security has trained an entire army, and she is in contact with some of the old Uprising militia members. Perhaps what we need is a street militia to deal with the task of rounding up the outlaws."

Grey looked at her in surprise. "A street militia?"

She smiled. "Who act within the confines of the law, as you say."

He considered this. He looked at Wolf and Younger. "Do you have any thoughts on this, gentlemen?"

They thought about it. "It wouldn't hurt," Wolf said. "At least until we have control of the outlands. It would be no different from the bounty hunter system."

Grey looked around at the assemblage. "Anna, is this sufficient for you?"

She thought about it. Finally, she nodded. "I think we should put this to a vote," Danny Chang, the representative from Sector 3 put in. "If we sanction a street militia, how can we be sure they won't abuse their power and march on the other sectors?"

"Their authority will extend only to the outlands and with respect to the fugitives," Petra replied.

Grey looked around. "All in favor of installing a temporary street militia in the outlands?"

Most of the table raised their hands. Grey nodded. "Petra, get Lux into contact with Anna and Wolf." He looked back down at his list. "Onto the next item, then."

The rest of the issues were more mundane: the quality of the drinking water; deciding what to do with the newly empty prisons and buildings around the city; public transportation; public schools, and appointing the headmaster of the lost children's home. Running a city, Grey had realized early on, was not as exciting as he would have expected. Most of it was tedious and time consuming.

Many of the representatives wanted to talk about money. Much of his time had been spent redistributing the money the King's people had seized from the accused. Scarlet had amassed a fortune during his reign, and most of it rightly belonged to someone else. Grey had set up a fund for the accused from his father's money and the money of the Nobles who had profited from the accused and their families, and he had been trying to make reparations. It took time to sort through all the claims.

Tru Haven, the representative from Sector 1, raised her hand. "The city center and the outlands are still overrun with violence. I want to make a proposal that we outlaw guns in Razor City."

This caused quite a stir. The representatives and the guests began arguing loudly. Some of them liked the idea of taking the guns away from outlaws. Others wanted to be able to protect themselves. Grey listened to them for several moments. Finally, he stood and faced them. "This is a serous issue, and we should take the time to share it with the people and get their thoughts. I agree that outlawing guns would seriously decrease the violence, especially in the outlands, but there is a lot to consider. If we outlaw guns, police and Marshals will still need to carry them for protection."

"The bounty hunters won't like it," Petra said.

"It might not actually be a bad idea," Cage remarked.

"What are you talking about?" Petra asked him quietly. "You have tons of guns. You don't want to give them up."

For a moment, his mouth twitched, but then he shrugged.

"I think this is an issue we should take to a city wide vote," Grey said. "Furthermore, I propose we table it until after the election. It's not a decision we should make lightly, and I think it would be best to wait until the people have made their decision about who will lead them."

The assemblage didn't seem to like it one way or another, but they agreed.

"Is there anything else?"

Now Erika Brana, the city prosecutor rose. She was a tall, slender woman with long, wavy dark hair. She looked grim. Grey suspected he wasn't going to like what she had to say. "The trials for Scarlet and the Nobles begin next week."

"Yes, I have heard."

"We're afraid it will be difficult to find impartial jurors," Chief Younger added.

Grey thought about this. "We will have to trust our citizens to act responsibly."

"They are all guilty," Danny Chang put in. "There is plenty of proof. The jury will not have much to decide upon. They already know."

"That is not the way the justice system works," Erika said, frowning.

"There is no justice system anymore," Anna Bane argued. "All that ended after the war. Why are we even bothering to try them? Why not just put them to death?"

Grey frowned. "Because that is what is old regime used to do. We are going to do things fairly. We will do what we can to give them a fair trial."

"Grey, we need to discuss whether or not executions will continue in Razor City," Erika said. "Do we wish to seek execution in these trials?"

Grey was silent a long moment. "I do not believe I can be trusted to make such a decision, Erika," he said finally. "I cannot be considered objective in this case. Despite his crimes, I do not wish to see my father dead."

"Perhaps we should give the people the chance to decide," Tru Haven said. "Call a city wide vote."

"There isn't enough time for that," Erika replied. "It would take too long to organize it, and we would have to put the trials off. No one wants that."

Grey sighed. "We have to put it to a vote, then. We have to decide."

Cage rose. "We should think about this rationally before we make an emotional decision based on what Scarlet and his Nobles have done to this city. We all want to see justice, but we have to ask ourselves if we are willing to start our new lives by killing the old regime. Showing mercy to the King and his people would be a message to the people that things have changed. We will punish the guilty, but an eye for an eye is the way of the old regime."

They all thought about this. "But Scarlet and his people reigned in terror. They killed hundreds of innocent people. They deserve to get paid back in turn," Danny said.

"Violence is not the answer, Danny," Tru told him. "This is the defining moment of the new regime. The way we handle this will decide what sort of city we'll have in the future."

"Yes, and we don't want to appear weak in front of the people. We want to prove we are strong enough to control the city," Danny replied.

"Showing mercy is not a weakness," Cage argued. "Scarlet and his people showed they were strong through violence and imprisonment. If we decide to execute them, we are showing that we are dangerously close to becoming exactly the same."

They all thought about this. No one else argued. "Are we prepared to put it to a vote?" Grey asked. He looked around at them. He lifted his chin, but his eyes were stormy. "All in favor of execution."

Danny, Brana, Younger and Wolf raised their hands. No one else did. The four were not enough. Grey's let out a long breath he didn't realize he was holding. He'd at least expected a tie. He was surprised Anna hadn't raised her hand, but perhaps she was not as cold and vengeful as she seemed. Perhaps she, too, simply wanted to live in a world where no one had to live in fear for their lives.

Those who had voted for execution didn't argue, but they did not look satisfied. Brana nodded a little curtly. "Fine. We will seek life imprisonment."

"This decision will send a positive message to the people," Cage said. "We are a society who punishes the guilty, but we show mercy."

Grey found his voice again. He looked around. "The final issue on the agenda is the election for city leader. Representatives, do you have candidates to present from your sectors?"

Tru spoke first. "Yes. We held sector-wide elections. Individuals were nominated by the people, and the nominees were voted on. The Sector 1 candidate is Neil Burns."

"The former city councilman from before the war?" Younger said.

Tru nodded. "He is a good man, and he is popular among the people."

Grey had expected the representatives to challenge him for city leader. None of them did. Anna presented Hansel Graves, a well-known bounty hunter. Danny presented Marshal Wolf.

Grey looked at him in slight surprise. "I hadn't realized you had designs on the city leadership."

Wolf smiled. "Are you concerned, prince?"

Grey wasn't offended by this. "I only want what's best for the city." He looked around. "Are there any other nominees?"

Randall Wiley lifted his hand. "Sector 2 presents Victor Harrington."

"Scarlet's business manager?"

"Harrington worked for Scarlet before the war. He was not part of the regime."

"How can he have worked for Scarlet and not have been part of his empire?"

"Simply working for Scarlet is not proof of guilt," Randall argued. "He handled his export business, but he was not a Noble. He was just trying to stay alive. He was quite gifted in his position, and he was skilled at keeping out of Scarlet's line of fire."

They all considered. "If there is no reason to believe he is guilty of crimes, he is as welcome to run for leader as anyone else," Grey said. "Campaigning will begin right away. It promises to be a very exciting race. It will, at the least, be a learning experience for the city and the regime."

"But you have not announced your candidacy, Grey," Anna said.

He looked around at them, then at Cage and finally at Petra. She smiled at him. "I have not been nominated," he said finally.

"But you are the incumbent. You do not have to be nominated," Cage told him.

Tru rose. "I nominate Grey for city leader."

He looked at her in surprise. He hadn't even fully decided whether he would run.

"I second the nomination," Anna said.

"All in favor?" Petra said quickly, before he could change his mind.

Everyone at the table raised their hands. Grey looked around at them for a moment. Finally, he smiled wanly. "Well. I suppose it looks like I'll be running, too."

CHAPTER THIRTEEN

Later, at the newly appointed Razor City Courthouse...

Grey was tense. Beside him, Petra folded his hand in hers. He glanced at her. A storm of emotion raged behind his eyes. "What are you worried about?" she whispered. "They didn't seek execution."

He sighed. "I know. And I know he will be found guilty. He is guilty. I agree with his imprisonment. It's just...he's still my father, Petra. It's hard to see him like this."

The trials for Ezra Scarlet and his Nobles had been long and hard. There were so many people who had been wronged by the King's reign, so many people who had been hurt. Erika Brana had not pulled any punches. Grey and Cage had been called to answer for their parts in the crimes, but their work to restore the city had protected them from punishment. They would, however, be paying reparations to their own victims for a long time. As far as Grey was concerned, it was only right. Cage, too, seemed eager to atone for his own sins.

The citizens of Razor City were happy to see the end of the trials. It was as though a heavy weight was lifting off their shoulders. It was as though the entire city had been suspended and breathless. Now, they could breath again. There had been a great public outcry about the decision not to execute the former King and his Nobles, but the media had supported the representatives' decision to be merciful toward the former regime. Eventually, the city had reconciled to the idea, though there were still protests even outside the courtroom that day.

The street militia from Sector 5 stood guard outside the courtroom. Anna Bane had argued over the loss of their presence from the outlands, but Grey had insisted. He wasn't taking any chances on one of the angrier citizens dispensing their own vigilante justice against his father and the Nobles. So far, nothing terrible had happened. Grey hoped the city would remain calm, even after the verdicts were read.

They were certain to be found guilty. They had carefully selected the jurors, but there wasn't a life in Razor City that hadn't been touched by Scarlet and his men. They would not get off easily for their crimes. No one believed they should. Except maybe Scarlet and his Nobles.

His father had not repented for his crimes. He'd reminded the citizens of the good he had done in the beginning, right after the world had been thrust in chaos and needed a heavy hand to unite the city. He'd insisted that his deeds had been just. Grey thought he almost seemed surprised to hear the droves of citizens testifying to his wickedness.

Perhaps he'd never been aware of the level of corruption he'd reached. Grey knew his father didn't expect to be found justified in his actions. He'd known from the beginning what would come of the trial. Grey hoped that, someday, he might actually understand the impact of everything he'd done.

"It's almost over," Petra told him in a low voice.

"I know. Once it is, we can finally put this all behind us. Maybe someday my father will learn from his mistakes."

"Perhaps it's more important that you learn from his mistakes."

Grey smiled wanly. "I like to think I have. But I probably have a lot left to learn."

She squeezed his hand. "Knowing it is what makes you better than him."

He sighed. "I don't know if I want to be better than him. He is still my father, and I think there is good in him. He simply went the wrong way with his power and his influence. Perhaps I just want to make better choices about how I handle them."

"You will. You already have. You started out on the wrong track, but you got rebooted. You got start over."

He smiled. "Rebooted. Yeah, I guess a bump on the head was exactly what I needed."

"Sometimes you have to shut down and restart. It usually doesn't work as well for people as machines, but this time it worked out pretty good."

"If not for you, I might have gone back and never known what I could have made of myself."

She considered. "Do you think you would have gone back to your father if the Uprising hadn't struck when it did?"

He'd thought about this a lot. "I don't know if I ever would have gone back to the way I was, but I don't know if I would have taken over the city by force, like I'd planned. At the time, I thought my father was trying to have me killed. When I realized he wasn't, I tried to make a fresh start with him. I thought maybe I could change him." He sighed. "I don't think I could have. I'd like to think I could, but

I don't think anything but a complete revolution would have changed him. I like to think I would have stayed good, but who knows what could have happened. I don't like to think about it."

She smiled at him. "You would have stayed good. Perhaps you would have reached a point when you realized you had to do something."

If he thought the same, he didn't get a chance to say. The bailiff called for attention. The judge strode into the courtroom. The spectators stopped talking and rose. The silence was tense and charged. The judge was a stiff-jawed man in his late fifties with steely grey hair combed back from his strong, humorless face. His dark eyes swept the courtroom with an uncanny alertness. He nodded and motioned them to sit.

Grey's breath caught. His grip on Petra's hand tightened almost painfully. She moved closer to him. The warmth and weight of her beside him was oddly reassuring. He wrapped an arm around her shoulders. His heart thumped. He watched the door for his father to enter.

The courtroom, too, sat back down to await King Scarlet. A guard brought him into the room from a side door. He looked grim, but he held his head high. Grey watched him as though he were the only person in the room. Scarlet had lost weight. His charcoal grey suit looked too large. His hair was combed back from his face, but it didn't look as flawless as it used to. It stuck up slightly in the back as though he hadn't been able to tame it. He looked as though he hadn't slept well, either. Grey had seen him since his arrest. He visited him often. His father had not yet forgiven him for helping to overthrow his empire, but they were attempting to reconcile.

Grey thought they were talking more now than they'd ever talked in his life. He wished there could be another outcome to the trial. There couldn't. Even Grey couldn't have let his father off for his crimes.

The judge was anxious to end the spectacle. "Has the jury reached a verdict?" he asked immediately.

"Yes, Your Honor."

The silence that ensued was deafening. The clerk passed the jury's verdict to the judge. He looked at Scarlet. "Ezra Scarlet, please rise."

Scarlet looked almost as though he might refuse this last indignity, but he finally rose. His attorney rose to stand at his side. The man looked as though he'd been through a terrible ordeal. He looked like a beaten, hopeless man. He'd tried his best. He was a good lawyer. There was no defending a man like Scarlet, a man who refused to show even the slightest remorse for his sins. Grey felt a little bad for the attorney.

"In the case of Razor City versus Ezra Scarlet, we find the defendant guilty. He will be sentenced to life imprisonment in a facility chosen by the city leader. There will be no hope of ever getting out."

Scarlet lifted his chin. His dark eyes were unreadable. The courtroom exploded in a cacophony of cheering and shouting. Grey closed his eyes. He didn't want to see his father dragged out of the courtroom in chains. He didn't want to see his face as they took him away.

"I'm sorry, Grey," Petra said beside him. She remained firmly planted in her seat, despite the pandemonium around them. "I know you wish it could be different."

He sighed. He opened his eyes and looked at her. "I do wish it could be different."

He glanced around them at the citizens in the courtroom. They were happy. They were happier than he had ever seen them. The man who'd been oppressing, terrorizing and destroying their lives for a decade was finally going to face justice.

"I wish it could be different," he said. "But it can't. This is the only way it can be."

Petra smiled wanly. "It's finally over, Grey. We can finally start over."

"Do me a favor, Petra."

She glanced at him in surprise. "Okay."

"Just make sure I don't end up in the same place in ten years."

He looked so serious, she couldn't bring herself to laugh. She patted his arm comfortingly. "Don't worry. If you start to turn into an evil overlord, I'll overthrow you long before you get the chance to wind up here."

"Thanks, Petra. I knew I could count on you."

* * *

Later, at a deeply depressing prison in Razor City...

The drab grey prison uniform did not flatter Scarlet, but he walked as though he were still a king among his subjects. The guards didn't like him, and the prisoners blamed him for losing his foothold in the city. Prison did not suit Ezra

Scarlet. There was something different in his eyes when he sat across from his son in the small, private meeting room in the newly minted Razor City Detention Center.

For a long moment, Scarlet stared at his son as though he'd never seen him before. Finally, he said, "You look good, son."

Grey inclined his head. "You look…"

"I know." Scarlet waved his hand. He sighed and leaned back in his chair.

"How are you?"

"I'm in the worst place I've ever been in my life, and it's never going to end," he admitted dryly.

"You are still alive."

"There are many who believe I should not be."

"Yes, there are. I'm not one of them."

"Was it you who vetoed execution, city leader?"

Grey couldn't tell if he was angry or if he was making fun of him. "No. I did not think it would be appropriate for me to make the decision. It was put to a vote. Against all expectation, your life was spared."

Scarlet looked somewhat surprised by this. "So that is how it is now in my city? The people make decisions together? They decide what's best for them?"

"It is. It is the only way a city can live in peace."

"People don't like being responsible for their own lives. They want someone to tell them want to do. They want someone else to take responsibility. They want someone else to blame when something goes wrong."

"They do not want to be told how to live their lives. They do not want to live in fear of stepping out of line or saying the wrong thing to the wrong person. They want to know that the decisions that are being made are in their best interest."

"Are you suggesting I did not intend to act in the best interest of my people?"

Grey stared at him. "Do you believe you did?"

He considered this a long time. Finally, he sighed. "I liked to think that I was acting in the interest of the people, but I think we both know the truth."

"Everyone knows the truth, Father."

Scarlet looked away. "It is a small comfort, Dante, but I am proud of you."

Grey blinked. He wasn't sure what to say to this.

"I made many mistakes during my time as King of this city. I did have good intentions in the beginning. I had good intentions throughout, but I am not a good man at my core. I was so sure you would go the same way, but I was wrong. You did what I couldn't do."

Grey smiled sadly. "I wish you'd realized your mistakes sooner. You will be paying for them now for a very long time."

"Yes. For the rest of my life, even if I am pardoned some day. But I will be able to see my son grow into the man I could never be."

Grey was so startled by this he did not speak for several moments. Scarlet, too, seemed not to want to say anything else. Finally, Grey asked, "How is Warin?"

Scarlet sighed. "I do not see him often. He hasn't given up his grudge against me. He doesn't leave his cell often. When he does, he won't speak to anyone much, least of all me." He frowned slightly. "I wish I could tell him I am sorry about Elia, but it's too late now, I'm afraid."

"He did try to kill me. Can't he call it even?"

Scarlet snorted. "I think not. I don't think he will ever consider us even. It's not something you can square."

An intercom buzzed beside the door. "Five minutes," a guard barked.

Scarlet smirked at Grey. "There's the warning bell. You're the city leader. Can't you bend the rules?"

"That not the way I run things. I don't bend rules. I have to set examples."

Scarlet smiled. It was a small smile, but it was genuine. Grey didn't think he'd seen it in a very long time. "I'm not surprised, I suppose. You are like your mother. She was always good. Perhaps if she had lived, I would have been a better man and none of this would have happened."

Grey sighed. "Things would have been very different for us both if she were still here."

Scarlet reached across the table and patted his hand. "Speaking of the city leader, I hear there is an election coming up."

"Yes. Now that the representatives have been elected, I thought it was only right the city get to choose their own leader."

Scarlet shook his head. He looked amused. "Who is the competition?"

"Neil Burns, the former city councilman from before the war."

"The man's past his prime. He wasn't any good when he was running the show. He didn't have the mettle to step in when the city was falling apart; now he wants to take over what he never earned to begin with."

Grey shrugged. "I hear he is very savvy in politics. He might put on a good campaign."

Scarlet scoffed and waved his hand. "Who else?"

"Hansel Graves."

His father laughed out loud. "Brilliant. That should be an interesting show."

"He does have quite a following."

"Among the outlaws and vigilantes. Is there anyone who will be competition?"

"Marshal Wolf is running."

"Ah. I am not surprised. I always suspected he had designs on power. I am not certain his reign would be any less tyrannical than the city considered mine."

"He seems like a good man."

"He is a wolf in sheep's clothing. If he gets control, it will only be a matter of time before things begin to look dark for your little rebellion."

"Victor Harrington is running."

Scarlet lifted his eyebrows. "My old business manager? Well, well. I never would have expected. He always kept his head down and his hands clean."

"Is he a good man?"

"He was a good business manager. Beyond that, I know little about him. He managed to keep his job and keep out of my way. Perhaps he's got something up his sleeve. I wouldn't trust him."

"I'm not sure I trust anyone who wants to be the leader of the city."

Scarlet laughed. "That is a wise position."

The intercom buzzed again. "Time's up," the guard said.

Scarlet sighed. He stood. Grey rose to meet him. Scarlet patted his shoulder. "Good luck, son. I hope you win."

Grey smiled humorlessly. "I'm not sure I want to."

"That's how I know you'll be good for the job; I would have wanted to."

204

The door opened. The guard strode inside to reclaim his prisoner.

Scarlet hugged Grey. It surprised him. It always surprised him, though his father did it after every visit. "Good bye, son. Good luck. Come see me again soon. It's the only entertainment I get in this place."

Grey nodded. "I will, Dad. Goodbye."

He watched the guard snap the shackles on his father's feet and wrists. Scarlet held his head high, but the weight must have been terrible. Grey sighed. If he was going to lead this city, he'd better do it right.

He enjoyed visiting with his father, but he didn't want to join him.

* * *

Later, in the dazzling courtyard outside the former King's palace...

The courtyard was teeming with people. They had been at the voting poles all day. Even those who had already voted gathered inside the gates and spilled out into the streets outside to await the results of the election. The atmosphere was festive and charged with excitement.

Petra and Cage stood on either side of Grey as he stood on the steps outside the palace, peering out at the crowd as though he was afraid they would scoop him up and carry him off. Petra held tightly to his hand. She was smiling, but Grey sensed that she was nervous. She'd worked day and night for weeks on his campaign. Soon, they would all discover the fate of Razor City.

A television news reporter stood in front of the podium outside the palace. She was a petite, pretty blonde woman in a hot pink dress. She looked as excited as everyone else seemed to be feeling. The news these days wasn't as thrilling as it used to be. Grey didn't showboat for the camera like Scarlet had. He almost never talked to the media. Now that the King was gone and no longer limiting the media to pro-Scarlet propaganda, they had to come up with their own stories. They were struggling a bit. The campaigns and election had been the most interesting news Razor City had seen since the trials.

If they spent a little more time in the outlands, Grey thought, they'd have plenty of news to report. Anna was still struggling with the residents of Section 5, but things were improving. It was the best they could hope for. At least the street militia seemed to be doing some good. The outlaws were a bit more humble than they used to be. Most of them even tried to keep their heads down most of the time.

The news reporter was speaking to the camera. "The officiators are counting ballots now, and in just a few minutes, the winner of the election for Razor City leader will be announced. This is the first city wide election in the history of Razor City since King Scarlet took control and reigned over the city for a long, bloody decade of terror and oppression. The candidates have run a long, intense race, and now we're facing the moment of truth. The people will finally make their own choice of who they want to lead them into what city officials are claiming to be a new era of peace, security and liberty."

She turned to jab her microphone at Grey. He didn't like speaking in front of cameras, but he'd gotten used to it over the course of the campaign. Cage nudged him forward.

"Prince Dante, do you have anything to tell our viewers before the numbers are in?"

"I'm no longer a Prince. You can just call me Grey."

The reporter smiled. "Yes, we've been hearing the name all over the city. How did you get the name Grey?"

He glanced at Petra. She wasn't paying attention to the interview. She was craning her neck to peer out at the crowd. Her long, pale blonde hair glinted in the sun. She was still as beautiful as the moment she'd leaned over him in that dark alley, but now she was more than that. He smiled. "It's the nickname given to me by a friend when I broke away from my father and decided to join the rebels. It seems appropriate."

He didn't know the reporter's name, but she had a nice smile. It never slipped from her face. "How are you feeling about the election, Grey?"

"I'm feeling good. All the candidates fought a good fight. I would be proud to be led by any of them."

"What are you planning to do if you win today?"

"If I win this election, I will do what I can to continue the changes we've been making in Razor City to make it a safe, happy place to live."

"Will you continue the city council system?"

"Yes. It's the only way to ensure no single person ever has too much power. It's the only way for the people to have a voice and help make the decisions that affect them."

"And it seems to be working. Crime is at its lowest in decades, and the citizens report that they haven't been as content since before the war."

"I'm very happy to hear that."

"How much of that do you think is contributed to your own vision, and how much is from the help of the advisers you like to keep so close?"

Grey laughed. "If you're asking if Cage Spears influences my decisions, he does, and there are many other people who give me help, advice and wisdom when I need it."

"What do you say to the rumors that Cage Spears is the true power behind Razor City?"

Cage stepped in. He was smiling. He almost never smiled, but he looked genuinely amused by this remark. "I can answer that one for myself, Grey." He turned to the reporter. "Grey is his own man. He makes his own decisions. The vision for this city was his. He told it to me when he came to the Uprising and offered his allegiance. He did the work to put it into motion. I offer guidance as a friend when he needs it, but I do not make his choices for him."

The reporter seemed to like this. She smiled radiantly at Cage. She might just have liked him. He'd become popular since his people had helped overthrow an evil overlord. She turned back to Grey. "Have you seen your father since the sentence was passed down?"

"Yes. I visit him regularly."

"Has he forgiven you for helping take down his empire?"

Grey thought about this. "It took time. It is still taking time, but we are repairing our relationship slowly. My father's reign was terrible, but I am trying to learn from his mistakes and avoid them."

"Does he feel remorse for his actions and crimes when he was King?"

"I believe my father has realized that he made mistakes and that he'd become corrupt and greedy. But I also think he has much more to reconcile and many more mistakes to admit to himself. It will be a process, and it will not be easy. My father is a proud and stubborn man. He believes much of what he did was well-intentioned. I think he reached a point at which he did not realize was too far."

"Well, he'll have plenty of time to think about his actions and his crimes."

"Yes. And I will do my best to help as I can."

"There are some people who think there is no help for him."

"I understand feeling that way. But he is still my father. I would like to think there is." He smiled. "I am, of course, extremely biased."

The reporter smiled and turned back to the camera. "There you have it, everybody. Rebel Grey. In just a few minutes, we will find out if he will continue as leader of Razor City. Stay tuned to Razor City News 2 where we will be talking to the other candidates before the final decision is announced." She slashed her hand across her chest to cut the camera. She lowered her microphone and turned back to Grey. "Thanks for the interview. Good luck with the election." She looked around as though she were afraid of being overhead. Then she whispered, "I voted for you."

Grey smiled as she strode away to jab her microphone toward Hansel Graves, who stood nearby in black jeans and a western-style button up shirt. A large, black cowboy hat topped his long, wild blonde hair. He smiled like a Wild West movie star, and he looked as dangerous as the outlaws.

Cage smiled and clapped Grey on the shoulder. "That was good."

Grey sighed. "I hate cameras."

Petra rolled her eyes. "Get used to them. You're the one who wanted to take over the city and make all these newsworthy changes. You have to face the music."

"I really don't think that I wanted to do any of those things."

"What you wanted doesn't matter. You did them."

Cage gripped Grey's arm. He nodded toward a young man in a blue suit. "I think it's about to happen."

The young man strode toward the sector representatives, who sat at a table set up on the lawn. He whispered in Tru Haven's ear. She nodded and glanced at the others. The young man handed her a piece of paper. She held it out to the other representatives. Danny Chang snatched it from her fingers and rose.

Grey's heart thumped. Petra slid her hand into his and squeezed it soothingly. She smiled at him. He felt a little better. Claire strode up to them. She looked very smart in her black suit. She nodded curtly to them all. "It's time, Grey. The count is in. They're announcing the winner. You have to go up to the podium."

"Just another minute?"

She rolled her eyes. "No. Go."

He sighed and glanced at Petra and Cage. "I guess that means it's time."

Petra gave him a little shove. "Go on. Good luck."

He smiled wanly and stepped up to the podium with the other four candidates.

They all nodded to each other. They were all smiling, and they all looked extremely confident. Grey felt very small and very young compared to them all, but he lifted his chin and tried to look as cool as they did. He suspected they really all felt as nervous as he did. It helped.

"Good luck, everybody," he said quietly.

Danny Chang marched up to the podium to speak into the microphone. He turned to look back at the candidates. He was grinning, and Grey wondered what that meant. He wasn't sure Danny had even looked at the slip of paper in his hand yet.

"Thank you all for coming today and casting your votes," Danny said brightly. He was a good speaker. The people liked him. "This is a historic occasion. You have all participated in the first ever city wide election in Razor City since the beginning of the great war. You have all listened to the candidates, and you have made your choice." He grinned and opened the slip of paper. There was a breathless silence.

"Razor City's leader for the next three years is..." He paused. The crowd waited. If they waited much longer, Grey thought, someone was going to start a riot. It might be him.

"Dante Scarlet, otherwise known as Grey."

The crowd exploded in cheers. For a moment, Grey looked around at them, stunned. Hansel Graves was the first to shake his hand. "Congratulations, Grey," he said. His voice was a low, gravelly growl. He looked a little disappointed, but he smiled all the same.

The other candidates stepped forward to congratulate him. Marshal Wolf looked a little sour, but he didn't complain. "I'll get you next time, kid," he promised, and then he smiled.

Grey smiled back. "I'll look forward to it."

"At least I still command the Marshals."

"I suppose the people have spoken," Neil Burns said a little coldly.

"I suppose they have," Victor Harrington added. He didn't look pleased. He turned on his heel without another word and strode away from the others. He leaned over to talk to Randall Wiley at the representatives table. They both glared in Grey's direction.

Grey didn't care. As the realization struck him that it was over, that the people wanted him to lead them, exhilaration thrilled through him. He strode toward

Petra and Cage. Cage looked a little surprised. He jerked his head toward the podium.

"Go on," Petra ordered, spinning him back around to face the crowd. "They expect you to make a speech."

"I didn't prepare one. I didn't actually expect to win."

"Are you kidding? After everything you've done for this city?"

Cage rolled his eyes. "Go on. You'd better make it good."

Grey sighed, but he stepped up to the podium. His voice was nearly drowned out by the cheers. "Thank you all," he said over the crowd. After several seconds, they quieted to listen to him. "It was a good race, and I would have been proud to concede to any one of the candidates. But I am honored and humbled that you chose me. I promise to continue to work toward the changes in the city. I promise to work with you to solve our problems and make this city what we want it to be. Most of all, I promise to continue to listen to you and continue to be the best leader to you I can be and make this city everything we know it can be."

The people cheered. They probably hadn't even listened to his speech. They were ready to celebrate. They deserved to celebrate. For the first time since the war, they had the sense that they were in control of their own lives. They'd waited long enough.

"Thank you," he repeated, and he ducked away from the flashbulbs and the television cameras.

Petra strode to meet him. She smiled. He sighed in relief. "Was that okay?" he asked.

"Yeah. It was good. How do you feel?"

"Pretty good, actually. To tell the truth, I was a little worried."

"Yeah?"

"I wasn't really sure if losing the post meant I had to give up the palace. I might have to write a provision about that."

Petra laughed. "Is that what you were worried about?"

"Well, there were other things too, and I suppose it wouldn't have been so bad to go back to the mall, but...well, I really like the palace."

Petra smirked. "Yeah, I like it, too. You can have Claire put it on the next meeting agenda."

"So, what do you say? Are you finally ready to leave the compound and move in here with me?"

"Whoa, buddy. I think the power high is going to your head."

He laughed. "I don't think so. Maybe the first couple times I asked, but not this time."

She smiled and looked around at the crowd. Everyone looked happy, even the losing candidates. The terror of Scarlet's reign was over. The city had a chance to rebuild. Everyone was feeling the excitement of a new era. She saw her brother in the crowd, laughing with Key, Beth and Lux. They were celebrating with the others. For the first time since she'd known most of them, they looked genuinely carefree. There was no worry in their faces.

Everyone was going to be okay.

Grey lifted an eyebrow. "So? What do you think?"

Petra looked up at him. His smile was so beautiful, and his eyes were so intensely, stormy grey, her heart skipped a beat. She threaded her fingers with his and smiled back at him. "I'll think about it."

END

www.ingramcontent.com/pod-product-compliance
Lightning Source LLC
Chambersburg PA
CBHW061220170626
46809CB00007B/2535